A ROAD TO HELL SERIES NOVEL

WRITTEN BY

A ROAD TO HELL SERIES NOVEL

Dance with the Devil

WRITTEN BY

Madison Chase

ALSO BY
Madison Chase

The Wolfblooded Series
Pack or Prey

The Road to Hell Series
Dance with the Devil
Devil in the Details

Short Stories & Anthologies
Tipping the Opal Scales
(from Rage is My Love Language: a Queer Feminine Rage
Anthology)

Developmental Editing by K.F. Starfell

Cover Art Designed by Madison Chase

ISBN:979-8-333-7441-1-1 (kdp) / ISBN:979-8-9927182-0-1 (paperback)

ISBN:979-8-9927182-3-2 (e-book)

ISBN:979-8-9927182-9-4 (hardback)

ISBN:979-8-9927182-4-9 (special edition)

ISBN:979-8-9927182-5-6 (audiobook)

AUTHORS' NOTE

This book contains scenes that may depict, mention or discuss: abduction, assault and violence, attempted murder, blood, gun violence, PTSD (Post-Traumatic Distress Disorder), animal attack, mind control, thoughts of self-harm, emotional and psychological abuse from a parent, divorce, sexually explicit content, and cynophobia.

This book also touches on religious themes and traumas related to certain mythologies/theologies. We have taken creative liberties with some of the origins of well-known figures from a purely entertainment standpoint. The views expressed within the narrative of this story do not necessarily align with the author's own viewpoints. This is a work of fiction. We understand that some may be upset by the strong opinions expressed by certain characters, but please know that our intention is not to offend anyone. If you cannot separate emotion from it, this book may not be for you.

For those healing from religious trauma this book *may* be for you.

If you've ever been told you were going to Hell, and you actually questioned if that was worse than spending eternity with those same judgmental assholes:

This book is for you.

We'll see you there.

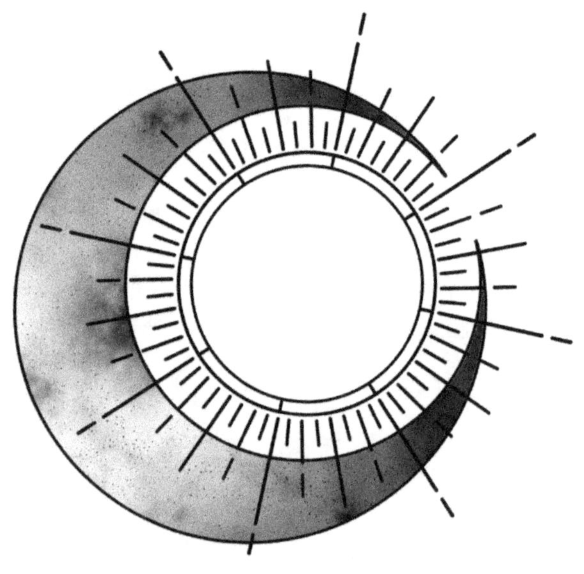

Prologue

"Do I HAVE TO wake up? I'd be perfectly fine spending the rest of my existence here." And I would be.

Here, in my little slice of paradise, I didn't have to worry about bills or jobs or grocery shopping or taxes or traffic... There was no room for broken hearts or chemical imbalances, fights or grief. There was just peace. Warmth.

Pleasure.

Who in their right mind wouldn't want to stay here?

He rewarded my question with a beautifully sad smile. "My darling, I would love nothing more than to give you eternity with me. But I can't. You know why."

I did, but it didn't make it suck any less. I turned over onto my stomach, rolling up in the silk sheet and resting my head on his chest. His eyes were closed, his face perfectly relaxed until he felt me staring at him.

Opening one green eye, he smiled a little wider. "What?"

"I don't know. You might have to convince me. Because, from where I'm sitting... there is nothing worth trading this moment for."

"Char–"

"No," I said, pressing my fingertips to his lips and stopping him from releasing what I knew would only be disappointing to hear. "I don't want to hear about having a life to live...people who love me...none of that Hallmark Channel bullshit. Everyone would be okay."

His hand wrapped around mine, slowly pulling my fingers away from his mouth so he could be free to speak. He leveled me with a devilish look first, bringing out another smile that somehow started deep in my belly until it stretched wide across my face.

"I want you. I want you forever. I want to forget about humanity, the world, existence itself, and see only you from this day until our last." He flipped my hand and placed a gentle kiss on it before turning onto his side so that we were facing one another.

"But we both know what it would mean for you to stay here. The dream world is no real world at all. You are asking to be locked away inside your own mind. Can you understand the sheer terror of such a notion?"

"I'm not scared here with you," I said.

"No, but I cannot remain here forever. Much as I wish I could."

I sighed, rolling my eyes and rolling to my back to stare at the warm summer skies above us. "I thought you could do whatever you wanted."

"Even the Devil has his limitations, my sweet. Who am I if not a realist?"

"Will I remember you this time?" The question fell from my lips heavily.

His hand cupped my cheek, making me look into his eyes. Making me see the sincerity in them. I knew what the answer was before he gave it.

"You won't. But you will have me tonight. And tomorrow. And every night for the rest of your life, if that's your wish."

"How many nights have I had you so far?"

He smiled but didn't answer my question. Instead, he quieted me with a deep kiss that made me shiver down to my toes. When we finally came up for air, I chuckled, draping an arm over his hip and pulling him closer to me.

"It's tragic to not remember kisses like that. You're doing a disservice to yourself."

"Perhaps. Such is the game we play."

Whatever. I was done wasting the few hours I had with my nocturnal lover on such sad thoughts. I sat up, slipping my leg over his hip and rolling him onto his back. I straddled him and leaned forward, taking his mouth into mine, allowing myself to drown in the taste of him. If I savored it longer, maybe I could remember it when I woke up.

Pulling away, I smiled down at the hunger dancing in his emerald gaze, feeling like a goddess with how he looked at me.

"Well then... Let's write some more tragedies."

Chapter 1

Charlie

EVERY MORNING, CHARLIE MADE her way to the little bakery on South Broad, determined to snag her some of that fresh-baked hope and steaming cup of delusion, counting on the sweet cinnamon and robust black coffee to uplift her weary spirits.

Especially after a night like the one before. She'd finally finished the Anderson case for good. It was by far the worst case she'd endured since being off the force, and frankly, coffee was just what she needed to set her head back on straight. Something about sticky cinnamon rolls and a hot cup of coffee really makes even the shittiest of days start out hopeful.

With a small brown paper bag tightly gripped between her teeth, she juggled coffee, a yellow envelope with paperwork from last night's case, and her obnoxiously large wallet while she fished for her keys out of her pocket. She was doing her best to not ruin her morning with a mess as she tried to unlock the door, the name *Brant's Catch and Release* screaming in her face in big black block letters. It wasn't a good name, but Bonnie had suggested it and seemed excited to help, so she just went along with it.

If she were being completely honest, Charlie hadn't paid too much attention to that sort of crap and just nodded along without really listening. Her first mistake.

Bonnie was a sweetheart, albeit a touch odd. Okay, maybe more than a touch, but nothing *too* crazy; just the weird-endearing-elderly-aunt kind of odd. She was in her late 60s, with wispy copper hair and a full face that somehow managed to retain her youthful charm over the years. Bonnie's entire personality seemed almost childlike at times, too, with her dressing like she had been playing dress up in her grandmother's closet, and deep affection and fascination with fairie lore and all the weirdness that came with it.

Bonnie's late husband had actually owned the business before Charlie. She'd been working with him on the odd job here and there, just trying to get back on her feet. When he'd passed, it was Charlie's name on all the paperwork having to do with the business.

It was a bit weird, but she never really questioned why he had left it to her instead of his wife. They hadn't had any children, and Bonnie wasn't exactly what one might call "business-minded." Still, Charlie hadn't been able to stand the idea of the widow sitting alone at home with nothing to do, getting into Lord only knew what kind of trouble.

Which is how she ended up with a bail bondsman business that sounded like a bait and tackle shop—something her brother Ben never let her live down—and an assistant who left little acorn caps filled with honey around the window sills.

The old door made the most awful squall as it opened, punctuated by the equally irritating cry of the small bell above her head. She'd been meaning to get some WD40 for the door hinges for months, but she was either too busy with work or she simply forgot about it. Promising herself she'd pick some up for the millionth time, she made her way to her desk and unloaded the burden in her hands, noticing the red light flashing on her answering machine.

Yes, she still used that archaic technology. She used pen and paper to take notes, too. She may have even still had her old Discman packed away somewhere. Crazy, right? So vintage.

Wondering what fresh case she was about to catch, she moved around her desk to play the tape, but before she could press the button, the door chimed and squalled once again. Her brows furrowed. Bonnie wasn't due for another hour.

Looking over her shoulder, she greeted her visitor with a terse, "We open at nine."

Business wasn't technically open for another ten minutes. Yes, she was that fickle about things like that, and it was a bit rude to barge in without any regard for business hours. Her customer service mask stayed off until nine sharp and if they couldn't handle that then that was their problem.

Her eyes scanned the figure standing in the doorway. His dark hair, though short, looked immaculately styled yet effortlessly natural all at once. The clothes he wore seemed to punctuate the sentiment. He was all well-dressed confidence and insanely green eyes as he stared at her from the shelter of her doorway, a rather arrogant smile spread across his face.

There was an air of meticulousness about him, and it didn't sit well with her. Or maybe she just didn't trust people who seemed that well-put-together so early in the morning. God knew she was barely human before eleven.

Aside from her personal bias toward morning people, something else seemed off about the stranger. Like the fact that he was standing there, holding her stare, and hadn't spoken a single word yet. Talk about creeper vibes.

Breaking the silence—and the impromptu staring contest—Charlie moved to her chair. "Can I help you?"

Her voice came out more irritated than even she expected, but she felt it justified. First, he barged in before she was even open, and now he was just standing there wasting her time.

"Yes, well, I'm looking for a detective, aren't I? Why else would I be here?" he said, finally looking around her humble little office.

His voice held a soft accent to it. Not British exactly, but nothing specific to any region of America, either. At least not one she could pinpoint. Articulate, concise, and unemotional. It was both unremarkable and unique at the same time.

Her eyes narrowed, not at all pleased with being fed a thick line of sarcasm before breakfast. When their eyes finally locked again, her spine immediately stiffened, a sense of great discomfort becoming overwhelmingly clear. This time, it was her who broke the stare, and she looked away from him, grabbed her coffee, moved some papers... whatever she could to look busy and not let him see her unease.

Clearing her throat, she gave him a brisk response. "If it's a detective you want, you'll have better luck at the police. If you're looking for someone to hunt down some asshole who broke their bond, then I'm your guy. My fees depend on the job. I usually ask for a retainer up front and after the job is done, you can pay the rest."

"Wonderful. Well, I do require your assistance, after all, Ms. Brant. I assume you are the one that owns this fine establishment."

"Fine establishment," she snorted, then licked her lips. "Right. So, what exactly can I help you with?"

"I'm in a bit of a pickle, with 'an asshole who broke his bonds', as you say."

He moved closer, easing himself into the chair in front of her. Her eyes followed his every movement, but her expression was anything but amused. Hands laced together, he propped his elbows on the armrests. With a tilt of his head, his expression slid from amused to intrigued.

"Interesting..." was the only word that came from him then.

"What is?"

"Oh, nothing." He sat back, relaxing in the chair as a grin spread on his face again and Charlie couldn't shake the feeling she'd become the butt of some inside joke. "I've lost my dear old puppy. I can't find him anywhere." His expression was very serious.

She could feel the tension pulling at her neck and head. What the hell was this guy's deal? Did he just wake up this morning and decide today was a great day to waste someone's time? To mock her?

Or maybe there was something more to it than that. It almost felt targeted.

The thought tickled at long-avoided memories. People looking at her with equal parts sympathy and concern. Old coworkers laughing, making snide remarks after *the incident.*

Was this guy buddies with one of the cops from her precinct? Had they concocted some plan to get a rise out of her? Realizing the claws of paranoia were sinking into her again, she mentally shook herself out of that line of thought and tried to remain focused on the issue in front of her.

Look at that, Dr. Hendricks. You'd be proud.

"You want me to look for your... dog?" She repeated and he quickly nodded his head. She took in a deep breath; her patience had run thin. "Look, sir, I hate to break it to you but that's not the sort of thing I do. Maybe try some fliers? Posting on a neighborhood social media page? Hire a child..."

The disdain in her voice was clear. She was trying to be cordial. She at least had to give herself that, but this guy... Charlie really wanted to tell him to get the fuck out of her office.

"This is much more serious than you might believe."

She waited for him to clarify, but there was no hint that he planned to add anything else. Charlie tilted her head to the side. She was at a loss for words. It was clear this was not what he expected from her, judging by the look he was giving.

"There are other resources out there besides me." Turning towards a filing cabinet, she rummaged for some old pamphlets.

"I see. Well, it was a pleasure, Ms. Brant." His tone went dark and Charlie stiffened in place.

"Pleasure is all mine," she said flatly, but her eyes were rolling. "Here, try this number. They pick up animals all the time, maybe they'll have..." When she looked back, she found she was talking to an empty room.

Charlie stood abruptly, looked around, then headed to the front door. The bell chimed above her head, and her door whined in that horrible way as she opened it again so she could look down the empty hallway. Her face scrunched with confusion. He wasn't there.

She shut the door, looking up at the little metal bell when it latched. Had the bell rung? She knew for a fact the door hadn't moved or else she'd have been greeted with that horrible sound it always gave.

What an odd guy. And not endearing odd, like when Bonnie rubbed an egg over her to "absorb the evil-eye" or whatever nonsense it was. Odd in the way that made her scalp itch and every nerve in her body go on alert.

For one, he'd almost seemed like he'd been toying with her. Coming in here talking about some lost dog as if she were Gertrude, the nosey neighborhood watch. Everything about him seemed to clash with the idea that he was searching for a lost pet.

His smirk, for instance, felt like he was laughing at some inside joke Charlie wasn't clued in on. His irritatingly perfect suit, completely clean of even a single stray dog hair, made her doubt he had ever come in contact with a dog, let alone owned one.

Dog people carried pieces of their pets with them. It was like a law. One that, honestly, had kept Charlie from indulging in pot luck dishes most of her life.

But if he hadn't actually had a dog, then what on earth could he have gained by invading her office to weave some unconvincing story about it? She didn't like that question. Not at all. And there were so many more swimming in her head.

Shaking her head, she returned to her desk and grabbed her coffee, bringing it to her lips to take a swig of the warm liquid. Her phone rang as the coffee touched her tongue, startling her out of her thoughts. A splash of coffee blossomed on the front of her shirt.

"Shit!" Taking in a deep breath, she set the cup down and batted at the fresh stain before reaching for the receiver and answering with a harsh, "*What?*"

"Well good morning to you too, sunshine. Get your ass down here." The voice on the other end was all too familiar.

Carmen Vega, her ex-partner and now Chief of Police. Carmen quickly climbed the promotional ladder, while Charlie got labeled as the town crazy. Definitely not how either of them envisioned their careers going.

"Well, hello, Charlie. How are you, Charlie? What have you been up to, Charlie? Have you been sleeping well? I mean usually, these are the questions you ask your only friend in the whole wide world." Charlie teased Carmen and she could almost feel the woman's dagger-like stare coming back at her from the receiver. "Alright, alright. I'm heading that way. Can you at least give me thirty minutes?"

"You've got fifteen." Before the phone beeped in her ear. What could she have possibly done wrong *this* time?

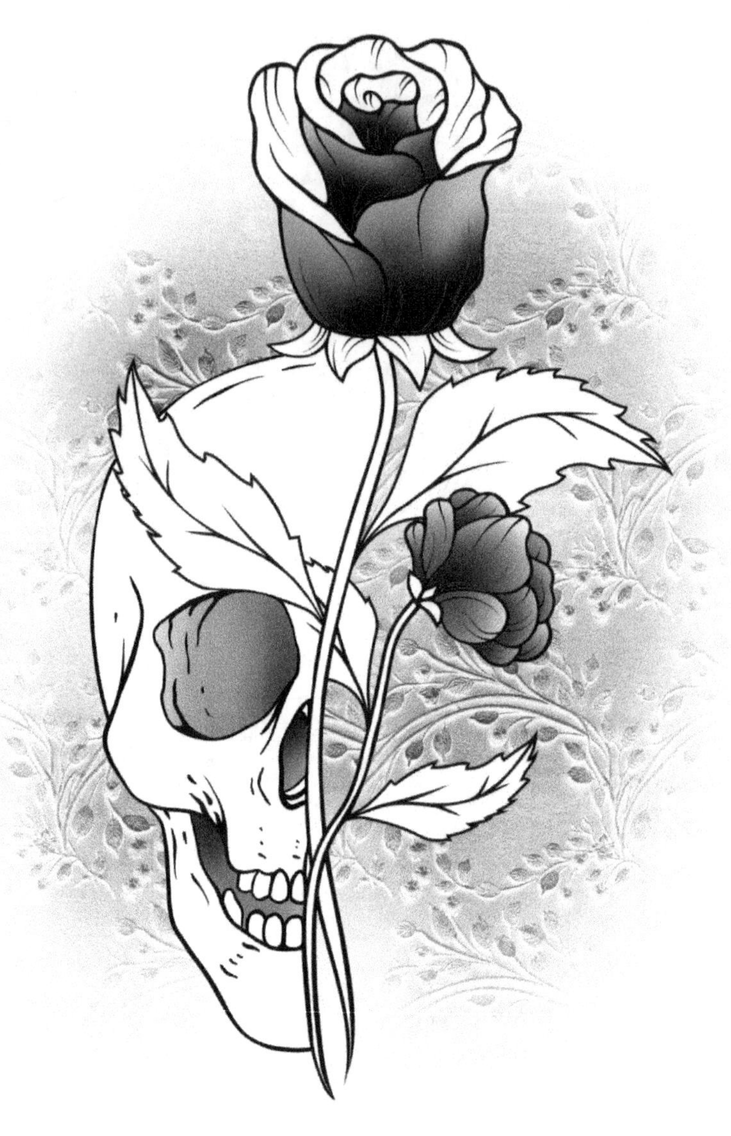

Chapter 2

THE WALK TO THE police station didn't take long, which honestly sort of sucked for her. The longer she could give Carmen to cool down from whatever fire had burned her biscuits, the better it would be in the end. Unfortunately, past-Charlie's brilliant idea to get an apartment within walking distance of the precinct was going to bite her in the ass.

Now, a measly twelve minutes of peace stood between her and the Carmen's legendary scolding, which was never a fun time for Charlie when she was on the receiving end. That was what best friends were for, though, right? They always pointed out your stupid choices; like the ones Charlie often found herself in as of late.

Job after job, she seemed to be getting into an increasingly alarming amount of trouble. Nothing she couldn't get herself out of, usually. And she had to admit she enjoyed the rush of adrenaline that came with the territory. The jobs were making her feel whole somehow. Alive. Even if they resulted in regular scoldings from her best friend.

Even now, Charlie had a pretty good idea what had gotten her an invite to Carmen's office. The last job had made even Charlie question herself. A first for her.

Dr. Hendricks—the therapist she'd seen briefly after the incident—had mentioned something about how people in her situation sometimes put themselves in danger as a means of like... gaining the control they didn't have before... or some head-doctor psychobabble bullshit like that.

Whatever. There was a reason she quit going to therapy.

Being psychoanalyzed over a trauma no one believed happened was not her idea of a good time. She spent enough time dwelling on the events as it was, and she didn't need to shell out her downsized salary to do so.

Charlie stopped in front of the precinct, eyeing the building. Maybe it wasn't too late to run. She knew how to disappear if she really wanted to. She could pack up and make herself a scarce memory, a nameless face, disappearing without a trace, just like her ex-husband.

Taking a deep breath, she pushed inside, knowing damn well that running was not an option. She knew exactly where she needed to go, shuffling her feet across the station with numerous eyes lingering on her like the pariah she came to be known as. The station used to be a home away from home. Though she wasn't technically a cop anymore, she'd pop back in every once in a while, with a runner in tow.

The problem was Carmen—sorry, *Chief Vega*—wasn't exactly keen on her doing the rest of the officers' jobs for them. Especially since perps were usually worse for wear and she was often reminded that the "real" police could bring them in.

She paused at the door, eyeing the golden letters as she sighed to herself, then knocked before entering Carmen's office. "Hey, partner."

A cheesy grin spread across her face but the moment those brown eyes fixed on her she saw they were not the happy ones that normally greeted her.

Well shit.

Charlie lost that shit-eating grin quickly and shut the door behind her. Nobody needed to hear this. Charlie wanted to keep what shreds of dignity she had left, few as they may be.

"Don't you fucking 'partner' me, Brant." Her voice slowly started to rise. "Sit your ass down." She pointed at a chair across from her desk.

"Well, since we aren't partners anymore, could you call me Charlie, then? Drop the whole buddy-cop schtick?" You could hear a feather hit the ground in the silence that answered her.

Yeah, that didn't make things any better.

A sigh of resignation escaped her. Instead of sitting down like she was told, Charlie stood with her arms crossed in front of her chest and leaned against the door. She didn't care who it was, she wasn't going to let someone order her around like some mindless soldier.

Not even her best friend.

"What did I do this time?"

"What *didn't* you do..." A growl rolled out as she pulled out a file and threw it across the desk.

Charlie's eyes followed the file as it slid dangerously close to the edge. The anxiety built up inside as it threatened to topple to the ground, and with a defeated groan, she moved to the desk to snatch it up and thumbed through it.

"You went into Dela Muertas territory, again, without proper backup or even letting someone know what you were up to. You managed to derail one of our undercovers that had been working his way in for the last seven months, pissed off one of the more influential businessmen in the city, and what else?" Carmen pretended to think about it, but Charlie already knew what was coming. "Oh, right, you left his son with a busted arm and a bullet hole in his kneecap! What the hell were you thinking?! Who do you think you are, the friggin' Terminator now? He was ready to press charges!"

"He called me crazy, so I showed him crazy." Charlie said with a smile. It was a joke, but clearly Carmen wasn't laughing. She shrugged her shoulders. "Look, he wasn't gonna press charges. And you're yelling at me, why? Because I did my job? Protected myself?"

"You're not a fucking cop anymore, Charlie. I can't keep bailing you out every time you wanna play vigilante. I don't know how you managed to get the charges dropped already, but your luck is gonna run out one day, *hermana*."

"One day?" Charlie's lips pressed into a thin line. "My best friend sailed while I sunk, my husband left me, my family's pissed at me, and let's not forget that I almost died. Oh, and my parting gifts for my service to this city?

"Mockery from my former coworkers, nightmares that keep me up all hours of the night, and a bottle of happy pills that don't work. I think the luck well is pretty fucking dry. So, excuse me for finally finding something that I get to look forward to."

The words spewed out before she could stop herself. Carmen leaned in; fingers spread out before sharply tapping against the desk. She was carefully picking her words. It was a weird chess game between the two.

Surprisingly, her glare softened as she looked at Charlie. "I know loss too, remember Charlie? We share similar scars."

Charlie glanced towards Carmen's left arm before quickly turning her gaze to the file in front of her. The thing was, Carmen knew exactly what she was going through. Of all the people in her life, she'd been the one that was there since before and was still there after.

Carmen Vega was a soldier who found a second life and excelled in it. She quite literally sacrificed life and limb for her country and refused to let it slow her down.

Carmen pinched the bridge of her nose. "I get it. You found a new gig and you're making good money. But I don't want you getting thrown into jail—or worse—by being so damn reckless. You're snooping around in places you shouldn't, and it's going to end up putting you in a ditch somewhere."

Little did Carmen know, the only reason Charlie knew the guy wouldn't press charges was because the man who hired her had the pull to cover her ass. He hired her to bring the shitbag in because most cops were afraid to touch him—if they weren't on his payroll already. A suspicion that sat heavy in Charlie's gut. The one good thing she could give her sudden career change was the freedom to get things done however she deemed necessary. Free of red tape—as long as she stayed smart about it.

She knew she'd narrowly escaped jail a few times. Hell, if she wasn't as careful as she had been, she was risking outright brutality. But she knew what she was doing. Mostly.

That being said, Charlie had expected her morning to go a bit different than how it was. She caught the bad guy. He got a lesson in justice. All she wanted was to reward herself with a damn cinnamon roll and have a relaxing day.

Was it a crime to bask in a win for once? Apparently so.

Growing tired with being talked at, Charlie let her attention wander around the office in an attempt to drown out Carmen's continued lecture. She fixated on the back of a head of clean-cut dark hair out in the bullpen. There was something about that head that looked way too familiar—as far as heads went anyway. She tried to place it as her eyes scanned down his figure. That build she knew... That body. Her heart seized painfully before her brain could even register who she was seeing.

"Are you fucking kidding me?"

Her sudden outburst managed to shut Carmen up mid-sentence. Charlie turned narrow eyes back to Carmen before pointing towards the guy on the other side of the window. "Why the fuck is Brian here?"

Carmen's eyes darted to the window then back at Charlie. The harshness quickly drained from her face, turning into something else. Shame? Guilt? Yeah, that was definitely Carmen's guilt-face. She'd seen it enough since her less than amicable split from the department.

"It wasn't my call. He was assigned here as of today. I was going to tell you but wasn't sure how yet. I thought he left for the day, or I wouldn't have ca–."

A laugh erupted from Charlie, but there was nothing happy or humorous about it. The sound was downright cynical. "So let me get this straight, you've had *this* little nugget of information, and you are now telling me that my ex-husband was hired onto the NOPD. After you literally scolded me for being reckless about my job because you were worried about me. Aren't you supposed to be my friend who always got my back?"

The laughter all but left, her voice rose higher as she yelled at Carmen, an act that was completely out of the norm between the two. The woman stood there, just taking it as though she knew she fucked up.

Carmen knew how Charlie felt about Brian. Hell, as far as Charlie knew, Carmen also hated the bastard as much–if not more–for what he did to her.

Rather than punch her best friend—which was incredibly tempting at the moment—Charlie stormed right out of her office and made a beeline right to Brian. Carmen called out for her, asking her to stop, but she ignored her. She didn't want to be talked out of saying whatever she was going to say when she got to him. The last time Charlie saw Brian he was walking out of her hospital room.

That had been five damn years ago.

He turned around as she stepped behind him. Whether he was surprised or happy to see her, she'd never know, because the second his stupid face came into her line of sight she swung a left hook. She shook her hand and stepped back as all the officers around them rushed in to see what had happened. Charlie could hear Carmen cursing as she pushed her way through the crowd, though she didn't seem to be in any real hurry to break it up.

Maybe her eyes were playing tricks on her, but she could have sworn Carmen was smiling for the briefest of seconds.

"You fucking asshole..." Someone snatched her by the elbow and tugged her away from him.

Brian leaned on the edge of his desk, wiping at the corner of his mouth; shock, hurt, and confusion written all over his face. When their eyes met again, she could already feel her fist clenching up again at her side. What the hell was he confused about? He knew what he'd done.

And if he didn't, she could give him another not-so-friendly reminder.

Only Carmen managed to stop her from swinging again as she grabbed Charlie by her shoulders and spun her to look at her. "God damn it, Charlie. You can't just go around punching cops!"

"Oh, he's fine. Put some ice on it, you'll live." Charlie said to him as she gave her hand one final shake, flexing the fingers to stretch the ache out.

Her whole body shook beneath her skin, amped up with anxiety or adrenaline... or maybe just reveling in finally getting some much-needed release. To be completely honest, she had surprised even herself at what she had done.

"I cannot believe you let that son of a bitch work here."

"Like I said, I can't control that. But I can keep my best friend from assaulting an officer in front of me. Even if he fucking deserved it." Carmen's eyes slid to Brian as she said the last, her volume raising a few levels to make sure he knew where her loyalties were.

Looking back to her friend, her demeanor shifted from authoritative, to concerned. "Go home, Charlie. Ice your hand, enjoy playing that moment back a few times if you gotta. God knows it was pretty fucking satisfying. But calm your shit down before you come back into my precinct. Okay? I'd hate to have to arrest you over a douchebag."

Charlie turned to Carmen and saw guilt still hanging on her face. She knew her friend was stuck between a rock and a hard place. On the one hand, she had to play by the rules. It was the price of being in her position. On the other, she knew Carmen was rooting for her deep inside. Or maybe not even that deep. Had they not been in the middle of a crowd of fellow officers, she might have taken a swing at him herself. Charlie stood there for a second, gathering herself before nodding in agreement and pushing past Carmen.

Chapter 3

Charlie

INSTEAD OF GOING STRAIGHT home, as instructed, Charlie made her way to Chartres and took the time to clear her head. Why did this kind of shit always happen to her? It was like she was the butt of one big cosmic joke, and everyone else was in on it.

As her feet led her through the Quarter, she passed by all sorts of people. Tourists already awake and looking for their first drink of the day, locals just trying to get through the masses to their jobs, bicyclists zipping past her far too close thinking they owned the streets and sidewalks alike, and groups of homeless people sitting along the sidewalks with their dogs.

She hated to see it, but it had become as common in the Quarter as the long-forgotten plastic beads hanging high in the tree branches. She kept going forward, ignoring the occasional request for change, until she finally reached the place she'd been heading for.

The Little Bar on Gravier.

Aside from the obvious perk of being a short walk from her apartment, it was a nice little dive bar that was often overlooked by the touristy-masses. New Orleans definitely was not short on options when it came to getting a drink. It was, however, short on options that didn't include a tidal wave of vacationers taking up precious space.

The bar itself wasn't big by any means, but it was cozy. A little dirty around the edges, but you knew the beer was good. She walked in and smiled at the breathalyzer hanging on the wall by the entrance. That had always been her favorite little thing about this place. If it was common for people to drive around the French Quarter, it might have even saved a few people from some DUIs or worse.

Of course, no one really drove around the Quarter. Not unless they were picking up a fare.

Lucky for her, the bar was fairly empty. An empty bar at 11 A.M. wouldn't be surprising in any other city, but New Orleans was all but overflowing with traveling alcoholics who practically brushed their teeth with Brandy Milk Punch. Charlie may have liked to drink her woes away, but even she had limits; she at least waited until McDonald's stopped their breakfast menu before taking her first shot of the day.

She wished she could talk to her mom, or even Ben. Get some outside perspectives on the situation, maybe even a little validation.

Sadly, she knew she couldn't go to them for advice. Her mom and dad would be thrilled to hear from her, no doubt, but she couldn't bring herself to talk with them right now. Not when she had felt like she was just starting to put the pieces of her life back together.

She already felt like a failure with everything that had happened, and the last thing she wanted to do was let her dad know she had fucked up. Again. Seeing as Carmen was currently on her shit list, she wasn't an option either. And Bonnie was in her own little world. Sometimes she was jealous about her ability to check out of reality. The bar seemed like the best place to empty out her sorrows. It wasn't the first time, nor would it be her last.

She slumped into an empty barstool and ordered herself a vodka on ice. She nursed her drink for hours, letting her brain devolve into a complete tailspin over what had happened.

Carmen was right—maybe she had gotten a little too cocky with the whole Anderson job. She didn't exactly have to get as deep as she did, but damn it, it felt good to feel like one of the good guys again. She missed being a cop. As much as she hated to admit it, they'd taken something important from her. To protect and serve, or some shit along those lines.

As the last drop of vodka rolled onto her tongue, she glanced at the bartender then tapped the bottom of her empty glass on the bar top in a silent request. When she glanced back down at it, she saw the years-old etchings in the wood peeking out from under it. With a gentle push on her glass, the words "Bullet or Watch" stared back at her, nearly erased by time.

The words took her back to nights with Carmen, grabbing a drink after a long day. Their rookie days. When everything felt alive and full of possibilities, and they were just starting out on their journeys as cops. Back when the only ways out were retiring or meeting a bullet in the line of duty.

As the bartender poured her another drink, those words stared at her mockingly. Worn and forgotten, just like her.

It shouldn't have gone down that way. Sure, being a cop came with its risks. Charlie had always worked with the understanding that any day she could meet the bullet that ended everything. They'd put her picture in the paper, they'd praise her heroics while she traveled in the motorcade, and they would send her to heaven to the tune of a twenty-one-gun orchestra. That was the end she'd always been ready to accept if it had come down to it. If only her father could have accepted that.

When she was a little girl, she wanted nothing more than to get her father's approval. He was always out hunting, always with her brother, never letting her tag along. She was always jealous of the comradery between them. For whatever reason she couldn't create that kind of bond with her mother, but she swore that she could have with her father if he'd given her the chance.

Instead, he treated her like a glass doll. All of them did.

Her family's disapproval over her career choices never deterred her from her dreams. She expected them to ventually accept it, in their own time. Not once, however, did she expect it to end with a pen stroke and a bottle of pills for PTSD. To be ridiculed and mocked by her fellow boys in blue while she rocked and shook, drenched in a cold sweat, during one of her episodes. To constantly have her sanity questioned when she tried to explain what she'd seen that night. It was mildly insulting, at best. Downright cruel at its worst.

Contrary to whispers around the bullpen, Charlie didn't blame Carmen for what happened. She blamed her superiors. They were the ones who failed her in the end. Charlie knew what she saw, even if she kept it to herself now.

A creature with eyes of black fire approached her best friend as they stood in position. They had tailed some sick bastard right to the old warehouse. Three young girls had just been pulled from a cellar in Algiers, but he'd slipped out. Both Carmen and Charlie knew they couldn't let him get out of there. They held position while they waited for backup, standing on opposite sides of the open garage door. Their guns were out, pointed up but ready to shoot if necessary. Their backup was taking too long. He was going to slip right through their fingers.

Carmen tossed a rock to grab Charlie's attention, shaking her head in a silent warning to not do what she was thinking about doing, but any thought of storming into the place slipped away in mere seconds.

The low growl caught Charlie's attention first. They hadn't seen any dogs, but it wasn't something they were wholly unready to deal with if the need arose.

As much as Charlie loved dogs, she loved her life more.

When the animal peered out of the shadows behind Carmen, it was unlike anything Charlie had ever laid eyes on. Huge, with a long tail and pointed ears. Not a cat, not the way it ran. Not the way it sounded.

It gave her absolutely zero time to think, but truth be told, she didn't need to. Carmen wasn't only her partner, but her best friend, and the mother of an adorable little girl. She never married, and as far as Charlie knew the dad wasn't even a part of their lives, so Carmen was all Camilla had in the entire world. Charlie had long ago come to terms with the fact that, should shit go sideways, she would do anything to keep Carmen alive.

As the beast went for Carmen, Charlie understood with extreme clarity that the day had finally come.

Luckily, she hadn't died that night. Scarred, sure, but not dead. The attack had left its impression on the young detective, both physically and mentally speaking, and she'd had more than a few "episodes" when she'd returned to work some weeks later. She was told it was to be expected. Eventually, the psychologist diagnosed her with Post-Traumatic Stress Disorder, and the chief at the time had managed to label her as mentally unfit, resulting in her being let go.

There were many rumors about what had attacked her. Her brother had even cracked jokes about it being a werewolf, of all things. But come the next full moon... nothing.

So much for the interesting theories. It just seemed to be another rabid dog on the streets. One that had nearly torn her shoulder off and haunted her almost nightly... but a dog, nonetheless.

By the time she climbed out of her own head, the windows had darkened and the buildings outside were lit up in alluring neon lights. Might as well call it a night. She paid for her drinks and decided to head home. Tomorrow was a whole new day.

A new day of shit, probably, but anything would be better than dealing with her ex-husband. Even though that left hook was pretty nice, she really didn't want to see him like that.

She walked on the sidewalk, bumping into people here and there before entering the Gravier Place Apartments. The lobby was already empty, everyone either already home for the night or out for the next few hours. A small favor. It meant she could grab her mail without the judgment of her neighbors seeing her walk of shame.

Taking the elevator up, she moved down her hallway and stopped in front of her door. Home sweet home. The moment she entered and shut the door; the silence swallowed her up. She dropped everything from her hands. Mail scattered around her feet, keys and wallet on the other side. Charlie fell back heavily against the door and slowly slid to the cold floor below.

She dropped her head into her hands and cried fat salty tears. Those tears had been aching to escape since she'd seen Brian, but she'd kept them locked away while the anger took control instead. She hated being so fragile, and had spent five years building herself back up from that pitiful mess she had become when he left her. She was not weak. Not for him. Not anymore.

He'd lost the privilege of affecting her in such a way when she signed the papers. Her teeth clenched painfully at the mere thought of that day, and the tears turned bitter.

Five minutes. She allowed herself five minutes to let out all the pent-up emotions, all the anger and heartbreak, before she wiped her face on her sleeve, sniffled, and forced herself to stand up. Charlie used the door as support, slowly getting her bearings back in order. She straightened out her blouse, which she just now realized still had coffee on it from earlier.

She'd paraded around the city like that. All day. Fan-fucking-tastic.

Charlie looked around the living room and forced out a puff of air before heading towards the kitchen. She didn't even bother turning the light on, letting her muscle memory lead her around her apartment.

In an almost zombie-like state, she moved to her selection of wines gathered on the counter. She pulled a glass from the cupboard and poured herself a generous cup, not really paying attention to how much went into her glass, then made her way back to the living room.

Plopping on the couch, she laid her head back and took a few moments to breathe and regain her senses. She stared at the glass in her hand as if it had magically appeared there. When she finally took a drink, she didn't stop at one leisurely sip but drained the entire glass in one go.

She was done with the day. It was as simple as that. She needed to decompress, get ready for bed, and reset all the static in her head. It sucked being alone in your own head on days like this. Without someone else there to distract her thoughts, she knew it would be harder to keep herself from falling back into that all-too-familiar depression.

Leaving her empty wine glass behind, she made her way to the bedroom and talked herself into some sleep pants before nestling into the seductive pile of fluffy blankets on her bed. Calling it for the night, early as it may be, was the only thing that would fix the situation in her mind. Luckily enough, the wine was making her feel just right and she was able to drift off slowly to sleep. She could deal with Carmen and Brian tomorrow.

Chapter 4

SOMETHING WOKE HER FROM a deep sleep, forcing her eyes open to stare up at the ceiling. The feeling of safety, comfort, and even happiness washed over her like a fast-acting drug as she came to. The heavy weight of an arm laid across her, which garnered a sleepy smile. Though her eyes were still blurry with sleep, she knew exactly who that arm belonged to.

Brian was one of her favorite things to wake up to. She missed him so violently while he was deployed, like a part of her body had been ripped away, but when he finally came back home, everything was right again. Everything was amazing.

Charlie turned to find him sleeping peacefully beside her. She took in every detail of his face before landing her gaze on his relaxed jawline. There was stubble growing in from the night before. He'd shave it clean after he woke, going through the deeply conditioned motions of military life, but she always wondered what he'd look like with a beard. One of those really long ones that tickled you during kisses. The thought of it made her chuckle softly.

They still had decades ahead of them. A future of gray hair and slow living. She would just have to wait and find out.

Blue hues flickered open as they lazily looked up at her. "Morning, handsome."

"Good morning, beautiful." A soft smile appeared on his face as he reached up to caress her cheek. Charlie grabbed hold of his hand and kissed it gently.

She never wanted this to end, but knew she only had a short time with him. He was never home enough for her liking. She may have had a piece of his heart, but the rest of him belonged to the Marines. This was the price they both agreed upon. She got to do her detective work, while he finished his career in the military. And one day, they would both retire, belonging to no one but each other.

Brian scooched closer to her as she pushed up onto his arm, giving her a soft kiss on her forehead. The gentle gesture sent waves of butterflies fluttering in Charlie's stomach. No matter how many times he showed her these little affectionate moments, she'd always be wonderstruck by them. When he moved back, he lowered his head to look into her eyes and study her face as she'd done his moments before.

She bit her bottom lip, and a low growl came from him. "You know how that makes me feel."

"What?" The word may have sounded innocent, but Charlie knew exactly what she was doing. A playful grin spread across his face as his hand moved from her face down to her chin, he lifted her up just enough, so his lips crashed into hers. Her eyes closed as their tongues danced together in a familiar dance that made her mind beg for more.

She sat up more, pushing him back towards his side of the bed as she kissed and moved one leg over him. Her fingers moved over his muscular figure as she sat on top of him, exploring the familiar paths with renewed fervor. She could go blind tomorrow and still she would know him just by the feel of him.

Brian's hands snaked around her hips and grabbed a handful of her behind, pulling a tiny yelp from her, before she moved her hands to the hem of her shirt and lifted it over her head, tossing it to the floor below. Bare-breasted, she smiled impishly at Brian, and let him feast on her with his eyes. The way he looked at her sometimes made her feel like a goddess—like she was the only female on earth and everything she did, everything she was, was divine.

The longer she stared down at him, though, the more she noticed something was not quite right. His eyes—usually calm blue pools of tranquility—had darkened into rich emerald jewels. Though strange, she found herself fascinated by it.

Inch by inch, Brian's entire form changed beneath her. His broad, round shoulders narrowed, his impressively built body shrunk down into smaller, longer cuts of muscle, and his entire body seemed to morph into a newer leaner figure. His physique had completely changed from body-builder mass to a lengthened athletic form.

The scent of rich cinnamon filled her nose, its spicy aroma tickling her sinuses in the best way, but underneath that earthy spice was something more. Almond? Vanilla? It was a sweet almost floral smell she knew but struggled to name. Sweet, with a tease of smokiness.

Poppies.

Her intrigued gaze moved up the strange new body to find a more angular chin, high chiseled cheekbones, and darker skin making those suddenly green eyes seem even brighter than naturally possible. Charlie sucked in a breath as she finally recognized the new face staring up at her.

The man from her office.

A wicked grin stretched on his face as he held her hips, ready to hold her in place if she tried to move. Strangely enough, the thought hadn't even crossed her mind. Rather, she felt the most wonderful sense of calm as she looked down at him.

"So, tell me," He whispered, "What happens next?" A thrill shot through her body before he flipped her under him. His hands traced delicately down her arms and encircled her wrists, guiding them above her head and pressing them gently into the mattress. "Is this what you wish, Ms. Brant? Is this what *moves* you?"

Her voice was lost to her confusion. Or maybe it was her desire. At that moment, she couldn't tell the difference between the two. Should she have been scared? Or, at the absolute *very* least, annoyed? She wasn't. Truth was, she was fascinated. Enchanted, even. Logic and reason would not take root, no matter how much the back of her brain itched.

"I can make your fantasy come to reality."

The man moved down the length of her body ever so slowly, his breath making her skin prickle with goosebumps. He hovered over her left breast, his eyes rolling up to look at her face before his mouth consumed her flesh. Charlie's back arched, pushing her breast further into his eager mouth. She moaned as his tongue wrapped around her nipple teasing it into a tight bud. She craved for more. He nipped lightly at her causing more of a reaction than she'd care to admit.

He relented, leaving her body silently screaming for him to come back, to keep going. Instead, he gave her another grin. "I can have you squirming for more. If you'd like, that is."

Yes.... yes, she would.

Instead, she asked, "Who are you?" Her voice was weak, her question half-hearted at best. Her heart was beating against its bony cage, begging to be let out, fearing it could no longer stay in its confinement.

He never answered her. Instead, he slid further down until he came to the part of her that was aching most. She lifted her head, looking down the line of her body and the wicked grin he rewarded her with.

It wasn't until she tried to reach out to him that she realized she still couldn't move her hands.

He was too far down to be holding them. In fact, now that she was no longer lost in sensation, she realized his hands were resting on either side of her hips. The logical side of her brain clawed its way back into control, bringing with it a little more lucidity. Twisting her head upward, she looked back at her wrists and found them bound to the bed.

With a quick jerk, she tugged at the restraints. "What is this?"

"Oh, you know, just a sweet little dream," he hummed, gleefully.

Charlie could feel his hands on either side of her legs as they moved downward, grabbing the thin sides of her panties and sliding them off her before pausing briefly.

"Well, a wet dream really." Another grin pulled at his features, and he tossed the blue silk over his shoulder. "I promise you'll enjoy it. And I always keep my promises, dear Charlotte." Her name rolled off his tongue like he'd said it a million times in a million wicked ways.

Her heart continued to race. A part of her did enjoy this whether she admitted it or not.

"I want you to be a good girl, for me. If you moan too early, I'll stop what I'm doing and start all over."

He leaned down between her legs, those green eyes fixed on her before he met her sex with his tongue. Charlie's head dug back into the pillow as he tasted her. A gasp left her and he paused. She could feel the heat of his body moving back up her form. He was looking down at her, a wicked grin resting on his face.

"That didn't last long. Looks like I get to start from the beginning."

He did exactly that, but this time he trailed kisses from her chin down her neck before moving over the top of her breast. She bit the bottom of her lip, trying to hold back any sound that threatened to spill out of her, but when his teeth nipped at her nipple another gasp escaped her. He chuckled against her flesh before hovering overhead. "My goodness, Ms. Brant. You're a vocal little minx, aren't you? This is exciting. Let's begin again, shall we?"

Charlie could feel her nose flare. Cheeky bastard. The desire that had been swelling within her gave a little more space to irritation at his teasing. It brought her back to her senses just enough that she pulled at her restraints.

His self-satisfied laughter stopped seconds before teeth bit harder into her. She managed not to give in to the moan of pleasure that wanted to leave her, but only just. Apparently satisfied with her restraint, he trailed lips and tongue down her body until he reached her depths, his hot breath tickling her womanhood.

Falling into a slow rhythm, his tongue danced across her clit. Her body squirmed around him, legs wrapping over his shoulders and pulling him and his wicked tongue further into her. Two fingers slid inside her as he continued devouring her, lapping her up and sucking gently on her clit until her head spun. Charlie lost her fight, and she cried her pleasure out. To her relief, he didn't stop.

It didn't take her long to reach the threshold of pure pleasure. To be fair, it had been years since she'd been touched this way. Each nerve ending radiated from below, sending electric shocks everywhere. When her body finally stopped moving, she released a deep satisfied sigh, opening her eyes as he lifted himself back over her. He smiled down at her, giving her a soft peck on her forehead.

"As I said, I keep my promises." Leaning towards her left forearm, he kissed it gently and rubbed his thumb over the soft skin. Before untying her bound wrists. "A parting gift. Have sweet dreams, Ms. Brant. I'll know if you don't."

Her eyes flickered open. She was lying on her side facing the closet door. Her skin sung with the afterglow of good sex, like live wires sparking under the skin. Charlie ran a hand across her face, trying to force herself to wake up fully.

She was going mental.

At least, for the first time in a long time, she'd had a good dream. A *really* good dream. Featuring the strange, but undeniably good-looking nameless dude from her office yesterday. If his tongue-work was as good in reality as it was in dreamland, she could see him being slightly less irritating.

Slightly.

Chapter 5

Charlie

GOD, SHE SERIOUSLY NEEDED to get laid. Fast.

Charlie grimaced as she stirred awake. She so wasn't ready to wake up. Not with the happy little remnants of such a delicious dream still clinging to the edges of her subconscious. Waking up to reality after *that* seemed so cruel.

As she stretched, she caught sight of her forearm, and through blurry eyes saw a strange black symbol written on her skin. What club had she gone to last night? She didn't recognize the stamp, and she'd seen her fair share through work alone. With one eye open by sheer force of will, she tried rubbing it away with her thumb.

Not even a smudge.

She flicked her tongue across her thumb and rubbed it harder, but it still laid perfect against her forearm. Sitting up straight with panic, she had a horrible thought. She hadn't gotten *that* drunk. Did she? The night before was definitely a blur, she couldn't even remember exactly how she got home, but she'd remember getting a tattoo. Right?

She stared at the ink, mentally retracing her steps. She'd gone to the bar... had a few drinks... maybe more than a few... she had planned to walk home and get some dinner...

This was where she drew a complete blank.

"The hell?"

Charlie rubbed the mark so vigorously she thought she might start a fire. It didn't even hurt. Fresh ink would hurt, right? She never got a tattoo before. Everything she knew about them she'd learned from Ben's friends.

Her thoughts slowly went back to the dream, those tender lips pressing on her skin before she woke. No, that was impossible. That was the hangover talking. Binge drinking in your thirties was definitely harder to recover from, but this was pushing it. She stared at the mark and tried to make sense of it. It looked like a cup but not quite. Not something she'd want to get for her first tattoo anyways.

An abrupt knock startled her. Charlie was by no means a morning person, and the thought of someone coming to her apartment this early quickly turned surprise into soul-deep agitation. The fact that a hangover was beginning to sink claws into her brain only served to amplify her ire.

She grabbed her cellphone from the nightstand and checked the time. It was seven-in-the-goddamn-morning. Who in their right mind showed up at people's homes so God-forsaken early? Growling to herself, she violently shoved her blankets off her and tip-toed to the door. Peeking through the eyehole, her heart instantly skipped a beat. This literally couldn't be happening right now.

On the other side of the door was none other than Brian. Why the hell was he here? So many questions, so damn early, and she hadn't had a sip of coffee yet. Charlie debated on opening the door, almost satisfied at letting him tuck tail and go away, but the knock came again, and his persistence quickly turned the irritation into actual anger.

What do you say when your greatest regret is standing on the other side of the door?

Sighing deeply, she finally unlocked the door and swung it open. A thousand words wanted to escape her mouth as she came face-to-face with him. Her eyes narrowed as her arms crossed over her chest. Why waste the breath?

"Charlie." The way her name rolled hesitantly off his tongue, as though he were afraid to even utter it, only pissed her off more. Was that guilt? Shame? Pretty late for that. "I-"

"Let me stop you right there." Charlie raised her hand, already done before he even started. "What gives you the right to show up at my house, at seven-in-the-god-damn-morning, wanting to—What? Talk?"

"Charlie, please." She stared at the red swelling at the corner of his lip. A grin would have surfaced but she didn't want to send the wrong message, so she just kept her glare. He fucking deserved it. "But I do want to talk. I want you to know what happened between us."

"There's nothing to talk about, asshole." This time the fakest smile spread on her face. "I don't want to know. I don't want to know where you went, I don't want to know what made you send me fucking divorce papers instead of helping your hurt wife like any decent man would, and I sure as fuck don't need to know why you're here now. I. Don't. Want. To. Know."

"We *need* to talk..." His voice was soft as he looked up at her with uncertain eyes.

Fuck that. Charlie knew what he was doing; working his charm on her like he always managed in the past. Too bad for him, she was long over it. She couldn't care less if he was hurting.

Sucks to suck.

"No, we really don't. Bye, Brian." She slammed the door in his face and locked it.

She stepped back from the door as an overwhelming sense of sadness struck her. This was not how she wanted to start the morning, especially after such a good dream. She glanced down at her arm, remembering the strange mark stuck to her skin.

If it even *was* a dream.

Charlie closed her eyes and drew in a few slow breaths, pushing down the swell of overwhelming emotions with every inhale and trying to blow away the bullshit with every exhale. There was a small part of her that really did want to talk to Brian, but she was so far beyond forgiving and forgetting. The hurt and betrayal had taken root deep within her bones, growing into real hatred.

Yes, there were still parts that wanted to love her best friend from childhood, to forgive everything he'd done and go back to eagerly waiting for him to come home and kiss her. But what good did wishing do?

She'd wasted days, years even, trying to figure out what she had done wrong. What fatal flaw she could have fixed in herself to keep him from leaving.

Not today. She wasn't going to let her heart suffer again by falling down that dark sucking hole of self-pity. Not right now, and hopefully not ever again. What she *needed* to do was cure the angry hangover pawing at her brain. Everything else could come after.

Her phone rang from the other room, giving her a much-appreciated break from the dark twisty place her thoughts were leading her to. Taking one final deep breath, she went to her bedroom and snatched it up.

Unknown Caller. Not totally unusual given her job. Sometimes the people that gave her tips preferred to be unknown, which meant lots of private numbers.

Shaking her arms, she tried to loosen up and center herself before answering. "Hello?"

"Good morning, Ms. Brant."

Her eyes grew as that gentle accent registered in her brain. Charlie wasn't exactly sure what to say but could certainly feel her cheeks burning red hot.

"Cat caught your tongue?" A soft chuckle came through. "Or perhaps something else is bothering you?"

He sounded so innocent, and yet somehow not all at the same time.

Charlie rolled her eyes, trying to ignore the unsettling feeling growing in the pit of her stomach. "No, I'm fine. Just trying to understand why in God's name everyone insists on talking to me so painfully early."

"Oh, please," he said, almost sounding disgusted, "don't bring *him* into this. I was hoping for a pleasant conversation."

"*Him*, who?" Charlie asked, looking back to the door she'd left Brian behind.

"God."

Charlie stood silently for a moment, before moving to her kitchen. It was becoming obvious that coffee would be a serious need for this call. Anything to wake her up and put as much distance between her and last night's steamy dream as she could manage.

"I told you yesterday I can't help you, so why are you calling?" She walked her coffee pot to the sink and filled it up.

"Straight to the point. I like women who know what they want..." he prattled on. Charlie could almost see the grin spreading across his face right now. After her dreamy exploits, his face was practically burnt into her brain. Whether she liked it or not. "Just like last night."

Water sloshed out of the top of the carafe as she jerked to an abrupt stop at those words. Charlie's eyes narrowed. "What did you say?"

"I'd like to invite you to talk." His voice was less playful than it was moments ago. Unease crept over her, making it hard to concentrate.

She was still dreaming. That explained the weirdness of the morning. First, she was in her old house with Brian, then she was getting down and dirty with some weird, albeit cute, dude that showed up at her job.... Brian randomly showed up first thing, and now the guy again... She was still asleep, and all of this was some weird kind of lucid dreaming.

Dreaming brought on by a serious need to get laid, as Carmen would put it.

"I didn't lose you now, did I?" That hint of playfulness was back, and Charlie looked at her phone. Was this guy for real? Even in her dreams, he was obnoxious as hell.

"No..."

"It's not, you know."

"Not what?"

"A dream," he said simply. "If it were, the phone would be in bed with you, and you'd be telling me all sorts of naughty tidbits while I..."

The phone clattered to the floor as she took a step back, barely managing to put the coffee pot down without making a mess. She stared at it lying there like it was diseased, or would turn into a frog, or some other impossible shit that was one-thousand percent more possible than what was happening right now.

How had he known she was thinking that?

Or... maybe that's exactly what would happen in a dream.

Or maybe she was simply losing her shit.

Yes. That.

When the phone didn't throw itself at her with a shiny new set of razor-sharp teeth, she let out a shaky breath and picked it back up. She was almost afraid to put it back to her ear, staring at it as she slid into a kitchen stool. When she finally did, his calm and casual tone greeted her again.

"Meet me at the Cathedral. I'll be waiting." The phone beeped as the call ended.

Charlie stared into space for a good long moment, letting it all soak in. This was just not possible.

She set her phone down on the counter and continued staring at it. Maybe everyone was right. Maybe Charlotte Brant had finally cracked... living in some weird state of insanity she would never be able to claw her way out of.

No, forget that. She wasn't about to allow some freak show to undo all the progress she'd made.

Was this a good idea, meeting this creep somewhere? No. It probably wasn't, but how could she possibly walk away without getting answers. What she needed was logic and reason and facts. Needed to make sense of the nonsensical. Or she could go on thinking she was crazy.

He had her, and he knew it. Luckily for her, he'd opted for a public place. Point for him. Still, she couldn't fully shake the unease gnawing away at her.

"Fuck." Charlie snatched up her phone, with its lovely new crack on the screen—because of course--and headed to get dressed.

What does one wear when meeting their dreamland sex toy at a church anyway?

Chapter 6

Charlie

OF COURSE. WHEN SHE wanted to get somewhere quickly, that was when everyone and their mother decided to take a leisurely walk through the streets of NOLA. Charlie weaved her way through groups of bodies loitering around the sidewalks, taking pictures, waiting in ridiculously long line for mediocre food, or just too drunk to know what direction they were going. Fucking tourists. The joys of living in a vacation hot spot.

Not that she really wanted to do this, but then when was what she wanted ever taken into account? The Fates were funny like that. Between not knowing what was waiting for her, the strange black mark on her arm, her Pornhub-worthy dream, the hangover, and Brian's bullshit visit this morning, she had more than enough reasons to be distracted and disgruntled.

The hangover alone should have kept her home and flipping the world off. If this was any other situation, she was certain she'd laugh it off and do just that. However, that curious cat deep inside Charlie wanted answers and wouldn't let her brain rest until she had them. It was downright irritating.

She spent her walk volleying back and forth trying to convince herself that all this was some weird illusion, that she was being tricked by some sort of street magician.

There was also a somewhat less solid theory of her being pranked by Carmen on some weird TV show. The more she entertained that particular theory, the easier it was to dismiss. Carmen was by no means like that. Not at all. Plus, the whole Brian thing? Yeah, she couldn't find any rhyme or reason in all of it so Charlie hoped that this dude had some sort of answer to all this mess.

Charlie stopped in front of the Saint Louis Cathedral, craning her neck to stare up at looming steeples. She was in no hurry to get inside, but what good would it do her to stop now? She had to face this demon eventually.

An ironic thought, seeing how she was going into a church. Charlie was by no means a religious woman. Sometimes she was spiritual, but that was as far as it went.

When your mother is very spiritual and extremely anti-organized religion it tends to flavor your upbringing. Her dad was all about guns and hunting, which he passed on to her brother. They always got to go hunting together while she stayed home with their mom, never allowed to go.

It was the whole reason she ended up as a detective. Sort of a friendly "fuck you" towards her dad for not letting her into their special boys club. She went and joined one of her own.

The grand entrance of the Cathedral was impressive architecturally speaking, but it didn't really make Charlie awestruck like most of the tourists that were often found inside. To some it was a holy wonder. To her it was just another room.

She scanned the sanctuary, taking note of how un-usually empty the place was until her eyes came across the familiar suit standing near the pulpit. He had his hands shoved into his black suit pockets, staring up at the center statue raised above the pulpit. Charlie remembered it as one of the three virtues that looked down upon the congregation, the middle one being Faith.

A soft snort escaped her before she could stop herself. With a guilty glance around her, she checked if anyone had noticed. Realizing no one had heard it, she took a deep breath and headed towards him. Her chest was going wild as the fight or flight crept in.

He seemed entranced by the statue as she walked up behind him. When he finally moved, it was to slide his hand from his pocket and lift it. She wouldn't have expected him to be the religious type—then again, she was really only going off of a dream guy. A literal figment of an overactive, wildly impaired, and seriously sex-deprived imagination.

She stopped moving, giving him a moment to finish the Sign of the Cross. It was one of many Catholic things she didn't understand but figured it would be rude to interrupt. At least, that's what she had thought he was about to do, but his hand continued to raise higher until his arm was fully extended towards the virtue of Faith. His middle finger followed suit shortly after.

Well, alrighty then.

"Ms. Brant."

Her eyes were already wide as she watched him give the statue the one-finger salute, but they grew even larger when he called out her name.

"Glad you could join me." He turned, and it felt like it was slow motion, and flashed her that devilish grin.

"What can I say, I'm a sucker for intrigue... or whatever." Her voice was flat and emotionless, belying the words and attempting to drive home just how unamused she was at the whole thing. "So, are you going to give me a name?

This is the second time we've met, and I still don't know what to call you."

"Second?" he asked, his grin curling even more. "Did our last encounter really leave such a forgettable impression, Charlotte?"

Again, the fact that he seemed to know she'd dreamt about him unnerved her. More confused than ever, she glared at him, quickly growing tired of the mind games. On the plus side, she wasn't exactly freaking out. Yet.

"Who are you?" she asked again.

"Getting existential, are we? I mean, does anyone really know who they are?"

Charlie turned on her heel and started heading for the door. She was done. He was walking her in circles, and she still had no clue why. Scratch that. She didn't care anymore.

"Do you really think you could handle it?" His voice called out to her, stopping her a few feet away. "You've had hints already. Tiny microscopic truths just waiting for you to riddle it out. Come *onnnn*, detective. Detect."

Her hands strangled the air in front of her and she whipped around again, locking onto him and closing the distance once more. As she reached him, her finger lashed out, poking him hard in the chest.

"Enough. I barely know you and I am already sick of your shit. Tell me who you are or I am out of here and I promise you the next time you contact me you are gonna need more than pithy words to hide behind."

He stared down at her finger, his grin unwavering. "Feisty. You know, I'm beginning to think maybe you can't handle it after all."

"Try me." The way she said it was not the confused woman that approached him before. No, she was pissed and wanting to go home and forget about the last 24 hours.

He chuckled as he stepped closer to her, pushing back against the finger still poking him, but Charlie stood her ground. His head tilted to the side as he scanned her face. "Be very careful what you ask for. You just might get it."

Her jaw tightened and for a brief moment, she regretted asking. It faded as quickly as it came. As far as she was concerned, ugly truths were better than pretty lies.

A scream echoed in the sanctuary, bouncing off the high arches and gilded walls. The few people with them inside the cavernous church began moving, crowding around the source of the noise. On instinct, Charlie turned to see what was going on as the small crowd's voices of alarm began overlapping with one another.

"Is that blood?"

A Deacon shouted, "Dear God! What evil is this?!"

Her feet automatically began to move toward the crowd, but before she could take more than a couple of steps, a hand grabbed her waist. She turned back to look at the man. His eyes had turned a golden hue, shining like the tiny flames on the candles surrounding the pulpit. It was quite alluring to see, like something out of a cheesy fantasy novel.

Her breath caught in her throat as he pulled her closer to him. She didn't get the chance to pull back before darkness swallowed them up.

Charlie pushed at him as she stumbled and fell on her ass. They were now in a new place, somewhere she didn't recognize. The room was quite grand with red cascading curtains covering the tall windows. The tiled floor surrounded her with intricate designs that spiraled toward the center of the room. A strange chair sat on a dais, beside it a very large fireplace blocked off by an iron gate. A burgundy carpet, stretched toward the chair. There was only one way to describe this room: a throne room fit for a king.

The man moved behind her, pulling her attention away from her surroundings and back to him again. He held out a hand towards her and Charlie wasn't sure if she should take it. Her mind felt scrambled as it tried to understand that she was no longer at the cathedral and now in some weird room with only him. She took in several breaths before finally caving at the patient man who had his arm outstretched towards her still.

"My name is Lucifer."

Now standing, Charlie snatched her hand back as she continued to stare at him. He had a smile on his face as he turned and walked towards a tall cabinet near the fireplace. He set out two cups and started to pour a golden liquid into each glass.

"Wow. Your parents must have really hated you. Okay, *Lucifer*," she said in a deceptively calm tone. In truth, she was far from calm. "Where the fuck am I?"

It seemed like a more logical question to bring up instead of further inquiring about his name. She was still looking around the room, not quite sure what the hell was going on.

"The Morningstar?" He turned to face her, the bottle hesitating momentarily over the second glass. His eyes fixated on her, as though he were waiting for a reaction.

A laugh burst out of her, short and abrupt. "Right. Okay. I get it now. Nice to meet you, *Lucifer Morningstar*. Oh Boy. So, is this some kind of cosplay thing, or like... one of those Live Action Roleplay things? I mean, I get it, it's a pretty good show and all, but I didn't expect someone your age to be such a serious fanboy."

His face was void of any and all amusement as she went on, that twinkle of mischief he always seemed to carry nowhere in sight at that moment.

"Fanboy?" He groaned, setting the bottle back down with an unceremonious *thunk*, rolling his eyes up at the sky. "I really should be getting some sort of royalties. No one is ever going to take me seriously again."

"Alright, so... Have fun with that. Hope your little fantasies were played out to your liking. I'm just gonna... find my way home and pray I forget all of this. Thanks," Charlie said, looking around for the exit.

Man, he really put a lot of time and money into this staging.

"Mmm, not quite. This is not the type of fantasies I'd want you to have. As I told you before, I keep my promises. And I never lie." Lucifer wagged his finger side to side as he approached her with two glasses in hand.

"No, see, this can't be real." She said flatly as she stepped back away from him. "Because Lucifer—the Devil—he's not real."

He was suddenly in her face, staring down at her with a look of impatience.

"I'm very real, Charlotte," he said, his voice even and neutral, yet somehow still incredibly menacing.

It stunned her silent for a brief moment, and she had to mentally coax her heart out of her throat. He was lucky she controlled her fight mode. She could have easily decked him in response—and were it anyone else she might have—but flight was definitely winning that particular race.

"What do you want with me?" Her tongue flickered across the bottom of her lip after mustering the courage that was trying to hide away.

"Ah, well, I want to get to know you. You're quite the interesting girl."

He held one of the glasses out to her and she grabbed it carefully, as if scared it would explode at her touch.

"An interesting *girl*? I'm sorry, do you see me in pigtails skipping rope right now?" The flash of a grin he gave made her hold a finger up between them, stopping whatever it was he might have been gearing up to say. She might not have known this guy long, but she'd picked up on a few things about him.

His inability to refrain from saying something inappropriate, for one.

"Allow me to save you a lot of trouble. I'm not interesting. I'm just someone who goes to work, goes home, and occasionally diverts from that eternally looping cycle to grab a drink. If you're looking for interesting, go stalk someone else. I'm no one. I'm just... *me*."

"I think we both know better than that," Lucifer said as he stalked away from her toward a large throne.

There was a throne. Of course there was.

"Okay, then clue me in. What makes me so interesting to the *Unholy One*?" She didn't even attempt to hide the snark as she said it. As he moved to sit, she set her glass down on the floor and walked closer.

Why would the Devil take notice of someone like her? She wasn't evil. She wouldn't even call herself evil-lite. Good grades, pretty good child growing up, kind to animals, an officer upholding the law.

Well, at least she used to be.

She hadn't killed anyone, not even in the line of duty. Her marriage had been a loyal and committed one. She had earned everything she had with blood, sweat, and tears.

Maybe a little too much blood and tears if she were being totally honest.

If Charlie was guilty of anything, it was how badly she doubted herself. She was the one who nearly got herself killed. The one who allowed her emotions to drive her over the edge and cost her the job she loved...the man she loved. Why would the Devil himself care to get to know such a spectacular failure like her?

Lucifer stared down at her from his perch, a grin sliding on his face. Apparently, he didn't want to share that information with her and that stirred up another twinge of anger.

Charlie stepped forward. "Fine, don't tell me. But you had no right abducting me to wherever the hell this is. I don't care who you are, you should be ashamed. Kidnapping, invading my dreams..." her face flushed a bright shade of red as the words fell out.

"My dear Ms. Brant; Shame is not exactly a word one would associate with someone like me. Besides, you didn't seem to mind my presence last night." He brought the glass up to his lips as he unfolded the truth like dirty laundry. "This may come as a surprise, but I can do whatever I want."

"Because you're the Devil? You like to torment people?"

"I love how mortals paint such a darling picture of me–" He pinched the bridge of his nose as though fighting off a headache. "No, Charlotte. Because I marked you and therefore that makes you mine until I see fit."

"*Yours*? I may not be some devout Christian, or Catholic, or whatever, but I'd hardly say I deserve eternal damnation. I'm not something you can just claim because you're bored, *Lucifer*."

"You invited me into your dreams and happily accepted what I offered. More than happily, actually. Dare I say, you've always welcomed me with wild enthusiasm. You sort of did this to yourself."

"*So* didn't invite you. And I hardly think I accepted it, considering we don't exactly have control over our dreams."

"Of course you do. It's your brain, isn't it? Your subconscious? What you do in your dreams is always embedded in some form of truth; abstract or otherwise. I may be able to pop in and out as I please, but I find it much more entertaining to let you humans take the wheel. See what decadent little adventures you're hiding deep in that psyche of yours."

Charlie glowered at him, meeting his self-satisfied smirk with a bemused frown. He was hardly discouraged by it. If nothing else, his smile seemed to curl even more as he pushed himself from his seat and casually stepped back to her, hands tucked in his pockets.

"Come on, Charlotte. Admit it. You've had a taste, but you want the full meal. Your soul is begging me to expose parts of you still trapped by shame and propriety. Parts that have been hiding an insatiable appetite for darkness in all its delicious forms. All you need to do is ask and I will rip your shame open and leave your truth bare to the world."

A sharp metallic click echoed around them, the barrel of her gun pressing to the underside of his chin. They both stilled instantly, locking eyes.

"When I tell you that I am *done* with this shit..." she warned through gritted teeth.

Lucifer's eyes wrinkled in the corners as his smile returned. "Ballsy. You really do underestimate how incredibly interesting you are." His hand wrapped around the barrel, positioning it for a more proper kill shot. "Pull the trigger. I dare you."

"Think I won't?" she asked, her voice shaky. She swallowed past the tightness in her throat, feeling her pulse race painfully in her chest. Could she actually do it?

"I think you *can't*."

The explosion echoed painfully in her ears, pieces of plaster raining down behind him. She breathed hard and measured as she stared at Lucifer, his eyes stretched wide in surprise. When she pulled the gun away, there was a tiny hole left in its wake. No blood. The hole quickly closed up, leaving the skin fresh and unmarred. The bullet had gone right through him and he was smiling down at her with a crazed look.

"Yes!" he shouted on the edge of a laugh. Charlie turned away from him, trying to calm her breathing, her gun held loosely at her side. Applause erupted behind her in slow, steady beats. "That... dear Charlotte... is exactly what makes you so intriguing. However, I think you've had enough truth for today, wouldn't you say? Hopefully, our next date will be just as exciting. But for now..."

He grabbed her hand, making her turn around to face him. With a soft press of lips to her knuckles, he grinned. "Get some rest. Take a bath, clear your head. You'll be hearing from me again soon enough. Then, we can talk business."

Chapter 7

Charlie

NO MATTER HOW TIGHTLY Charlie gripped her steering wheel, she couldn't stop the uncomfortable shaking in her hands. The moment she'd appeared in her car, she'd distanced herself from her own gun, throwing it in her glove box like a dirty secret. Her knuckles went white from the sheer grip she had on the wheel, and she tried to clear her mind of everything that had happened.

One minute she had been with Lucifer and the next the electric vibration of the French Quarter was zipping around her and her car, business as usual.

This day had been an absolute nightmare. One that never seemed to end, and it wasn't even noon yet. Just when she thought she'd dealt with the most unnerving thing she would—Oh would you look at that, it got worse. Surely meeting the actual Prince of Darkness was it. She had finally hit peak what-the-fuckery.

A flash of red and blue appeared in her rearview mirror. Apparently, she had not. Of course. Why not?

Defeat left her on the back of a deep sigh. She went through the motions: pulling the car over, grabbing for her wallet, pulling out the things the cop would need, so on and so forth, but as she looked towards the side view mirror her mouth dropped. Aggravated as all hell, she pushed the button and waited for the window to roll all the way down.

"Are you stalking me now?"

"We seriously need to talk, Charlie," Brian pleaded, leaning on her car to face her.

"Everyone wants to talk today..." She said under her breath. A morning visit from Brian, a little light kidnapping from Lucifer, and now back to Brian. She leveled him with an exhausted stare. "You really like to abuse your power don't you. First, illegally getting my address, and now pulling me over just so you can catch up with an old flame."

"Actually, you were going about 10 under the speed limit." He risked a grin as he said it, his tone made it clear he was getting impatient with her. On the bright side, if there was one, a small part of her was glad to see him. Brian had always been her knight in shining armor, and after the experience she'd had with Lucifer a familiar face was more than welcome.

"Fine, we'll talk." Charlie hated caving in, but he really didn't give her any choice. She was exhausted and the familiar throb of an oncoming hangover was rearing its ugly head. She wanted to run away from all the bullshit. Maybe get away from the city for a day or two and collect herself. But leaving town could wait until he was done spewing his guts. He finally wanted to what, talk? Fine. "Where?"

"I was hoping over dinner? My treat."

Her eyes flashed toward him with full-on rage and he must have taken notice because his hands quickly shot up in front of him as a means to halt her from saying anything else.

He clarified, "Not a date, just friends having dinner and talking."

"Friends... not the word I'd use to describe our current relationship." She glared at him before looking away. Charlie hoped her words stung whatever wounds he may have had. Brian's body language screamed "victim" which made her blood boil.

He was the one who left. He was the one who ripped her heart from her chest and danced on its remains. The victim here was not him, and though she may have been at one point since this whole mess began, she was never going to let herself become one again. Not if she could help it.

She spotted a burger joint down the street. "How about lunch," Charlie's head nodded towards the direction of where it was located. "We'll have it there."

Fifteen minutes of silent glaring later, Charlie was sitting across from Brian. As much comfort as he once was, there was nothing comfortable about this whole situation, and she was getting increasingly agitated with having to deal with it. If he was going to stay silent, then she had better places to be. Places far from pissed off best friends, infuriating exes, and psychotic devils. She waited for him to expel his grand apology, but he sat there practically twiddling his thumbs.

Her knee bounced under the table; arms crossed over her chest as her brows knitted together watching him. Every second of silence only served to nudge her closer to the edge of completely losing her shit on him.

"Look–"

"Finally, he speaks!" She steamrolled over him, not allowing him to finish whatever it was he had been working up the courage to say.

He'd had plenty of time—well beyond the last fifteen minutes they'd been sitting there—to figure out whatever it was he wanted to say. The fact that he had jumped headfirst into having this little talk, without even having prepped for it, only told her that in the last five damn years he'd been gone he had not once thought of apologizing. Or even explaining why he did what he did.

If it had been her—and let the record show it *never* would have been—she'd have at least had the courtesy to feel like a piece of shit for hurting someone she loved. She'd have known, in great fucking detail, exactly what she would want to say to him. So yeah, maybe she wasn't being very forgiving. He could get over it.

Those blue hues turned icy as they narrowed in on her. Finally, anger. Good. Seeing the boy scout act like a wounded animal was getting pitiful and if he was going to get rowdy, it gave her all the more reason to unload on him guilt-free.

Of course, much to her annoyance, Brian waited for a moment and let the anger in his eyes seep away before continuing, "I know you paint me as the enemy. You have every right to. I really wish I could explain more, Charlie. I need you to know it's not your fault."

"Are you fucking kidding me? I've been waiting for five years and," she looked at her watch, "fifteen minutes for you to finally, *finally*, explain yourself. You literally wasted my time, dragged me on this little "friend-date" to tell me you *can't* explain the bullshit you pulled? Then, like it's some consolation prize, you have the audacity to tell me it's not my fault? Well, guess what? I *know* it's not my fucking fault. And I'm not fucking consoled."

Carmen would have applauded her for finally letting him have it, and for calling him out for the bastard he was, but Charlie couldn't find the joy in the moment. Not when she was still reeling at how clueless he seemed to be.

"You know Brian, I spent months, *years*, dealing with what happened. I tried to figure out what I did wrong. Why I deserved to be abandoned by the one man who promised me he'd be with me forever. You know... *Through sickness and health*."

"I hurt you and I regret it every day, but you have to accept that I didn't want to." He was going stony. Un-readable. She hated that probably more than she hated him looking hurt.

Charlie had been a good wife. She never questioned Brian, never thought she needed to. She remained loyal even in those painfully lonely moments that had made so many other military wives break. No matter the struggle, her heart stayed fully in their marriage. So, seeing him act his abandonment was no big deal...it was the worst sort of betrayal.

"I don't have to accept shit from you. You're not my problem anymore." Her tone was very even as the waiter came over to fill their glasses. She still hadn't ordered any-thing. It wasn't exactly like she was hungry. Though the thought of ripping into a cheeseburger—rather than his throat—was probably not a terrible idea.

"Problem? Is that what you really think of me, then?" he asked.

She'd hoped to hear even the slightest bit of hurt in his voice, some kind of sign that she had managed to hurt him as he'd hurt her, but his voice remained neutral and steady. He was acting like a light switch, flipping between hurt and emotionless. She was annoyed, then immediately hated herself for wanting him to hurt so badly. It wasn't in her nature to be cruel, even to someone she pretended to hate. She just didn't have it in her.

He didn't want him to hurt, not truthfully. She wanted him to own up to what he had done to her. To do more than just say he was sorry. Charlie wanted real honesty. A real answer.

"Look, I get it. After what you went through... what you must be thinking..." His eyes wouldn't meet hers, focusing intently on his untouched water glass.

"You have no idea what I went through, Brian," Charlie said softly. She could feel the lump growing painfully in her chest. "You'd have had to stick around to know that sort of thing."

"I wanted to," he said, and the lump shot into her throat. "But things happened and–"

"And you decided you couldn't handle it. Answer me this, though: You and I both had an understanding. An agreement, before we even got married. We knew what we were getting into, knew our jobs came with risks. We promised each other we could handle it. Was all that just empty words to you?"

Brian licked his lips as she talked, and she found herself staring at them a little too long, a little too longingly. What she wouldn't give for the last five years to have been nothing more than a terrible, awful nightmare so she could wake up and kiss this man again. But it wasn't, and she couldn't.

Charlie did, however, reach for the glass of water and took a sip. When she sat it back down, she left her arm on the table and began to fool around with a napkin, trying to distract herself from reaching over the table and kissing him... or choking him.

"When did you get a tattoo?"

"Oh, you know, a wild night in Vegas, hanging with the girls, getting white-girl wasted and then making more regretful mistakes seeing as I have all this free time now." She made no attempt to hide the sarcasm that dripped off her tongue as she presented a sweet delicate smile that did not match her tone.

His face hardened, his eyes glued to the intricate symbol sketched on her arm. Feeling self-conscious, she tried to pull it towards herself but he grabbed hold of her arm and held it in place. His thumb brushed against her soft skin, skimming over the geometric markings like he'd recognized it.

"What is it?" she asked.

"We need to go."

Her brow rose as she looked at him like he lost his damn mind.

"We? Since when were we a *we* again? You're free to leave anytime you want. God knows you have plenty of practice. In fact, fuck you. You don't get to boss me around anymore." Charlie pulled her arm back from his grasp. "And I sure as hell am not going anywhere with *you*."

Brian abruptly stood up, towering over her. He tossed a few bills down before making his way towards her side of the table and grabbing her hand. She jerked it back, but he flashed her a look she'd never been on the receiving end of before. It was his stubborn you're-gonna-back-down-before-I-will, no negotiations look. It matched one of her very own.

After a few seconds of silently glaring at each other, he offered his hand and waited for her to accept. The way he was acting there was no doubt in her mind that he'd throw her over his shoulders if he had to. He'd done it before, playfully. But that was then, this is now. There were zero hints of playfulness behind that stoney face.

Cursing under her breath she stood, smacking his hand out of the way, and headed towards the front door. He was tailing behind, practically herding her towards the exit. "I can take my car."

He ignored her completely, blocking her from moving to her own car and using his body to direct her towards his. With a roll of her eyes, she stopped at the passenger door and crossed her arms. He opened the door and silently guided her inside.

When she got settled in, she turned to glare at him but got no reaction as the door was shut in her face. Charlie did *not* appreciate being ignored, especially with her anxiety starting to climb. Even more so, she hated being bossed around, whether verbally or non-verbal.

When he got in, he locked the doors and her anxiety spiked, smoothing over some of the irritation to make way for a growing concern. "Brian, what's going on? Where the hell are we going?" She could hear the panic in her own voice, which only made everything feel worse.

"Charlotte." He tossed a glance her way. "For once, be quiet... please."

The fact he used her real name gave her pause. She could see so many emotions swimming around on that face of his, so for once, Charlie actually stayed quiet as he peeled out of the parking lot. Whether she liked it or not, she was stuck with him for now.

The drive was filled with even more silence, Charlie's arms crossed over her chest as she stared out the window of the car, her fingers brushing idly over the mark that had set Brian off in a tailspin.

How exactly do you tell someone you met the Devil? The *actual* Devil. Lucifer had said it when they were in his little throne room. He'd marked her. She was *his*. What the hell did that even mean? How was she expecting to explain any of this to Brian when she herself barely understood? Then again, did Brian even deserve to be looped in? Mr. Absentee Lover, swooping into her life when she had finally found the smallest shred of normalcy again?

What did it say about Charlie that she couldn't tell who was the worst option between her ex-husband and Lucifer himself?

Her patience was running very thin and she found it increasingly harder to hold in the anxiety building inside. She watched the world outside the car window change from city to marsh, then to god-knows-where. She chewed on the bottom of her lip again, hoping to keep her internal tirade from spilling out a little bit longer, until she realized she was tasting the metallic sharpness of blood. She'd been doing that a lot lately–a nasty nervous habit that the past several hours had sent into overdrive.

Switching to biting on the edge of her fingernails to give her lip a rest, she tried to center herself with a deep breath that just wasn't doing the job. They had been driving for over a half-an-hour already and she wasn't sure if she could handle the silent treatment another minute.

"Dude. Where the fuck are you taking me?" She finally broke the silence.

Brian pulled up to an old run-down shack that raised more questions than answers. The car had hardly parked before she got out. Okay, *stormed* out.

The building across from them looked long-forgotten. Untouched in ages. It was the polar opposite of everything she knew about her ex-husband: Run down, disorderly, a mess. Why the hell would he be hiding out in a place like this?

Hands on her hips, she turned and stared at him over the top of the car. "Listen, I am not going into that death-trap. Not until you start fucking talking."

Brian simply grumbled in response and came around the car to meet her unmoving form. Unmoving, that is, until he literally grabbed her and threw her over his shoulder.

"Put me down!" she screamed, kicking and hitting his back. It was like hitting a statue.

He groaned lightly in protest of her hitting him, but all-in-all seemed mostly unphased by it. "Will you just shut up for a damn moment?"

Brian had never told her to shut up before. Part of her felt he was lucky she didn't have her gun on her, while the other half was stunned silent. He seemed to take it as a small victory.

Charlie, however, had grown mentally exhausted by all this abduction today. When the fuck did, she become Princess Peach?

He carried her through the rotting door of the shack, down a set of cement steps darkened with years-old mud and grime. The confusion was enough to keep her obediently quiet until they reached the landing. Brian set her back on her feet next to a large metal door that seemed extremely out of place among the surrounding building, then proceeded to place his hand on a small screen on the wall next to it. The door hissed as it unlocked and opened for him, revealing red flickering lights that saturated the room in a foreboding way. He grabbed Charlie's hand and tugged her inside before a disembodied voice boomed overhead.

"Welcome back Major Hart, armed and ready for execution lockdown. Tango. Zulu. Foxtrot. Tack. Zero. Zero. One. Shall I proceed?" The voice was robotic while somehow still sounding human.

Brian cleared his throat before speaking, "Negative. Abort operation."

Charlie literally stood in complete shell-shock as she witnessed the whole thing go down. When the lights turned white, lighting up the room to actually see where things were, her mouth dropped even further. Along the back wall were all sorts of assorted weapons, things that even a Marine shouldn't have access to. She couldn't even decide where to look, but her eyes finally locked in on a bookshelf filled with old books. Again, something Brian had never really been into.

She seemed to be discovering all sorts of things about the man.

On the other side of the room was a small kitchenette with a table for two. Closer to the center of this windowless room there was a plain white couch. She noticed a door in the back and imagined it led to a bedroom, or bathroom, or both.

"Now what?" she said as she continued to check out the strange surroundings. "You have me all to yourself. You gonna chop me up into bite-sized Charlie pieces or go Buffalo Bill on me?"

Large, muscular arms, wrapped around her, and she tensed instantly. She had only been joking before, but the instant he grabbed her, her mind jumped to the thought that he was actually about to go full blown serial killer on her before she registered the gentle nature of his embrace. As her panic started to slide away, she found herself loosening up a little.

Those warm and cozy feelings she got when he held her started to come back. For a brief millisecond, it felt right, but she quickly broke free and turned to face him. "You've seriously lost your damn mind."

"I'm sorry." He was a little too calm for her comfort as he spoke again. "You'll be safe here for now."

"Safe?" Charlie raised a hand to her face as she tried to hide a hysterical laugh from escaping.

If only he knew who she had met earlier today.

His face contorted with confusion, as he tried to reach his hand toward her. She jerked her shoulder back, not wanting to be touched as the tears started to seep from her eyes. She finally hit it. She finally hit her breaking point.

Brian was persistent, however, and he stepped forward wrapping his arms around Charlie again, holding her tight. Her head nestled into his chest. Fuck it. She needed something familiar to let it all out. If she had her bed, she'd be hiding there with all her blankets and pillows. For now, Brian would have to do. He wasn't exactly soft, but he had the best damn hugs that made her feel like nothing could ever harm her. She missed this the most as she inhaled his scent. He still had that earthy scent, one that smelt like rain.

"Shh. Shh. It's ok Charlie." His hand rubbed softly on her back as fat tears spilled out of her.

She hated feeling so helpless around him. Charlie made herself believe she was no longer that woman that he had fallen in love with, that she was less than her former self. The woman he had married was a fierce, formidable force of nature. Very little scared her and even less stopped her when she set her mind to something. Now, she was a shell of that woman. And so much scared her, but nothing scared her so much as herself.

With his gentle gesture, she was transported to the past. To a time when the world made absolute sense. For someone who wanted the divorce, he sure wasn't acting like he hated her. It was confusing at best.

The tears eased into hitching gasps as she pushed back a little to look up at those sharp, yet familiar features. The ocean blue eyes that had swept her heart away among the currents long ago stared deeply into her. She could almost melt in his arms right then and there. He was once her kryptonite.

And maybe still was.

"So, umm... what exactly are you keeping me safe from?" There was a very half-hearted attempt to lighten the mood and an attempt to distract herself from doing something stupid.

"You're going to think I'm crazy." He gave her a half-hearted grin.

"What's new? Oh wait... Nevermind that's me." They both chuckled. Not because any of this was funny but because this was probably the most awkward situation they found themselves in.

Had he heard about Charlie's "mental break" after he left? He had been in and out of the precinct for who knows how long before she discovered him. Certainly, someone would have questioned him about what set her off.

"I want to tell you everything, but if I do, you'd be worse off from whoever put that mark on you." He caressed her cheek, and she pushed her head into it on instinct.

This was going to get dangerous quickly, and exactly why she'd have preferred to meet in a public place. She could control herself in public. Privacy made all those old feelings feel so much more alive, so much heavier and harder to ignore. Swallowing hard, she moved her head away from his hand and stepped back.

"All these secrets. Is it really best to keep me in the dark? Is it actually going to keep me from the bad shit if I don't know what to watch out for?" Charlie avoided his eyes, not wanting to be swept away again.

When he didn't answer, she pushed more, waving her hand around the room around them. "Clearly, we are in some sort of James Bond 007 safe house. Neat." She stepped forward to the bookcase and read some of the book titles. "You've also seemed to take a shine to reading about the occult."

Turning back to him, she jammed all the obvious pieces of the puzzle together, knowing she was about to risk sounding absolutely insane. "Super-secret spy stuff... niche research topics. I guess you fancy yourself some sort of paranormal researcher? You know. Vampires, werewolves, all that oogie-boogie stuff."

The place gave her an overwhelming sense of Déjà vu. The fact was as she looked closer it wasn't too unlike her dad's office back home. The few times she'd managed to sneak in there, she had seen more than a few weird things.

Her eyes swept over to the array of weapons on the wall again. Some were incredibly advanced-looking, others looked like they could fall apart if the wind blew right. Relics.

"No. Not a researcher," she said way more calmly than she probably had any right to. "Hunter."

"You've always been good at your job." He rubbed his jaw nervously. His poker face was excellent, but she had managed to make him twitch a little.

"Or I watch a lot of TV." Her eyes rolled rather dramatically as she made her way to the couch and plopped down on it.

"You seem strangely okay with the idea," he said carefully, mirroring her movements around the room until he stood at the end of the couch. "Shouldn't it freak you out? The idea of monsters like that existed?"

"Like I said... I've watched a lot of TV shows, read a lot of books. That's a lot of the whole 'oh, no, this can't be happening' reactions in the face of irrefutable evidence. Gets kind of boring. Predictable."

"Predictable. Well," Brian said, a soft smile forming, "no one could ever accuse you of being that."

Charlie simply outstretched her arms as if to say she accepted the statement. She was, however, very well aware that Brian had yet to affirm or deny her suppositions. "Look, I could freak out, deny the wild things that are clearly happening, pretend to be completely oblivious, or I can process it and move forward. This has been one of the strangest weeks I have ever had, and all this? Well, to be honest, if I'm right it makes me feel a little less crazy. Besides, would it do me any good to freak out?"

"No. No, it wouldn't."

"Exactly. So, okay. Let's get on with it. You're a monster hunter. Monsters exist." *Clearly*, she thought to herself as her mind went back to her meeting with Lucifer.

Out loud, she said, "I've known this since the night I was attacked. What I don't understand is, if you knew this the whole time, why didn't you have the balls to back me up? Why leave me looking like the village crazy?"

He had the grace to look embarrassed. Finally.

"I didn't want to. That's the last thing I wanted; I swear on everything. But Charlie, it's so complicated. I–" He sighed heavily. "Like I said, if I told you everything, I'd just put you in even more danger. I couldn't risk losing you, so I–" He stopped again, though it looked almost physically painful to do so. With a shake of his head, he looked down at the arm of the couch, leaning against it. "I can't put you in harm's way. I won't."

As if all the pieces started to finally fall into place, her brows knitted together, and she turned to look at him. "Brian? What exactly did you do?"

"I did what was best for you, to make sure you survived. Even if that meant selling my soul to the Devil."

She snorted and turned away. Charlie highly doubted Lucifer had any hands in any of this. Meddlesome as he may be, it just didn't track. Unless...

Her mind was a sudden whir of thought, pulling every odd thing that had happened and laying them out for her to dissect. Brian disappearing. The dream. Brian's sudden return at exactly the same time that Lucifer decided to annoy the shit out of her.

Maybe...

Leaning over with elbows on her knees and her head resting on the palm of her hands, she closed her eyes. The couch sagged beside her and she knew Brian had sat down.

"It's not what you want to hear but..."

She looked at him. He looked so conflicted right then and there.

"I never stopped loving you." He was looking at her now, the pain in his eyes telling her everything.

Charlie sat up and stared at him as if he grew a third limb. But as she stared, she realized how well she knew him, well enough to know that he was telling the truth and maybe, with all that she had seen today, he really did still love her.

All this time she thought he'd grown tired of being with her and seized an opportunity to detach. After all, being married to the town crazy surely wasn't the reputation anyone would want to be saddled with. It made the most sense for him to bug out while he could. But if he was being honest now—that he still loved her and that he felt he did the right thing by leaving when he did—Jesus, what had he actually gotten himself into? Her heart ached at the revelation. Such a truth was so much more painful than anything she'd speculated on. He was right, she didn't want to hear this.

What was she supposed to do? How was she supposed to react? The pain in her chest grew with each sharp breath. Deep down, she never stopped loving him either; it grew into hate so she could stop hurting. When he left it destroyed her, but now that she figured it out it made her feel so much worse.

"Charlie..." He said softly as he leaned in towards her. The sharp pain seemed to dissipate as the butterflies began to flutter their wings in her stomach. She didn't move, practically frozen in place from what was going on. She could feel the heat building on her face the closer he got. This should not be happening, but yet here he was closing the distance.

"Whoa there, buddy!" she exclaimed as she shot up from the couch and put as much distance between her and Brian as she could.

The butterflies in her stomach were practically doing somersaults as she stared at him, trying to keep her thoughts in check. No easy feat considering the fact that she knew every single inch of that body.

"See, this?" she said, gesturing between them, "This can't happen."

He was on his feet walking towards her, his stride slow and careful as though he were approaching a skittish fawn. Or a threatened porcupine ready to stab him if he got too close.

"Why?"

"Why what?" she shot back, taking another step back. Distance. Distance was good.

"Why can't it happen?" He cut her off before she could say exactly what they both knew. "Unless... you're seeing someone else?" He said it carefully.

Intense green eyes popped into her mind, staring up at her from between her thighs while she lost herself.

No. Get that thought out right now.

"No. I'm not seeing anyone."

A boyish smile pulled at his lips, the answer seeming to encourage him to take another step toward her.

"That doesn't mean it's game on between us," she said, taking another step back.

"It's never been a game, Charlie." His voice was soft as he said it. Almost pained. He stopped in front of her, his hand raising to push her hair from her eyes. "I've missed you. I know you've missed me."

"Gee, maybe you should have been a detective." Her sarcasm slipped out of her mouth before she could stop it, but rather than get irritated, Brian simply smiled. Though she tried to fight it, she couldn't help but smile back.

Damn him.

His fingertips brushed down her cheek, sweeping under her chin so he could rub his thumb over her lower lip. He'd done it countless times before and she had taken it for granted each time, never believing it would have been the last. Now, knowing what she did, it meant so much more.

She wrapped her hand over his, closing her eyes and letting go of a wistful sigh that she'd been holding onto far too long. She hated to admit that she'd been thinking of this moment since the day he'd left. Hated that even after all the heartbreak and suffering he put her through that one simple touch could bring her right back to sleepy Sundays and twisted sheets.

If she was a stronger woman, she'd shut him out of her life and her heart for good. But he smelled so good, and his lips—which were drawing closer—she craved those even more than her favorite morning cinnamon roll.

"Tell me you don't want this, and I'll stop," he whispered. "We can just go back to awkward conversations and mutual resentment, and maybe eventually work our way back to being friends."

"I don't want to be your friend," she breathed out in the barest whisper.

She stared up at him, seriously contemplating his offer. Tell him to back off, go back to business only while wallowing over him, and focus on figuring out the mess she'd found herself in with the crackpot Lucifer guy. That would have been the smart thing to do.

"What the hell," she breathed before grabbing his face and pulling him in for a long-overdue kiss.

His arm snaked around her waist, pulling her tight against him. He held onto her with an ironlike grip while she devoured his mouth, letting all those years of pent-up feelings pour into him with every flick of her tongue. Everything about this was a bad idea, but sometimes loneliness was so much more unbearable than the consequences.

He was the same as she remembered. The smell of his soap still clung to him so that she was brought back to a sense memory of sandalwood-scented lather sliding over both of them as she joined him in the shower. She could live off of the scent of him, roll around in it, and keep it with her. She would never admit it—not to herself, or least of all Brian—but she had missed it so much.

He smiled against her lips, knowing he'd won himself a small victory.

How long had it been since she'd taken a breath? She couldn't remember.

Releasing his mouth, she pressed her forehead to his, staring into his blue eyes, trying to catch her breath. She swallowed hard.

Five years. Five long, cold years apart. Each year stretched on longer than the previous.

His hands moved to her shirt while she remembered those lonely years without him, and the memories of the hell she'd gone through alone was like a bucket of ice water dumped over her head. She grabbed his hands in hers before he could get the shirt too far up, and shoved them away.

"No," she whispered.

The word felt like a razor cutting up her throat, digging in and not wanting to dislodge, willing to tear her apart to keep from being spoken. Brian, ever the decent guy, had dropped his hands away from her as soon as she uttered it. His face, however, showed clear unfiltered hurt.

"I don't want to be just friends. But I don't want this."

"I don't want you to not be in my life anymore," he said.

"It hurts too much, Brian."

"So we heal. We work on it until it doesn't hurt anymore."

Charlie huffed a bitter laugh, "It's that easy, is it? It will be... for you. But it's gonna take a lot more for me to just get over everything. If I ever do. You hurt me in ways no one else has ever managed. When you left you ripped my soul apart. I'm still picking up the pieces, trying to find a way to be whole again and you think we can talk it out and be okay? That we can jump into bed together and, what? It heals everything? You aren't stupid, Brian. You know that's not how it works."

"I know it's not, I'm not saying that's what we should do," he said.

"Well, actions speak louder," Charlie countered, gesturing to the space where they had just been making out. "I am barely back on track with my life. I have so fought hard to get to this point, and I am barely hanging on with rubber bands and glue. If we were to—I can't. I owe it to myself to find my happiness again and not have it be reliant on someone who could do what you did."

Charlie watched Brian carefully as she hit him with the truth. Falling into bed with Brian would have been so much easier, but then what? It wasn't worth compromising all the work she'd done for herself. Not when she couldn't be sure he wouldn't just take off on her again.

The idea of that shattered her more than the first time. To go through what she had and work so hard to find herself again, only to allow him to wreck it all in the span of a night...

No fucking way.

"So now what?" Brian asked.

She felt a breeze of relief blow through her that he wasn't going to argue with her. Taking a deep breath she crossed her arms in front of her and shrugged a shoulder.

"Dinner?" She suggested.

"I have to admit, I've kind of lost my appetite."

She gave him a look, and he shrugged back at her.

"Fine. I'm tired anyway. Should probably go home and get some sleep."

"Well, that isn't happening," he said, and Charlie looked at him like he'd lost his mind, because obviously he had. Before she could argue though, he continued. "I'm only saying, I would feel a lot better if you stayed here until we can hash out whatever is up with that mark."

Charlie glanced at her arm, remembering the events that brought her there in the first place. Right. Whatever was up with the tattoo Lucifer had given her, it rattled Brian. Which meant he could find some more answers for her. And if there was information out there, then maybe a way to get rid of it, too.

"Right. I guess you're right. Okay, I'll crash on your couch tonight. In the morning, we talk. For real this time."

He stared at her for a moment, nodding.

"I mean it. You know more than you've been letting on. I deserve to know what the hell I've got sniffing at my doorstep."

He at her as though he were weighing his options.

"Fair enough," he said finally. He dropped his shirt back onto the couch and walked up to her, tracing his fingers over the top of her forehead then down behind her ear. "But I should warn you, the couch is shit. You can sleep in my bed. I swear, I won't do anything you don't want me to do."

His boyish grin made her roll her eyes. Oh, yeah. So much innocence in that one. Still, it wasn't the worst offer. She walked past him, moving toward the bedroom door and opening it.

"You're right," she said, before shutting the door between them and locking it. "You won't."

Chapter 8

LUCIFER DIDN'T WORK HIMSELF up over humans, but there was something about Charlotte Brant that got under his skin. She had become the one human for which he made great exception. Well—close enough anyway.

In the hours following their little meeting, her emotional state had run high. He could accept blame for that. Perhaps he had been a little much with the theatrics, but she had seemed like the sort of woman who needed the truth shoved in her face before she would accept it. Actions over words.

But in the last hour or so, her energy had gone from loud and clear to absolute dead quiet. As much as he tried not to admit it, the sudden silence made him anxious. So naturally, he set about looking for her. He'd searched in all the usual places he assumed she might be but came up empty.

She was a clever woman; it was one of the things he liked about her. Maybe she'd figured out a way to remove his mark?

How annoying.

Just as he was trying to think of other more creative ways to track her, he felt a stirring. A tugging sensation in the back of his skull. She had entered the dreamscape.

"Well," he muttered to himself, "that makes things easier."

Without knowing exactly where she was, it was easier to pull her to him than to go to her. Lucifer set a scene that would be most familiar to her: a local bar that she often visited when in distress. He'd spotted her the moment she entered. After a good solid moment, those hazel eyes met him and though he gave her his most charming smile, she froze in her spot.

"We are not doing this again," Charlie said as she stepped away from him.

It truly pained him to see her react that way to his presence. He may have been *perceived* as a monster, but that was far from actually being one. Granted, he had his days, but who didn't?

The beginnings of a headache prickled at his skull. "I feel like I say this often but, you wound me Charlie."

"Apparently not enough." The woman stared at him with the deadest of expressions.

He shrugged his shoulders before gesturing to the empty table beside him. "Just a chat. Nothing more, unless of course that is your wish."

She still didn't return the smile he gave her, but then he was starting to understand that about her. Charlie was a suspicious woman. Suspicion rarely allowed one to have a sense of humor.

A chair scraped along the floor as she pulled it out, choosing the seat furthest from him. At least she was trying. That felt like a win in his book. He grinned and snapped his fingers, her favorite beverage appeared in front of her. "So, where have you wandered off to?"

A bewildered look crossed her face. "I'm right here." She gestured to their surroundings.

Lucifer couldn't help but let out a soft chuckle. He often forgot how mortal Charlie was. Unique, yes. Heart-stoppingly beautiful, without a doubt. Infuriating, absolutely. But still painfully and regrettably mortal.

Her face shifted into irritation and his smile faded slightly. He knew that look all too well. Clearing his throat, as he adjusted his tie, trying to bring back some composure. "Right, sorry. I forget sometimes that you are only human."

"Lucifer—"

He held a hand up to stop her before she continued. This woman was a complex and layered creature. Both a blessing and a curse. Some dreams she was scared to death of him and he got nowhere with her. Others she was ready to wring his neck—possibly the truest side of her now that they'd had a real face-to-face meeting for him to compare it to.

Other dreams, however... well. Let's just say, there were some fun, spontaneous, and downright sexy versions of this woman.

Either way, it took Lucifer quite some time, and no small amount of luck, to get a level-headed facet of Charlie. This was the woman who would hear him out, who could have long serious conversations with him without emotions bungling things. It would appear, he lucked out again with her tonight, as she sat and simply accepted the drink in front of her.

"I mean, where are you in the real world?"

She stared at him; it was apparent she was contemplating her answer. "Actually, I don't know."

Lucifer perked up in his chair. He dissected each little thing, her mannerisms, the tone, and the words. She wasn't pulling his leg, wasn't being coy or outright lying to him. She really had no idea where she was, which was unsettlingly alarming to him.

Especially since he couldn't find the answer through his mark.

It was as though something was causing interference between them. Like static on a television screen. If he were being completely honest with himself about it, the white noise unnerved him more than a little bit. A lot more than he was willing to let her know. In fact, he was still smiling gently at her as his worries filtered through his brain, pushing forward a face of undisturbed peace.

"No matter, really. Was curious as to what you were up to. You left in such an uncomfortable form the other day, I wanted to be sure you were alright."

She stared at him with her eyebrow lifted suspiciously. He probably earned that.

"So!" he said with a jovial grin, rubbing his hands together eagerly before grabbing his drink. "Now that I have assured you, I mean no harm, how about you let that guard of yours down and enjoy our time together? With innocent conversation." He added that last part as she looked like she was ready to argue.

"And the Devil's idea of an 'innocent' conversation?"

Lucifer stared at her with careful contemplation. "Tell me about your family—mom, dad, even little Spot?"

"Spot?" Charlie pulled a face as she grabbed for her drink. "That's one of the worst dog names ever. Just under Fido." She let out a soft chuckle.

Finally, she was relaxing. He stared at her, waiting for her to come up with a response. In the meantime, he nursed his Bahama-Mama. Some would laugh at the choice. In fact, Charlie had in a past dream. But let's be real, mixed drinks came with a punch if you had the right bartender.

"My parents... I'm sure you know their names being an all-knowing being–"

"If I was all knowing, I'd have you all figured out by now." A flirtatious grin spread across his face, especially when he saw Charlie squirm in her seat.

"As I was saying," She tossed a glare his way, but at least the smile didn't falter on her face. "My parents had been together forever, then they had Jenna. I know my mom was excited to have kids. Her kids are her pride and joy. My father is a bit different. He's a bit of a tough love sort of mentality. Then my brother, Ben, came as a surprise. Less than a year between him and our sister. They call that sort of thing Irish Twins." She let out a soft chuckle before shaking her head.

"Why is that humorous?" he asked in genuine curiosity.

She waved a dismissive hand. "If you knew how different they are, you'd understand."

"And what about the infamous Charlotte Brant?" He wiggled his brows still sporting the grin from before. "How alike or different is she?"

Though her smile stayed in place, he watched as it slid out of her eyes.

"Well, I definitely had to one-up Ben when it came to surprising everyone. Apparently, when my mom was close to her due date, they had an ultrasound to see if I had turned the right way, and..." she huffed a soft laugh. "Well, the doc had to inform them that I'd died."

Lucifer leaned forward, feeling his interest spike. "Obviously, he was mistaken."

The smile returned to her hazel eyes and she nodded, taking another drink. "Yep. Turns out I was apparently only playing dead."

"Playing dead?" His brow rose.

She giggled into her glass before taking another drink. Clearing her throat, she said with a horribly reenacted accent, "I was only *mostly* dead."

"What on earth are you talking about?" Lucifer asked, looking genuinely confused...and concerned.

A soft flush pinkened her cheeks and he watched as her entire body language shifted from almost silly confidence to embarrassment. "It's from a movie—you know what, forget it."

"No, no," he said, the corner of his mouth beginning to twist up slightly. "Please tell me."

She stared at him over her glass and he could tell she was fighting with herself whether to continue or drop the whole thing. Luckily for him, she chose to continue.

"Princess Bride? I loved that movie when I was little. I probably watched it a hundred times with my mom and Ben. The Dread Pirate Roberts is tortured to death–"

Lucifer's eyes stretched wide. "This is a children's movie?"

"—and they take his body to this woodland elf guy named Max. So, Miracle Max is like, 'He's not *dead* dead, only mostly dead,' and brings him back to life with a chocolate pill."

He watched intently as she described the scene to him, and there was great joy in her eyes as she relived the memories. That spark was exactly what he found himself fascinated by. Even if the movie sounded absolutely absurd.

"Anyway," she said, cutting herself off and redirecting the point of the matter, "as I was saying, the doctor told my mom that I had no heartbeat, and she would have to give birth because of how far along she was when I supposedly passed, but as you can see," she gestured over her very much alive self, "I popped out breathing and kicking and with a strong pulse. Gotta love when doctors scare the living shit out of you for no reason, right?"

"Right. That does sound like an ordeal," he said, though he obviously would have no experience in such things. He couldn't even remember having a runny nose.

"Right? But, obviously, it must have shaken my parents cause God forbid I scraped my knee, or like... sneezed. Shit, sorry," she said as he cringed once more at her use of his Father's name. "I did it again, didn't I?"

He paused at that, taken by surprise by her sudden concern over his comfort. That was a new one. And certainly not something he'd have expected from real-life Charlie. Though, he supposed, there was at the very least a sliver of a human's true psyche in their dream states, wasn't there?

An interesting theory to think upon.

"It's perfectly alright. I know it's a habit of yours, so no harm. Thank you for," he struggled to decide on the right word, "caring."

She rewarded that with a flippant wave of her hand as she drained the remainder of her drink and waved the empty glass in the air. "Whatever. Anyway, is that all you wanted to know?"

"No, Charlotte. I dare say, I'd love to know every little boring detail about you."

She squirmed again and he pretended not to notice as he smiled into his own glass.

"So, what else would you like to know?"

He set his own glass down, hers refilling while still clasped in her hand though she didn't take notice of it. The bartenders and other patrons were, after all, Dream Shades. Not actual living breathing beings, as realistic as they might be. Dream Shades more often than not were to blame for the chaos that happened within human dreams. They were bound by no sense of reality, and though they could make an interesting dream to think back on once the human awoke, that was not exactly how Lucifer liked for these meetings to go down. Sometimes it was for the better to keep them in the background.

"What do they do? Your parents? Are they cops, like you were?" A rather undignified snort erupted from her nose, catching him off guard. "I'm sorry, I didn't think that was that unrealistic of a question."

Charlie smiled as though she were holding onto an inside joke. One she wasn't sure she was ready to let him in on as she waved her hand dismissively in front of her face.

"No, just... definitely not cops. Mom is more of a..." she stared off at some far off point on the ceiling as she mulled it over. "I mean she's a housewife. Maybe I could consider her an activist of sorts? She likes to help people, in her own weird little way."

"What is so weird about it?"

"Well, I mean... she fancies herself a witch for one."

Lucifer gave her an impressed look. "Really? A real one?"

Charlie looked at him strangely. "As opposed to fake ones?" She thought that over a moment. "Sure. I mean she really has a bunch of weird books, she grows random plants, can't walk ten feet in our house without tripping over some sort of 'psychic rock'," she actually made finger quotes at that. "One year, she sent me a satin pouch and told me I wasn't allowed to open it—ever—but that it would protect me on the job. I still have no idea what was in it but it smelled to high heaven. There was no way I could carry that on me at work every day. I had to pitch it, though I'd never tell her that."

He cringed inwardly hearing that, but fought to keep his face neutral.

"My sister's into that stuff, too. Couldn't do it myself."

"Any particular reason why?"

"Honestly, for starters, they kind of wouldn't let me? I guess they didn't want my skepticism to ruin whatever it was they were trying to do. Fair."

"And your dad's into the witch stuff too?"

"Oh, HELL no. He couldn't grow a fungus if he left food out back on a summer day. Besides, I'm pretty sure Mom shooed him out of the room more often than not when she was working on things. No, Dad was more of an action guy. Not a cop—he hated them—but an outdoorsy type. Lots of long trips away from home. He'd drag my brother along for a lot of them."

"Are you the outdoorsy type?"

"I wanted to be, but nope. Like I said, I scared them too early on for them to let me do anything they considered dangerous." Her voice dropped into a strange sort of mockery at the word, though he could tell it was a sensitive topic for her.

"I would think being a detective is plenty dangerous," Lucifer said.

She rewarded that with an almost sly grin. "Oh yeah. Definitely."

That was one of the looks that tugged at him. That defiant self-satisfied grin that told him she was a woman who knew what she wanted and would get it. Especially if you tell her no. There were many sides to Charlie. She didn't often show them all to any one particular person.

"So, you're not with your parents right now?"

"No, I don't see my parents often. They were so on top of me and everything I did as a kid, and I know it was out of love, but there's a certain level of disservice done when a parent babies their kid so much. I wanted to prove I was fine taking care of myself. That I wouldn't break if I made mistakes and met life head on like any other kid. So, I try to be more self-sufficient and aways made a point to not run to them for every little problem. Especially after Brian."

"Ah, yes, wonder boy." He rolled his eyes at the mention of Brian. That damn soldier boy that pops into her dream worlds sometimes. Lucifer may have been biased, but he didn't like the asshole very much. "I rather dislike him... moving on. So, who do you rely on?"

"Uh, myself?" She looked at him with her face scrunched up as if she was also implying that it was obvious.

"Of course. What was I thinking? My apologies." He took in the last sip of his drink before he decided to get ballsy, a wicked idea dancing around in his mind. He stood up and out of the corner of his eye he could see Charlie tense. Lucifer pushed his luck as he approached her, offering his hand. "Let me see you out."

Lucifer could see the wheels turning in her head, for a split second he thought she'd turn him down. Instead, once again caught by surprise, she took his hand.

He couldn't help but wonder if this version of Charlie was the one who wanted to be free of those mundane choices. That she was doing all the things she wished she would do in her waking life. Smiling like a fool, he gently pulled her to him. The moment she was in his space the bar around them melted away. In place was a night sky, glittering with thousands of perfect stars. Below them were puffy white clouds, pretending to be a solid floor.

He could see the all too familiar look upon Charlie's face as she spoke under her breath, "This is way too corny, even for you."

"Just trying to prove I'm not entirely a monster, dearest Charlotte." On that note, he guided her into a lazy waltz, moving in flowing, gentle, circles across the clouds. Music filled the space around them. When he pushed her away from him and brought her back, she simply smiled at him as her back landed against his chest.

"So corny." A soft genuine rumble of laughter escaped him, his head resting softly against the side of her face. "I don't, you know..."

He'd glance down at her perplexed at her comment. "Don't what?"

"Think you're actually a monster." She glanced up at him, all playfulness aside. His heart skipped a beat as he let out a soft sigh.

What he wouldn't give for her to remember this one. To remember how comfortable she felt with him. But he knew, deep down, that whatever had interfered with his mark would make this disappear as well. When he'd marked her, he worried about the implications of her easily remembering these dream encounters—a side effect of the connection between them—but in this exact moment, he felt differently about it.

He placed a gentle kiss on top of her head and she instantly went limp in his arms, asleep. "I hope you're safe, wherever you are. I'll be in touch."

Chapter 9

Charlie

CHARLIE GROANED IN PROTEST of her waking mind. For once she'd actually slept well: there were no haunting dreams that made her wake up in cold sweats or an annoyance intruding on her peace. Now that she thought about it she couldn't recall dreaming at all, which was a small blessing. A blissful smile spread ear to ear as she rolled over onto her back. Her restful brain started to collect itself slowly, then the rare smile on her face started to fade.

Like a horrific storm, the events that happened the day before flooded Charlie's mind. Her stomach instantly cramped, causing her to ball up. Last night, as hard as it was, she'd shut the door behind her, leaving Brian to his own accord, and passed out the moment her head hit the soft welcoming pillows. What the fuck did she get herself into this time?

It wasn't that she didn't enjoy what had happened. On the contrary, she felt ten times better than she had in a while. But the fact remained, she crossed a line. They both crossed a line. One she didn't think either could come back from.

Not to mention, she'd met the Devil himself. Which meant all of that religious dogma she'd spurned was real. What else was real?

Brian was allegedly some sort of monster hunter. Though, technically, he'd yet to confirm or deny such a thing. If hunters were real, then there were things that needed to be hunted.

"Fuck." Charlie wanted to cry her eyes out right then and there. However, she wouldn't let herself.

No more.

She'd cried enough in the past few days to last her for a while. What she could really use right now was some air. Her chest had tightened all of a sudden from being in this tiny room. She needed to get the hell out of there, but Brian wasn't going to let her leave. He wanted her to stay and be safe under his watchful eye. It sounded ideal on the surface, but Charlie was getting claustrophobic.

She tossed the blankets off her and climbed out of bed bending over to pick her boots up. It wasn't a good idea to slip them on just yet, noisy as they were on the marble floor, so she carried them as she cracked the door open.

Charlie peeked through the slit, seeing Brian still snoozing on the couch with a book laying across his chest.

What time was it exactly? She hadn't looked at her phone yet to see the time but she imagined it was earlier than six. Brian used to always wake up at that time.

Biting the bottom of her lip, Charlie decided to go for it. The longer she loitered about, the higher the chances she'd wake him. She tipped-toed as quietly as she could through the giant space. When she got to the archway that led towards the stairs, she stopped.

Charlie turned back, taking one last glance at Brian's sleeping face. Despite everything, the idea of walking away from him still left an unsettled feeling in the pit of her stomach. She never wanted to hurt him, but this was too complicated. All of this was happening too quickly. She didn't think he'd understand but she just couldn't face him right now.

Getting home was no easy feat. She had to walk a good bit to get back to some sort of civilization before her phone got any service. It was five in the morning, she had no cash on her, and she doubted there would be any sort of understanding uber driver this early to come get her from the middle of nowhere, so her next best bet was Carmen.

She hated to do it, but Carmen always said to call her if she ever needed anything, no matter what the time was. Time to test that theory.

There was no doubt how pissed the woman was when she pulled up to collect Charlie from the side of the road. She was almost certain she was going to have an earful from Carmen. She even held her breath in fear of causing her friend to snap. But to her surprise, Carmen didn't say one damn word. It felt like a disappointed mother picking their child up at a party they weren't supposed to go to. The feeling was very uncomfortable, to say the least.

Charlie barely breathed the entire trip in fear she'd lash out. Aside from waking Carmen up at five in the morning on her day off—something that would have had Charlie flipping her shit—there was an underlying reason she was pissed. Sadly, Charlie couldn't exactly pin that reason down. She didn't even bother trying. Carmen was always going to be her best friend, her sister. And that meant she would be annoyingly overprotective.

When they arrived at Charlie's complex, Carmen pulled up to the curb. Charlie slid out of the vehicle and looked back at Carmen who looked to be struggling to say something.

"Thanks, Carmen." Her lips curved into a subtle grin, one that was apologetic in nature.

"Noon. My House. Better not be late."

Well then. Charlie simply nodded her head in response, shut her door, and watched Carmen drive off. At least Carmen was holding back her rage for now.

Once inside, Charlie made a beeline towards her bathroom. A scalding-hot shower was in order. She would have taken one back at Brian's, but she didn't want to risk sticking around too long.

As she mindlessly went through the motions to get it all ready, Charlie's phone went off and her heart skipped a beat. Her first thought was that it was Brian, who she didn't exactly want to talk to yet. But then she remembered that Brian wasn't much of a texter. She gulped, reached for the phone, and unlocked it.

And where have you been, Ms. Brant?

Her eyes rolled as she read the message. She knew exactly who it was, and she didn't want to talk to *him* either. Still, her fingers seemed to have a mind of their own.

Finding you a room in the loony bin.

Hitting send, she tossed the phone on the counter before she proceeded to hop into the shower.

She must have been in there for a good hour or so to let the heat soak down to her bones. Clean and cleansed, at least physically. Charlie's next step was to hunt down the car she'd left behind the night before. If it hadn't already been towed away.

If that was the case, Brian was going to owe her big.

The plan was to get out of her apartment before Brian discovered she'd left the safe house. No doubt he would be hunting her down once he figured out she'd left. He wanted to keep her safe and Brian was one of those hero-type men. Real white-knight syndrome. It used to be romantic, the idea of him coming to her rescue. Now it was downright obnoxious.

Now that she was in the middle of the Quarter, there was no short supply of Ubers. As they drove through the city, the idea of skipping town once again sounded like a real valid choice for Charlie. Of course, would a change of location even deter friggin' Satan? Not likely. She might escape Brian that way, but Lucifer was a little bit trickier. And by a little, she meant a hell of a fucking lot. No matter where she was, she would eventually have to face her demons.

No pun intended.

Once her car was in sight, Charlie felt instant relief. She hated leaving it sitting overnight somewhere she wasn't too familiar with. The worst part was, like an absolute idiot, she'd left her gun in the glove box. However, the thought of her gun coming back into her possession after the incident with Lucifer did send a chill creeping down her spine. It unnerved her how easily she'd pulled that trigger. Keeping it there, for now, wouldn't do any harm. She hoped.

"If you wouldn't mind pulling up right there, thanks." The driver nodded and stopped the car where she'd pointed. Waving the driver off, she turned towards her vehicle. It was a sight to see, tow tag and all.

Before she even reached the driver's side door, she felt more than heard someone approach her from across the street. He looked sort of familiar, but she wasn't sure where she'd seen him before.

"Ms. Brant?" "Who's asking?" she asked as he stopped not more than five feet away.

"I'm Detective Noir." He smiled brightly as he held his hand out to Charlie.

Ah. That was it. She'd seen him around the police station. He showed up about six months before, if she recalled. Her eyes scanned his face as she held her hand out to shake his.

"What exactly can I do for you, detective?"

"I need your help identifying someone. I believe you may know this man." He pulled a picture from his pocket. It was a little blurry but there was no doubt who was in that image.

Lucifer.

Conflicted emotions coursed through her body, but Charlie held her poker face well. What would happen if she told the guy she knew the man in the photo? Would this be the end of her troubles with Lucifer? Or the end of the detective. That thought made her cringe on the inside. "I'm afraid I can't help."

"Can't or won't?" His face was as still as hers and it was nerve-racking.

"Excuse me?"

"There were reported claims that he was in your workplace. Ms. Brant, I don't know how you know him, but you should know this man is dangerous. He has multiple harassment claims against him; pretty, young women whom he charms into submission and takes whatever he can get." He let his eyes scan over her, as if trying to make a point. "It's also believed he's a part of some cult. Real death and debauchery type stuff. Obviously, you're a much smarter woman than most. So, if you have any information at–"

"Let me stop you right there," Charlie interrupted, sliding her sleeve further down her arm as the thought of Lucifer's mark entered her brain. "I know how this shit works, bud. I used to be in your shoes. I don't have any information to give. If you know where I work, then you also know I rent the space. Meaning, while he may very well have been in the building, there are also a plethora of other offices outside of mine he could have been visiting."

He smiled. A self-assured, cocky grin that raised her hackles. "I'm well aware who you are, Ms. Brant. Your ex-husband is my new partner."

Charlie's eyes narrowed. His face was practically emotionless as he spat that information out.

That was probably how he found her to begin with. "Not exactly winning me over now, are we? You know my ex. Great. Doesn't mean you know shit about me." He took a slight breath, gearing up to respond but she wasn't giving him the chance. "I'll tell you what. I will keep my ear to the ground about this guy. If I hear anything I'll make sure to let Brian know. M'kay?"

Without waiting for his answer, she dropped herself into her car and slammed the door. As her key turned, a knock erupted on her driver's side window. The guy was pushy. And clueless. Didn't he know that was his cue to leave? She pushed the button to roll the window down without turning her eyes from the road in front of her.

"Be safe out there, Ms. Brant." The guy leaned over to talk to Charlie.

"I can take care of myself, Mr. Noir."

He smiled at her before he finally turned around and left for good.

BRIAN

The first thing Brian saw when he woke was the book lying on his chest, *Grimorium Verum*. When Charlie had gone to his room, he'd hoped to distract himself from the many intrusive thoughts her presence always seemed to bring about. Sexy, tempting, frustrating thoughts that he knew would only lead to more trouble than he was willing to cause right now. Instead, he dove headfirst into a little studying until he drifted off to sleep sometime after midnight.

The marking on Charlie's arm sent him straight to the leather-bound book in the lowest part of his shelves. He knew he'd seen that symbol before, and it turned out his fears were not entirely misplaced. The mark was the symbol of Lucifer. But why was his ex-wife of all people carrying it? It made absolutely no sense. Charlie was completely non-religious.

When they got married, they had to have a meeting with a priest just to be allowed to use the church they wanted for the ceremony. It was odd to the both of them, and the entire experience brought about lots of silly jokes and complaints from the pair. In the end, they decided to rebuff the church and had a beautiful ceremony in Audubon Park under the famous "Tree of Life." It had turned out a hundred times better than any stuffy church could have offered.

Religion, and anything related to it, was just not something Charlie ever cared about. So why would she suddenly carry a mark associated with one of the most infamous religious figures known to man?

Had she really changed so much over the years?

Brian grabbed the book off his chest and tossed it gently onto the floor. Sitting up from the uncomfortable couch, he groaned and stretched his arms overhead. A yawn escaped while he rubbed his eye with the back of his hand. Sleeping on the couch was the worst, but he didn't regret forcing Charlie into his bed. He hoped she rested better than he had.

The next thing on his list was the attempt to stand up, knowing his hips were most likely stiff from sleeping in an awkward place. He reminded himself he'd slept in the worst places before. Being in the military had definitely trained him for things like sleeping on lumpy couches. They were like heaven compared to the alternatives.

He needed some coffee, and unless she had changed literally everything about herself since they separated, he also knew Charlie would need some too when she woke.

Brian didn't attempt to check on her after the coffee was brewing. The last thing he wanted to do was prematurely wake the woman. He smiled a little as he remembered the grouchy little gremlin she was pre-caffeine. He'd give her a few minutes to let the aroma of the dark roast make its way into the bedroom and coax her gently awake.

Last night was unexpected, but it wasn't regretful by any means. There was a part of him, deep down, that wanted to rekindle things with his wife. Ex-wife. The problem with that though was his connections. If he attempted to work things out with her, he'd be risking her safety. He closed his eyes as he tried to pause his mind. She was obviously already in some sort of trouble. He couldn't help but take some of that blame. If he could just tell her the truth without that fear of her becoming a target, then he would spill his guts to her.

Not a day had gone by that he hadn't felt like shit for what he had to do. Her life was on the line, and he chose to save her, even if it meant letting her go in the process. Seeing the pain on her face, even to this day, cut deeper than a natural wound. This cut into his soul. At the end of the day though, she was safe.

Or he'd thought she was.

Brian narrowed his eyes. *They* promised nothing would ever happen to her if he obeyed and complied. He did everything for *them.* He was leaning over the counter as his mind played it all out. He had been loyal, and they betrayed him. A loud crack echoed through the tiny space, snapping him back to reality. He stepped back to assess the damage he'd done to his counter.

"Shit, that's going to be hard to explain."

Looking over his shoulder at the door, he was half expecting Charlie to storm out of it. When she didn't, a wave of unease crashed over him. He moved through the space quickly only stopping at the door. There was no way he could barge in without some sort of resistance from the woman. So, he knocked on the door lightly. "Charlie?"

No response.

He knocked one more time just in case before he'd open the door. His eyes first landed on the messy bed, on which he expected her to be, but she wasn't there. He waited for a second to see if she'd emerge from the bathroom. When she didn't come out, he cursed under his breath.

"Damn it, Charlie."

Brian should have known. He should have heard... Hell, he should have turned his damn alarm on. He wasn't expecting her to leave considering she wanted answers. Dare he say, she could be a pain in the ass sometimes. Now she was a pain in the ass for leaving. When did she sneak out?

He growled under his breath as he ran a hand over his face. Brian was going to have to go track her ass down and haul her back.

Chapter 10

Charlie

Noon was ticking closer and Charlie didn't dare wait any longer. She drove her car straight to Carmens' after her conversation with Detective Noir. That guy gave her bad vibes. She wasn't sure if it was the way he questioned her, or just overall. He came off self-righteous, a quality she never liked. Guys who thought they were better than others, superior.

If Brian was smart, he'd put the guy in his place, and she'd not have to worry about him again.

Pulling behind Carmen's pickup truck, Charlie shut her car off and sorted herself for a moment. She knew once she got in that house a verbal ass-whooping was going to happen. Why was she being punished? First Lucifer, then Brian, and now this shit. The last two days had been the longest two days in a while and all she wanted to do was tell Carmen everything that had happened.

She wanted to vent to her best friend. The one person who was supposed to always have her back, even when she was being less than smart. Her ride or die.

Then she recalled telling Carmen about the big ass dog that had attacked her. *Dog*. That was no dog. It was a fucking monster, a fact she was even more certain of now. But Carmen had been like everyone else.

She couldn't do that right now. Not when she was already dealing with so much other crap. She quickly shoved that shit way down, getting out of the car to face the consequences.

Knocking on the door, Charlie stood patiently waiting. She had to knock again when a few minutes passed. It was very possible that Carmen was in the kitchen, she was always in the kitchen when she was ticked. Definitely not a good sign for her.

The door opened very carefully, and Charlie's eyes dropped down to see big beautiful brown eyes looking up at her. Charlie smiled and then the little girl smiled.

"Auntie Charlie!"

"Hey, kiddo." The door swung open as the little girl flung herself into Charlie. Charlie bent down to return the affection by giving her a proper hug before pulling back to scan Camilla. "Did you grow since the last time I've seen you?"

"Mhmm! And I lost a tooth, too. See!" Camilla gave the biggest, cheesiest, grin that a little girl could give just to prove that her tooth was indeed missing. Charlie couldn't help but chuckle.

"Is your mama around?"

Camilla got real quiet as she put her small finger to her own lips. "*Shh*, mama is very mad. You should run."

"She could try but she wouldn't get far," Carmen said as Charlie's attention snapped up to Carmen who was coming up behind Camilla. She could see her weighing Charlie with a stare that had stopped many punk shoplifters dead in their tracks back in the day. Without another word, Carmen opened the door more and walked away towards the kitchen, leaving the pair alone.

Camilla turned back to Charlie and whispered again, grabbing Charlie's hand and stuffing her G.I. Joe into her palm. "You're gonna *need* this. He has an M40 sniper rifle. He'll protect you."

Another chuckle came from Charlie as the doll got shoved further into her hand. Charlie looked at it long and hard as she bit her bottom lip before turning her gaze back at Camilla. She wasn't going to tell the little girl that the doll was not going to save her from her mother's wrath.

Instead, she gave the doll a hug and handed it back to Camilla. "Thanks, baby girl, but I'll be ok this time."

With that, the two walked inside with Charlie closing the door and locking it behind her. She knew how Carmen felt about her door. The woman was more paranoid than Charlie ever was, but she imagined it had something to do with Carmen's experience in the military. Which, in her opinion, gave her every right to be paranoid. She knew she'd seen a lot of screwed up things.

Carmen was fussing about something when Charlie walked into the kitchen. Without turning around, she said, "*Mija*, go to your room for a little bit and watch some TV. *Y no discutas conmigo.*" [1]

Looking a little disappointed that she couldn't hang out with them, Camilla sighed. "Yes, mama." She turned to Charlie then mouthed a secretive "sorry" before wandering off to her room.

When she turned back to see Carmen, she was moving about her kitchen in a frenzy. The verbal lashing was about to commence. When Charlie heard the girl's door click, that was when Carmen spun on her heel and slammed a

---

1. Charlie's Translation: Don't argue.

plate full of arroz congri on the table in front of where Charlie stood.

"You look like shit, eat."

"I love our little love-filled greetings." The sarcasm slipped out of her mouth, but she did slide into a seat without any hesitation.

She knew better than to ignore Carmen. Last time she had something thrown at her that looked deceptively like a shoe. Charlie knew Carmen meant well. At least she tried to remind herself of this countless times. Carmen was a mama bear—not just to her child but to Charlie, too.

The sound of the spoon clashing with metal did make Charlie look up to see Carmen leaning back against her counter, arms crossed, and staring right at her. "So, you're going to tell me exactly whose house you wandered out of this morning?"

Silence lingered longer than it meant too because Charlie had no idea what to say. So instead of giving her an answer Charlie shrugged her shoulders.

"*Esta perra tonta. Dios me impida saltar sobre esta mesa ahora mismo.*" [2] The Spanish flew out of Carmen's mouth in such intensity that Charlie didn't have to know what was being said to know that she was in deep shit. "You were with *him* weren't you."

"*Him*? There are a lot of guys out there, can you be more specific?" This was a dangerous game that Charlie was playing. It was like poking a beehive and not expecting to get swarmed. Charlie looked at Carmen's face and she could swear that she saw her eye twitch.

---

2. Charlie's Translation: You're a dumb bitch, about to kick your ass.

"Don't play like a dumb bitch. I don't waste my time with stupid people, and you know that." Charlie lowered her eyes to see Carmen gripping the counter and going white knuckled. She was impressed Carmen hadn't thrown something at her yet. "You've always been open with me so start talking and for the love of all that's holy, *eat.*"

"Do you want me to tell you or eat? Can't do both." She grinned at Carmen, but Carmen was clearly not having it so Charlie grabbed the fork in her hand and shoveled food into her mouth, knowing full well that Carmen was wanting to scold instead of hear her speak.

Charlie watched as Carmen pulled the chair out in front of the table and sat down across from her. She leaned back as the two locked eyes and had a weird staring contest. Carmen was the one that broke first and sighed.

"He left you, Charlie. When you were at your worst, he fucking abandoned you. Why would you open that door again?"

Charlie swallowed the food in her mouth and after a long pause she finally cracked. "I know..."

There was not really much Charlie could say. She knew she fucked up; it was one of the reasons she'd snuck out like she did. If Charlie faced Brian again, she had a feeling that more mistakes were bound to happen.

"I get you needed closure, but I didn't take you for someone who sleeps with their ex to find it." Carmen reached for a pitcher of what looked like lemonade and started to pour a glass.

"For the record, we didn't." She paused for a moment before adding, "Close, but I just... Couldn't."

Carmen pushed the cup towards Charlie and then proceeded to get herself a cup. "Eat," she said again. It wasn't a request, but the stern urgency of a concerned family member. Her eyes were studying her face again and Charlie almost wiggled in the chair.

"There's something else, isn't there? What aren't you telling me?"

Sometimes it sucked having a friend that knew you far too well. Charlie continued to stuff her face as she tried to find a way to explain the last day without getting into too much detail.

"There isn't anything else. Just had a weird-ass dream and then I met Brian out in town."

Charlie didn't think that Carmen would actually buy that, but when the woman's shoulders relaxed and her eyes softened, she held her ground. Her heart was racing but she kept calm. *No way.*

"Fine..." Carmen pushed herself from the table and headed towards the pot where the food was. She dished herself out her own plate before returning to the table. They sat for the rest of the meal in silence until Camilla came back out and everything seemed to go back to normal.

Thank fucking god for boring blissful normalcy.

Chapter 11

Lucifer

SOMETHING WASN'T RIGHT. SHORTLY after he'd sent Charlie on her way, he felt her energy moving through the world as it should, then in an instant, it stopped again. Not like before—not that white noise interference. It was just gone.

Severed.

If she had died, surely he would have known.

It made little to no sense, but even more importantly, it was starting to piss him off. Who in the seven hells was playing with his power like that? Lucifer sat upon his throne in deep thought, chin resting on his knuckles.

"Oh, Luci!"

"For the love of damnation..." His eyes rolled as the voice rang in his ears.

It was like nails to a chalkboard, one of the worst forms of torture. He would know, he's tortured a few souls now and then. His own personal form of torture was about to walk through the door. He did not need this right now.

A burly lumberjack of a man walked around the corner. A joyful smile spread across his face the moment his eyes locked on Lucifer. The King of Hell pinched the bridge of his nose, knowing this encounter was going to cause a massive headache even for the Devil.

"Go away, Asmodeus."

"But sir, I have exciting news for you."

Lucifer couldn't tell what was worse, the Prince of Lust constantly flirting with him or the sing-songy-voice he often held. Truth be told, he much preferred Asmo's female form. Not only was it less annoying, but he could at least be distracted from his mindless prattle by the presence of enormous pillowy tits.

"What news could you possibly bring that won't ruin my day any further?" He turned his head in time to see Asmodeus walk towards him. Even his gait across the floor was light-footed. Far be it from Lucifer to question the demon's choices, but sometimes he found it hard for him to wrap his head around.

"Well, it may ruin your day, but it is still important for you to know." Asmodeus tapped his chin as his eyes drifted towards the ceiling. Like he was contemplating telling Lucifer in the end.

"Asmodeus... if you don't spit it out, I will personally send you back to the pits of hell where you can wait another century before I ever let you back into my palace and on earth."

The demon winced, clearly not liking that idea at all. "Okay, okay. Sheesh, don't shoot the messenger. You did say not to ruin your day further. I'm just looking out for you Luci."

"Will you stop calling me that!"

"Call you what?" He grinned playfully.

"You know what I'm—" Lucifer was growing short-tempered. He waved his hand as he said, "Get on with it already!"

"Right, so, there was a pride demon downtown getting coffee at this diner and he saw something, so then he told one of my lust demons the news—cause he figured it would be best coming from *moi*," he laid his hand on his chest before he continued. Lucifer rolled his eyes knowing this was going to drag on for a moment. "The lust demon eventually grew balls-" And just as he expected the story kept going on and on, Lucifer closed his eyes as he tried to think of something else until Asmodeus got to the point, "-so your brother is in town."

When the words left the demon's lips Lucifer sat up instantly in his chair. "What did you say?"

"Which part? I said a lot, so you have to be a *little* more specific..."

"Which. Brother." Lucifer stared at Asmodeus knowing that he was like a squirrel around a pile of nuts. He had to reign him in quickly or he'd go off on another tangent. Demons...

"Oh. Michael." He said with a smile.

Michael... What was he doing here? Sticking his nose in Lucifer's business again, no doubt. He never showed his face unless he was directed to. Michael was always the goody-two-shoes golden child.

Whenever God told him to jump. he simply asked how high and did it better than anyone for the sake of getting their father's praise. It was sickening. Yet, to Michael's displeasure, Lucifer was still considered the favorite of them all.

While being God's favorite son gave Lucifer no sense of pleasure, he did find amusement in Michael's reaction to it. That alone almost made it entirely worth it.

"So, what are we going to do, boss man?" Lucifer looked at Asmodeus who was still lingering around.

"I'll handle Michael. Just keep an eye out for other pesky little angels who might be snooping around."

The hint of Charlie's feelings rushed through him just then. Good, she was safe... at least he hoped. He pulled his phone from his pocket as he quickly typed out a message to her. He wanted to know where she had been.

He glanced up from his phone and noticed Asmodeus still hanging about. "You can go now."

"Right, sorry. Bye Luci!" And then Asmodeus poofed into the shadows.

Looking back at the phone, an amused grin curled his lips. Cheeky woman.

Chapter 12

As much as Charlie loved to hang out with her favorite girls, it was starting to get late. She watched Carmen and Camilla shrink away in her rearview mirror as she pulled out of the driveway, feeling as she always felt when leaving their house: warm, loved, and needing to go up a pants size.

Even when Carmen was chewing her out, there was an underlying layer of familial love behind it that she couldn't refute. She loved her blood family, don't get her wrong, but there was something especially sweet about chosen family. Especially when she had Camilla's sweet face to see.

The drive home wasn't terrible. There was some traffic, but Charlie was in no real hurry. It gave her plenty of time to let her mind get quiet, without the threat of yet another guy interrupting her solitude.

She had her radio turned up and had her windows rolled down, enjoying the rush of warm mid-September air passing through her car. She tried not to think about Lucifer or Brian. Instead, she enjoyed being in the moment, blocking out the thoughts of infuriating men or other beastly things that roamed around the world. It was just her and Breaking Benjamin blaring from her speakers.

Charlie eventually made it home, pulling into the parking garage and walking to her building. The visit with

Carmen made her see things a little clearer, so in the end she was happy to have her ass chewed out. Sometimes having a friend tell you the errors of your ways was just enough to give you a whole new clarity.

If only she could have told Carmen about Lucifer. Carmen always had the best advice with everything. It made her wonder what she would have had to say about him.

She had to climb two flights of stairs to reach her apartment door, and every time she reached her floor she strongly considered moving. She shuffled heavy, tired feet onto the landing and turned the corner, wondering how many more assholes she'd have to track down to afford a ground-floor apartment, when she froze.

Brian was waiting outside her door.

His face tightened when he spotted her. *Shit.* She stood there, not really sure what to do, but knew this confrontation would happen eventually. Charlie had hoped she could get a hot shower and a good night's sleep under her belt first.

They stared at each other across the hall, but neither one seemed to know what to say. She knew he'd be pissed about her taking off, but what did he expect? He couldn't hold her against her will—though she was sure the thought had crossed his mind. He had to know her well enough to know she wasn't about to let that happen.

Brian moved, finally, shifting away from the wall and taking a couple of slow steps toward her. Her heart pounded as he started toward her, and she mentally searched through a rapid fire catalog of what to say to him, but before she could settle on anything, she was overcome with the smell of cinnamon and poppy flowers.

A high-pitched sound started just to the right of Charlie, and she glanced at the wall sconce lighting up the stairwell, the sound growing louder and more urgent as the light also grew brighter, then flickered, before everything suddenly went dark and silent. A wall of darkness stretched between the pair and then the lights suddenly flipped back on and she loosed a startled yelp of surprise.

Standing almost directly in front of her was Lucifer.

"Hello gorgeous."

Charlie looked at him, then over his shoulder. He turned just a bit to see Brian standing a short distance away, his face twisted in fury.

"Well, well, well. What do we have here? The ex? My, you are quite handsome. I see what she sees in you—well, *saw.*"

"Lucifer." Brain's face was anything but amused as he slowly took steps closer towards both of them.

"Maybe." A grin stretched across his face as he looped an arm around Charlie's waist.

"If I were you, I would step away from her. Now," Brian said.

"Mmm, let me think... No."

"Lucifer–" Charlie started, already growing annoyed with the pissing contest they were starting.

"Don't worry, Charlotte. I won't hurt the boy toy," he said. He even sounded sincere, but the smile on his face was anything but trustworthy.

"I'm not the one you should be worried about," Brian said, taking another step toward them.

"Oh, trust me," Lucifer said, squeezing Charlie closer against his body. "I don't worry about you. Neither of us do."

Brian growled as he charged forward and before Charlie could even blink darkness surrounded them. The familiar unease in her stomach returned, and after a few moments the darkness cleared like so much smoke carried away on the wind, leaving them standing somewhere that was definitely *not* her apartment.

She stared at the empty space where Brian should have been. "Why did you do that?" Charlie quickly turned towards Lucifer. He still had that smug look on his face as if he'd won a golden prize.

"I wanted us to have a private conversation without the boy scout interfering." He shrugged his shoulders. Charlie's eyes turned into slits, glaring at him. A look of painful confusion crossed over his face. "Was this not what you wanted?"

"No, it wasn't. I wanted to go home. I really wanted to have a nice quiet evening without worrying whether or not I was losing my fucking mind, but you and Brian won't leave me alone!" Charlie stepped away from him practically throwing her hands into the air as she reclaimed her space.

She finally realized they were standing in a bedroom. A canopy bed sat pushed against the far wall, overburdened with a load of useless decorative pillows atop a giant comforter that all but seduced her with promises of cozy warmth. Heavy velvet curtains draped over the windows in deep swags, making the room feel even more lush. A fire crackled in the fireplace next to her, flanked by two chairs and a small round table between them. She looked back at Lucifer and he smiled at her.

She hated that stupid smile.

For a moment, she entertained grabbing something heavy and smashing it against his skull, but if a bullet at point-blank range hadn't even left a scratch on him then she doubted there was much she could do to him. Letting out a deep exasperated sigh, she flexed her hands at her side.

Charlie stared at him in silence for a moment and weighed her options. Attack? Run? Or just... Fuck it. If she ran, he'd simply pluck her out of wherever she went and put her right back. If she attacked, he'd laugh at her.

Or get a boner.

She tried exceptionally hard to push *those* thoughts out of her head and crossed her arms in the meager show of defiance she could manage.

"Whatever. Here I am," she huffed out. Charlie moved to the chair farthest from Lucifer and plopped down on it. "What do you want to talk about?"

Lucifer finally moved from his spot; a contemplative look on his face. He took the other chair and leaned on his elbow. He watched her carefully before he spoke, "You have a brother."

That caught her off guard. "You tell me. You seem to know everything."

"That would be my father. Not me. I'm not as omnipotent as people assume." A soft chuckle came from him. "But can you imagine all the delights if I was?"

Alright. Stepping away from that land mine.

"I have siblings, yes. A sister and a brother."

"Aren't they a pain in the ass?"

"Sometimes." It took her a moment to process what he was getting at. If she recalled, there were other beings out there like him. Angels... Demons... Obviously they were very real and that was terrifying to think about.

"My feathered fuck-boy of a brother is terrorizing me, yet again. Or plans to anyway. I was only just informed he was back in town, but it is a favorite pastime of his. What do you think I should do about it?"

Was he being serious? It was hard to tell the difference between humor and his serious nature sometimes.

Her brows pushed forward as she gave him a look. "Do I look like a fucking family therapist?"

"But what would you do with your brother?"

"My brother doesn't terrorize me for one. Sounds like you need to work it out."

"Hmm, work it out..." Lucifer repeated what she said as he seemed to drift off for a moment. The way it sounded, he acted as if he'd never considered it before. She half grinned and shook her head. This was why he whisked her away? To talk about family problems? It was weird to say the least, but again what hadn't been the last 24 hours or so?

While he seemed lost in thought she let hers drift back towards Brian. The cat was out of the bag now. Though, now that she thought about it, she supposed he had figured it out already, considering he recognized Lucifer when he saw him.

"Well this has been a nice little chat and all, but I think it's time to take me home now," she said, pushing herself to her feet.

"No."

She stopped mid-stance, hands on the arms of the chair, and stared at him.

"What do you mean, *No*?"

"Look, Charlotte. Normally I would be fine leaving you to your little life unbothered–"

"Doubtful," the word shot out of her, earning an annoyed glance from Lucifer before he continued.

"But with Michael popping up, and me having no idea what it is he wants, it's becoming increasingly clear to me that a little caution is necessary. So, you're going to be my guest of honor for a little bit. I hope you enjoy your room."

A look of horror spread across Charlie's face as she stared at Lucifer. She pushed away from the chair, moving closer to him as she exploded in a fit of panic.

"Are you fucking kidding me? Take me home, Lucifer."

"Honestly, have you been paying any attention?" he asked, his eyebrow arching with a glance around them.

He slowly stood up which caused Charlie to step back a little. She was inches away and she didn't exactly want to be that close to him.

"I don't think you appreciate exactly what you've gotten yourself into here. I vaguely recall telling you I can do anything. I meant it."

Charlie stared at him, a volatile mixture of panic and rage building in her chest. "I haven't gotten myself into shit. I was just going about my day, and *you* showed up to fuck it all to hell."

His shoulders lifted softly as he slid his hands into his pockets, walking around her in a slow circle. "You could say that again."

He smiled at her, but the smile vanished pretty quickly as he saw the look she was giving him. He sighed and leveled her with a serious stare, stopping his stride. "Look, all jokes aside, it's for your protection. I promise. I truly don't know what it is my brother has planned, but I do know that he is aggravatingly persistent once he sets his mind to a task. I would just feel better if you were somewhere I could get to you if you needed help. What better way than having you as my personal house guest?"

"Yeah, you still haven't gotten around to the whole 'why it's my problem' part..."

Lucifer scratched the side of his nose idly, deep in thought. The longer it took him to spill, the more irritated Charlie was going to get. And the more likely she would find something hefty to crack against his skull.

Remembering their first meeting at the church, Charlie quickly decided against it. Mostly because she was afraid, he might like it.

Finally, he grabbed her wrist and pulled her arm between them, pushing her sleeve up to reveal the black sigil on her forearm. As she stared down at it, she realized it looked alive. An ethereal energy emanated from the solid lines, making it appear to shimmer and move. The closer he pulled it to himself, the more electric it became, like the energy was reaching out to its source, wanting to go back home.

"Because of this," he said. All traces of playful humor were gone. "This is basically a beacon for trouble and trust me when I say... its signal is being heard loud and clear. And not by someone you want to get in the way of."

Charlie stared at her arm like it was something completely foreign. In that moment, a thought was born and slipped from her head to her lips with little effort. "Your brother would connect me to you because of this?"

Lucifer smiled, but it didn't reach his eyes. "Indeed. The original narc with a temper as strong as he is ugly." He smiled a little wider, appearing to find some sort of joy in insulting the Archangel.

Charlie leveled a look at him, trying to decide if she was supposed to take him seriously.

Realizing he was still holding onto her arm, Charlie pulled it away from him, relieved that he didn't try to hold on to it. "So. Your brother—Michael—is looking for you and is willing to take out anyone who gets in his way."

"You do catch on quick."

"And he knows I know you because he's drawn to this mark. That *you* put on me."

Lucifer's smug smile faltered when he saw the look in her eyes. His mouth opened and he stuttered for a moment before finally saying, "Oh, look... How was I supposed to know he'd jumped on the first train to Earth? It's not like I keep tabs on him. No, he's the stalker of the family if we are being completely honest."

"Are we?" she asked, wondering if he was as truly unaware of himself as he seemed to be. Getting back on topic, she added, "So take the mark off."

"Yeah, well, it's not always as simple as all that is it?" He looked slightly embarrassed at the admission. "There's the magicks, and the energies, sacrifices to appease those I would have to awaken.... You know.... Pain and logistics."

"And you really have no idea why he might be after you?" Charlie asked, cutting him off before he went on another tangent.

"Who knows. Normally when I spend a little too much time up top, dear old Dad sends Michael after me. See, the demons tend to get all antsy if I'm gone too long, and they start following me up here—which I personally think they should be allowed to stretch their wings a little now and then, but they have a nasty habit of causing chaos and destruction. Then he has to send out pest control to clean up, feathers and fangs fly, and it gets really messy."

Charlie watched on as he explained, noticing how animated he was becoming as he did. "Any time I try to have a little fun, he sends Big Brother to ruin it all. Dick brain could kill a wet dream."

"So he's coming to send you home."

"Now, you see, that's the weird of it. I haven't been out of Hell long at all. On the contrary, I just came from there. So, having Michael sent after me doesn't really make sense. Unless of course he's just looking for a fight. I imagine he's getting tired of being the errand boy. But what can I say?" He flashed her another grin. "I enjoy ruffling his feathers."

"So, you and your brother are like every other fucked up family. Can't say I'm surprised. What I don't understand is why you've decided to put me in the middle of your game of divine hide and seek?"

"Well..." He stopped and looked like he was really thinking about it. "Yeah. Yeah, I guess that's pretty much what happened, isn't it."

"Tell me why I shouldn't just call up ol' Mikey and tell him exactly where to find you? Do us both the favor of getting you the fuck out of here and stick you back where you belong?"

The sudden glare he gave her was a clear, unspoken warning. Those vibrant green eyes burned into her, the real danger of what her threat would cause him to do unspoken yet unmistakable. Ice crept up her spine. Perhaps threatening him with that—however empty it may have been—was a bad idea.

He must have felt satisfied that she'd understood how bad of an idea it would be, because his face quickly relaxed again, and his eyes softened.

"Well for starters, it wasn't intentional. You have to give me at least that much credit. I couldn't have possibly known he'd choose now to come pay me a visit. However, you have just demonstrated reason number two of why I feel it is in *my* best interest to keep you here. You're not the only one I'm protecting here, Ms. Brant."

Charlie's arm dropped heavily to her side, and she stared at him, then the ceiling as she tried to keep her anger in check. What she *really* wanted to do was knock the smug ass grin right off his face. Maybe collect some of his teeth for good measure.

Instead of provoking an all-powerful devil, though, she breathed deeply until the urge subsided. When she thought it was safe to do so, she looked at him again and spoke as calmly as she could manage.

"How long?"

It was as though she had said the magic words. His mood lifted visibly at her apparent concession. "Splendid. Don't worry, I don't plan to keep you for eternity. There's time enough for that. Let me figure out what Michael's angle is. Negotiate some terms that guarantee you are left out of the family drama. If all goes well, I'll take you home in a day or two. You have my word."

"Fine. Just keep your hands to yourself. I'm not here to play footsie with you. Once you get me home, and figure out how to remove this stupid mark, I'm officially done with you and all this insanity." Charlie held her finger towards him to emphasize that there was a line that he better not step over.

She doubted he'd listen, but dammit she had to try.

"I promise, I'll keep my *hands* off. At least until I'm certain you won't hack them off if I don't."

That made her roll her eyes.

With an amused chuckle, he bowed his head slightly in her direction. "Sweet dreams, Charlotte."

"And stay out of *those*, too," she warned.

With that, Lucifer turned and headed towards the door, a soft chuckle whispering from the darkness. He'd stop momentarily turning his head over his shoulder. A thought had crossed his mind.

"If I were you, I'd stay in this room," he said. "I'd hate for the others to mess with you. Food will be brought to you, so you won't have to worry about that. Think of this as a mini vacation." He paused for a moment staring at her as a wicked grin filled his face.

"On second thought, you're the type to skip out before daybreak, aren't you?" Chuckling, he stepped out the door and Charlie heard the deadbolt slam into place. She ran towards the door and started banging on it, shaking the handle.

"Bastard," she whispered.

She hadn't planned on leaving after telling him she'd stick it out, but if she were being brutally honest with herself, she hadn't planned to skip out on Brian earlier either. A part of her wondered if she would have been better off staying with him, if leaving was the stupid move now that she was stuck in Lucifer's care.

A light bulb lit in her head. She reached for her phone in her back pocket. She could call Brian. Maybe he could get her out of here. But as she patted her back pocket, she found it was empty. That sneaky son of a bitch.

Who was she kidding, though? What would Brian be able to do to get her out of here? It's not like she knew where she was. Sure, Brian was resourceful but considering how fast Lucifer was snatching her out of the hallway. Brian probably wouldn't be able to stand a chance. The last thing she wanted was to send him to an early grave.

Feeling defeated, Charlie shuffled to her new bed. She fell face-first into it and grumbled, "What the hell did you get yourself into?"

What, indeed. All she had been trying to do was move through life with as little drama as possible. She'd had her fill of it. Had her fill of crazy shit happening to her, shit that no one believed. And now she got to add this to the growing list of what-the-fuckery.

Girl meets guy, guy annoys girl, guy kidnaps girl, guy reveals he's the Dark Underlord, girl shoots guy, girl nearly hooks up with ex-husband, guy kidnaps her again. It couldn't have been a more ridiculous scenario if it had been the plot of some book. One where the author had to be off her freakin' nut.

Chapter 13

Michael

THE CITY OF NEW ORLEANS was rather peaceful at night, considering its tourists who naturally party day in and day out. They were obnoxious, sinful, and ignorant and their aimless shuffle through their short meaningless lives made Michael feel...restless. Uneasy.

He remembered what the city was like when it first flourished. The promise, the excitement. People flocked to it with hope. The city grew at an impressive pace, holding onto its strange otherworldly charm as it did. But as with anything shiny and new, the humans quickly tarnished it and warped it into something darker and more oppressive.

Still, Michael had a soft spot for this city. He couldn't explain the pull, not entirely. It was the same pull he imagined other creatures above humanity had. New Orleans, for whatever reason, had become a mecca for powerful creatures, enticing them in in droves. Their influence, for better or for worse, had shaped the cityscape and nurtured life within it.

With all the advances of humanity, technology was one of the few things Michael found useful. It was easier to track people down through the many resources a police officer had. That was how he got Charlotte Brant's information. Pretending to be a cop, putting Brian in a position to distract Charlie. It should have worked. He had hoped Brian would distract Charlie a lot longer. So many promises but nothing delivered.

Unfortunately, that plan didn't work so now he needed to think of something new. A more aggressive strategy.

Safely out of eyesight on the empty roof, Michael was free to let his wings stretch as far as they could. It was a relief to let them air out. He hated having to hide them, but the humans would have likely lost their minds if they'd seen a man with wings walk down their streets. Mortals were fickle beings...

He heard footsteps crunching behind him and he gave an annoyed shake of his head, bringing his wings back into his body so that they absorbed into his back.

"You're late," he said, disapprovingly.

"Is that so?"

The voice was not what he was expecting. Michael whirled around to see a man he did not know. A wave of malice flowed off the stranger as he stopped in front of Michael. He stood unphased at having seen a literal angel. Dark veins scrawled up the man's neck, reaching towards his bloodshot eyes. Thick black slime oozed out of his ears and down his neck. Even the air itself struggled away from the man, as though trying to keep from touching him.

From touching pure evil.

"Impossible..." The word was low, even, but with an edge of growing anger.

"Is that all I get after all this time?" the man asked.

"You're supposed to be locked away in the pits of hell." His words rushed out of his mout and Michael could no longer hold back the anger rising inside him. His hand reached for his belt, and he magically willed forth a flame-bladed weapon.

The man clicked his tongue at Michael and tilted his head. "When the light fades, darkness will always find its way." He smiled. "Did you think you all could keep me locked away forever? Your father forgets who I am... Have you learned nothing after all these years? He's turned his back on you all."

"Enough of this." Michael stepped forward, gripping his sword ready to swing, but the man held a hand up and it was enough to make Michael stop in his tracks.

"Did your father send you on another mission, Michael?" He was met with silence. "I see. And did he tell you everything? Did he tell you all the sordid details about my incarceration? About the things he's done in the name of...well... himself? Did he tell you what will happen when you fail?"

"I won't fail. I never have and I never will."

"Oh, sweet boy, you amuse me. I'll give you a hint, firstborn son. You will fail, you will come crawling to me begging, and then you *will* fall, Michael. Then you will be the same as me. A pitiful creature who is only asking for another chance."

"Lies!"

"Have I ever lied to you? Unlike *Him*." His grin stretched ear to ear. The Darkness, for all his evil ways, had never lied. But that didn't mean he wouldn't start now.

The man's self-satisfied laughter filled Michael's ear, and his grip tightened on the hilt of his great sword. He rushed the man, plunging the sword right through the center of the dark creature. Michael sneered.

"Take your false promises back to hell with you."

When he pulled the blade out, it was coated in a thick foul substance, its holy fire smothered out. The man clutched Michael's shoulder, stumbling into him with a grin that chilled him to the core. He didn't fight. He didn't antagonize him. It was just what it was. This angered Michael. The creature had always played games, but he never actually lied.

Michael pushed those thoughts out of his mind. He was a harbinger for good. For the light. He was to snuff out the darkness that tried to consume the world. It was his purpose.

"You... can't... suppress... the darkness."

Michael felt no pity as the man crumpled at his feet. Unfortunately, he hadn't killed the abomination that had been controlling that body. The mortal man it had been driving around had long been dead and there was no saving him. Releasing his physical body from its bonds was the only solace he could offer him. Sadly, the Archangel also knew that the man's soul would have suffered for the wicked games of that monstrous beast.

"You said you'd make sure she was safe!"

Michael's head snapped around to see Brian had finally arrived. He cleaned the dark goo from his blade as he walked towards his partner.

"What took you so long?"

"What took me so long?" Brian echoed, nostrils flaring. "I was watching my wife get kidnapped by your psycho brother, that's what took me so long. You told me she would be safe. Being in Lucifer's grasp doesn't exactly scream safe, does it? And what the fuck was that?!"

Brian waved a hand aggressively at the corpse lying at Michael's feet. Michael watched as Brian's face contorted. It reeked of old death; much older than the mere moments it had been. Like everything inside that unmoving shell of a body had been rotting for some time and was opened to the world by Michael's blade.

"You wouldn't understand. Your mortal brain would explode."

"Is that supposed to be a joke?" Brian stared at him with narrowed eyes before letting out an aggravated sigh, "You were the one that picked *me*."

Michael nodded slowly. "I did. Because you were a warrior at heart, and I was confident you wouldn't let anything get in the way of the mission."

A look of embarrassment crept over Brian's face at that. The angel already knew what had happened. Brian failed at keeping Charlie away until he sent Lucifer back. It was as simple as that.

"At least that's what I'd been led to believe. Now I'm not so certain."

Brian grumbled, shaking his head and looking out over the dark rooftops surrounding them. "You don't know Charlie. She's stubborn, pig-headed, confrontational, doesn't listen to a word I say."

"You still love her," Michael accused.

Brian paused, leveling the angel with an apprehensive stare. Of course, he still loved Charlie. Everything he'd done, he'd done for her. He knew she believed some terrible things about him, and about why he left, and he didn't blame her for it at all.

The last thing he wanted was to cause her pain. But sometimes you have to inflict a little pain to prevent a lot of suffering. This was the sacrifice he'd chosen. She might hate him forever, but he had been resting well knowing she was still alive and well enough to hate him. He'd done that for her.

Though after their night together, he was no longer sure she did.

"Yeah. Yeah, I do. But that doesn't change anything."

"You called her your wife just a moment ago. Not Charlie. Not ex."

Brian's eyes softened a touch as he pointed that out. He had his full attention now. Good.

"Love can change *everything*," Michael continued. "It makes you hesitant. Sloppy. Love has destroyed cities, crushed empires, and changed the course of human progression. Millions upon millions of innocent people have perished at love's unkind hand."

He looked down at the corpse lying between their feet. "With what's coming, we cannot afford to be anything but focused. You need to push how you feel down so you can see the bigger picture. Or all will be lost."

"Alright," Brian said, but it hardly sounded convincing.

"Including your wife."

Brian's eyes snapped up to meet the angel's hard stare. A silent understanding passed between them, and after a moment the fight eased out of Brian's posture.

"So, what do we do now?" he asked.

That was a step in the right direction. Though Brian finally seemed to be less interested in fighting against him, Michael could still sense the unease radiating off him. He was curious how much he could push the mortal before he cracked.

"Bring her to me."

There was a long pause as if Brian was weighing his options. Though he knew Brian was a smart soldier, Michael could feel the rage building up inside of him, barely held back by sheer force of will.

"That wasn't part of the deal. She's not to be used as bait for your sick games."

"Necessity is the mother of all change." Michael didn't show any sort of emotion as he stepped forward towards Brian.

"You told me she would be safe," he repeated his sentiment from before. "You said if I helped you that you would make sure she wasn't involved."

"She involved herself, already," Michael said flatly.

"The hell she did!" Brian snapped. "She doesn't want to be involved in any of this shit. Trust me, I know her. It's Lucifer who's dragging her into this mess. Just let me get her away, far away, and we can get back to work getting rid of this bastard."

"It's too late!" Michael's eyes glowed eerily in the dark. "She's in it. Deeply. She can't run from the darkness anymore, and she's the key to its defeat. Or its rise. We need to take control of the situation before we lose our chance to stop it."

"I won't betray her again," Brian said, taking a step back from the angel as he pressed forward.

"You will do what's necessary," Michael said. "Because you won't have a choice."

"Don't do this." Brian was pleading with the angel, but Michael had already made up his mind.

"You will comply."

Michael locked eyes with Brain and watched as his breath quickened, his muscles tensing from head to toe. The human strained, fighting against his own body, but the fight was futile. What he'd been able to learn from Brian and his superiors had been enough to figure out how to work this to his advantage.

He could hear his pulse even out, and watched all emotion drain out of his face, leaving a silent, empty, compliant shell. A robot waiting for orders.

"Good, now let's begin," Michael said.
"As you order."

Chapter 14

TWELVE LONG HOURS WITH nothing but the company of her own thoughts was not an ideal situation for Charlie. Her mind could easily stumble into a dark place full of cruel and unforgiving lies disguised as truths. They wrapped around her, bound her in place as they wreaked havoc on her nervous system. Peeled away everything good and happy and light that kept her going.

Being locked in a small place brought back unpleasant memories of being confined to a hospital room while the world moved on without her. While her husband moved on without her.

Granted the bed was absolutely the best thing she'd ever slept on, but it wasn't home. It wasn't *her* safe space.

After waking, she excluded herself to the farthest corner of the room, sliding down the wall and feeling the crippling anxiety taking hold of her chest. Charlie rocked back and forth, with her face buried in her knees, while her arms wrapped around her legs.

You're weak.

"No, I'm not."

You let this happen.

"The fuck I did."

You fail at everything.

"Actually... you're right."

"Charlotte?"

Now *that* voice wasn't hers...

Her head shot up to see Lucifer kneeling in front of her. The sympathetic look in his eyes took Charlie by complete surprise. His usual smugness and wry grin were nowhere to be found. Instead, he looked as though he actually cared.

She put her face back on her knees, worried that his look of concern would break something inside her and her emotions would just spill out, raw and exposed and vulnerable. She didn't want the Devil to pity her. How twisted was that?

Oddly enough, as he grew closer, she realized the voices had faded from her head.

"Don't like being locked away?"

"What could possibly make you think that?" She questioned, flatly.

"Well, talking to yourself as you rock in a dark corner tends to tip one off." A soft, soul-warming chuckle came from him. He grabbed her wrist and gently pulled her arm away from her knees, running a soft fingertip along the black ink in her skin making it shimmer again. "That... and I'm attuned to your emotions, remember?"

Charlie lifted her head again and he released her wrist back to her. So, he knew *exactly* how she felt. Another thing to add to the list of 'things that Charlie hates'. That list seemed to be growing quite long in an impressively short time.

"Lucky you. You get a taste of the crazy," she said, her voice edged with a resigned darkness. "Thought you weren't gonna touch me until you were sure I wouldn't cut your hands off."

"Call it a calculated risk," he said softly, obviously joking though his voice was soft and serious. "Tell me, Charlotte, no bullshit. What is happening inside that head of yours?"

Charlie grinned, though it felt strange. As though it were a mirage—there, but not quite real. "Wouldn't you like to know."

"Yes, I would," Lucifer countered, completely serious.

The smile dropped away easily, and she shook her head, looking back to her knees. She picked at the cloth covering them. Should she bother trying to explain it to him? What good would it do? Then again, what could it hurt?

"You know what sucks?"

"What?"

"When your kidnapper forgets your crazy pills." She flicked her eyes up at him. "Panic attacks. They, um.... They're fun in the most not-fun sort of way."

Lucifer apparently made another calculation, because his hand slipped over one of hers, holding it lightly. "You're not crazy. Not in the slightest."

Her eyes narrowed slightly, and she stared at his face for a heartbeat. There was no malice there, no joking nature to his features. He believed what he said in complete earnest.

"Yeah, well. My doctor, my old boss, pretty much every cop in the city, they all would probably beg to differ. Normally, these episodes aren't too bad. If I don't have my meds on me, I can usually find a way to distract myself until it passes but..." She pointed her index finger around them. "You don't really have a television or books or... I don't know... anything. So, it's just been me and the voices for hours. As far as company goes, they suck."

"I would have come sooner. I had some matters I had no choice but to attend to, but had I known..."

Charlie waved him off. "Nah., I get it. You're the King of Hell, right? I'm sure you have lots more important things to deal with than your human prisoner."

"You're not a prisoner here." He smiled before holding a hand out to her. She stared at it for a second then reached a shaky hand and took it. Lucifer lifted her to her feet but didn't release her hand. "Walk with me."

Charlie let out a deep sigh and nodded her head. Clearly, she didn't have a choice in the matter, so why fight? Lucifer led her through the hall, and she realized his home was so much larger than she'd originally imagined. Each room she passed was bigger than the last. She couldn't recall any property in New Orleans that could match its size. It was hard to tell where she was really, practically all the windows were covered by white curtains, blocking her view outside.

They eventually passed through a conservatory that was as big as the room that she'd been locked in. Plants of all assortments scattered the room, reminding her of a small jungle until they walked through two French doors. The moment they stepped through them, Charlie was met with a breathtaking view. She was right, she was definitely not back home.

The horizon rose to kiss the heavens, surrounding them with majestic mountain peaks. Charlie had never seen mountains in anything but pictures, but looking at them now, she could tell the photos never did them justice. A warm sunrise painted the sky behind the white peaks, looking far more serene than she thought she'd ever felt like in her entire life.

"Holy shit," she whispered. Any other words seemed to fail her.

"Glorious, isn't it?" Lucifer asked behind her ear. "I gotta say, I am a sucker for an exquisite view."

"Where are we?" Charlie asked, unable to tear her eyes from the horizon.

Lucifer moved past her, shrugging his shoulders with his hands clasped idly behind his back. "Now, you see, that part is a bit trickier to explain."

He moved to a small retaining wall at the edge of the walk-out patio and turned to face Charlie, leaning against it. "Technically speaking, you are at my home. And you are nowhere."

He looked at Charlie's face and smiled as she let him see the extent of her confusion. "What you see here is a replication. A pretty view I enjoyed once upon a time and decided to keep – you're still confused..." It wasn't a question. He nodded and stood to his full height again, reaching an arm out as though to beckon her closer.

After a moment of hesitation, Charlie complied, stepping alongside him as he led her down a stone path edged by hedges on either side. "There are very few places an angel, like my brother, can't pop in. One such place is my home in–"

"Hell," Charlie breathed as realization hit her.

"Yes. And no. But let's not be overdramatic about it. As you can see, it's not all sulfur and hellfire. It truly is just another realm of existence and one where I'm in power. So I can mold it to my liking. I happen to like the mountains."

She glanced at him and couldn't help but return the warm smile he gave her. Not wanting to linger too long, she quickly returned to looking around as they walked, taking in the finely kept lawns and gardens, the colorful blooms decorating the paths.

"So. I'm in Hell. Literally this time."

He chuckled beside her as they came upon a beautifully carved gazebo at the end of the path, and held a hand out as though to invite her to sit. "Yes. Well... technically we are on the *edge* of Hell. It's a hidden place for me to go and think. A loophole if you will. What do you think of it? I've been dying to get a real honest opinion of it and if I've learned one thing about you Ms. Brant, it's that you have no problem going right for my jugular with your brutal honesty."

Charlie tried to hide her smile from him by tucking her hair behind her ear as she walked under the canopy. On the ground, spread over large white linen, were all kinds of tasty-looking treats—cakes and cookies, crackers, meats, and cheeses, and a few different selections of wines. She quirked an eyebrow at him but said nothing as she lowered herself onto a tufted pillow waiting for her.

"Charlie," she said.

Lucifer was halfway down to the ground when she said it, and he looked at her as though he were taken by surprise. "Sorry?"

"If you are not going to go away any time soon, and you are damn determined to refer to me by name every five minutes... then the name is Charlie. Not Ms. Brant. Not Charlotte. Just Charlie."

"Ooh, does that mean we're friends now?" he said with a grin as he finished sitting down across from her.

"No," she said, but couldn't hide her smile from him this time.

Goddammit, this was not how she had planned to be with all this. She was supposed to be mean and surly and impossible to get to. Instead, she was finally starting to pick up on his charm through his infuriating exterior. It wasn't fair.

Lucifer didn't say anything, nor did his smile falter in the least. He popped a red grape into his mouth, chewing far too happily for her liking. Rather than exhausting herself with a battle of wits—as always seemed to be what happened with him—she decided to just go with it today.

Tomorrow, if he didn't take her home, then she could go back to her normal pissy self. Today, she had to admit she was starving and the little picnic laid out before her was winning her over.

For now.

Lucifer -1. Charlie - 0.

"So, what can I call you? Luci?"

He went green around the gills at that suggestion, his smile vanishing with the blink of an eye. Swallowing hard, he cleared his throat and forced the smile back into place, though she could tell he was not completely sincere in it. "No. Please, let's just... not."

The sudden change in demeanor only piqued her curiosity. Oof. She'd touched a sore spot it seemed. Did the Devil himself get bullied as a child? Now that was an insane, but interesting thought.

"Not a favorite of yours?" she asked, though the answer was already pretty clear.

"Let's just say that family can really eat away at you after a few lifetimes. Especially when one particularly annoying relative likes to torment you while lazing about every home you acquire and leech away your very patience." He said it as his eyes glanced at the stoney front of his home, before rolling and returning his attention back to her.

"Another angel?" Charlie asked, curiously.

"Not as such," he said, grabbing a bottle of white wine and opening it. "We'll call it... a cousin. From the other side of the family."

Charlie stared at him a few moments before it hit her. "Oh! Oh, you mean demons?"

At this point, nothing seemed to surprise her. What else could once you've been kidnapped by the literal King of Hell? He confirmed her guess with a nod and poured them each a glass.

"So, you have demons living with you," she said, taking her glass.

"That goes without saying. Most just pass through from time to time, but there are a couple that tend to over-stay their welcome. Asmodeus and Abaddon are especially hard to shake off when they get bored." He put the wine back and grabbed his glass, bringing it to his mouth before whispering, "Fucking leeches."

"Asmodeus and Abaddon," Charlie said softly to herself. "Why do those names sound familiar?"

"Mm. Well," he offered her a plate of crackers and brie, "because they are some of the most prolific demonic entities, I suppose. Even those not well-read in the occult have at least heard their names in passing. See, where I'm the King of Hell, they are two of the princes. Asmodeus, the Prince of Lust—terrible gossip—and Abaddon, the Prince of Pride. To be fair, of all the rest they are probably the two I can tolerate best. Though that's not saying very much."

Charlie tried to focus on eating and taking in the information he offered. Pride and Lust. Fun. "So that leaves Envy, Sloth, Gluttony, Wrath, and Greed," she listed off. He nodded. "So which sin belongs to you?"

A slow grin spread over his face at the question, and it made her squirm slightly in her own skin.

"Well, I thought that would be obvious. All of them do, Charlie."

That put a bit of a pause in the conversation. She wasn't sure exactly what Lucifer meant by that, and to be completely honest, she wasn't sure she was ready to dig much deeper into it. The way he'd said it made her feel... strange. He already had a strange connection to her thanks to the mark he'd put on her, making it impossible to really hide what she was feeling. That motivated her to keep her emotions in check, and quickly.

If all the sins belonged to him then what could he do with them? The dream from the other night sprang to mind with such ferocious intensity that she nearly released an involuntary sigh. When she glanced back at Lucifer, she found his rich green eyes staring at her over the rim of his wine glass with a mischievous sparkle in them.

"Felt that."

Swallowing hard—and trying even harder to shove the memories of that dream back into their box—she drained her glass and set it down in front of her. "So how did you fall?"

The question fell out of her mouth so unexpectedly that even Lucifer hadn't seemed to be prepared for it. The sparkle in his eyes disappeared, his face going stoney and lifeless. A long silence stretched between them before he finally reached for a silver tray of sweets and held it out to her.

"Have you ever tried Baklava? It's delicious. I have it imported from a little cafe in Greece..."

"You can literally feel everything I'm feeling," Charlie said firmly, not taking the bait. "I think you owe me some personal baggage, Lucifer."

He stared at her over the offered tray, the muscles in his jaw tensing. Finally, he huffed and broke eye contact with her, setting the tray down with a soft *thunk* to the ground. "Fine. Fair's fair."

He shrugged his jacket off his shoulders and tossed it aside, his movements a little jerkier and more hot-tempered than she'd been used to so far. He bent his knees, pulling them to his chest and resting his arms on them. The whole thing looked much more vulnerable than she'd ever expected from the King of Hell himself.

"They have it all wrong you know," he said, finally. "All the books. The bibles. The stories. Just one long-played game of telephone. Stories pass from lips to ears, over and over until the truth loses its entertainment value and what's left is a tangled and manipulated mess. So many versions of 'truth' are out there now that the word no longer holds value."

Charlie understood what he meant. There were lots of stories, many of them contradicting each other. Even she found it hard to trust organized religion and Charlie wasn't even sure if she believed in any of it. Christianity, paganism, whatever. She'd seen such horrific things in her line of work and the idea of any powerful deity existing and simply choosing to ignore its worshippers in their time of need? It was inexcusable and made not believing in the existence of any of them the more comforting choice.

But how could she continue to not believe they existed when one of them was sitting across from her, eating Baklava and looking so wistful?

"You want to know how I fell?" A bitter smile graced his lips as he finally looked at her again. "I didn't. How many religions do you think I could crumble to dust if they were to learn of that?"

"Well... all the Abrahamic ones, at least," Charlie answered, though she knew he hadn't really been asking.

"Right. Well, the story is a lot more pathetic on my part, I'm afraid. So, all of their little dogmatic beliefs, everything that keeps them feeling safe and cozy in their beds when they finish their prayers, are safe. The real truth isn't one I'm proud of. I'd rather the whole of existence keep believing my father's truth—that I'm a monster. It keeps them thinking of me as something to fear. I'd much rather have their fear than their pity. It's less complicated that way."

Charlie tried not to simply hear his words but really take in everything he was saying. A person's body language often told her more than their words, and she was surprised to see that the Devil was no exception. He was so drawn in on himself, comforting himself within his own embrace.

He only trusted one being. Himself. What a lonely existence that had to be.

Without thinking, Charlie reached out and rested a hand on top of his arm. He stared at it like it was a deer he was afraid to frighten off by moving too quickly. His eyes carefully swept along the length of her arm until they reached her face. She rewarded him with a soft smile.

"Maybe you need someone to hear your story. The real story," she suggested. Sitting back on her heels again, she shrugged. "I mean, why waste a captive audience?" She could see him debating the idea. "What do you have to lose?"

His smile tugged at one side of his mouth. "Are you sure? I'd hate to completely dismantle your faith on the first date."

"This isn't a date," she said a little too quickly. Clearing her throat and trying to ignore the humor in his eyes she pressed on. "And trust me. You can't damage it more than it already is."

He mulled that around for a moment and she watched nearly imperceptible changes shift across his face as he pondered whether to tell her or not. For a moment, the solemnity in his eyes had her believing he'd deny her the story, but something new kindled within them. Something resolute, but worried.

Finally, he pulled the flirtatious mask back on, hiding his hesitancy from her, and leaned into her. The sudden closeness of him made her throat tighten, but she managed to hold her ground and not run away, even as his wicked grin grew even closer.

She licked her lips as his face stopped inches away from hers. Fingertips slowly grazed upward from the crook of her elbow, breaking her skin out in goosebumps. They traced the curve of her bicep, up and across her collarbone. By the time he reached the hollow of her throat, his eyes had her ensnared.

"As you wish."

Chapter 15

"WHAT DO YOU GET when you merge pure darkness and pure light?" Lucifer knew that his eyes started to glow into that golden hue that she was familiar with. He also knew what it was doing to her as she sat there. Her lips fell apart as she sucked in air.

"I'm not sure, what?" she asked as she looked at him with curious eyes.

"A god-killing weapon." Acting like this was common knowledge, Lucifer shrugged. He took notice that she was a little confused by his statement, so he added, "I was forged by God to kill his brother."

"Wait, God has a brother?"

"And a sister." He nodded his head and added that little fact, happy to find he held her interest now.

"When God created me, he set off an imbalance of nature. He took the light he controlled," he held out his left hand as a glowing orb grew from his palm, "which is what the angels were made from. And then, that naughty father of mine stole a bit of his brother's darkness, the very core of Hell itself." He mirrored his left hand with his right, but this time a dark shadow swirled about in his palm. "Then, the old man smashed them together," this he demonstrated with the shadow and the light, pressing them together between his palms until they swirled in a beautiful dance that was near hypnotic to watch, "and made me, a Nephilim. The first of my kind."

Charlie couldn't tear her eyes from the swirling orb in his hand. With a smile and a flick of his wrist, the orb disappeared, freeing her gaze.

"You mentioned something about a weapon," she said finally.

"Yes, I did."

He stood lifting her up with a hand as they started to walk down to an entrance of a garden maze. However, once they stepped through the hedge, the world around them disappeared until they were walking on literally nothing, surrounded by even more nothingness.

Charlie's eyes widened and Lucifer couldn't help but smile wider as she seemed to move a touch closer to him. He wondered how a mortal brain might handle what was happening now. Even in dreams, the humans were determined to create some semblance of reality.

In the vast nothingness, a diffused light spread throughout, drawing her attention to the distance. "As I said, I was created to kill his brother. My father is nothing if not... petty. Paranoid, one might even say. He and his siblings were rulers of their own domains. God, the Creator. Gaia, of Nature. And then there was the Darkness. The Destroyer. With the three of them, there was true balance to life.

So, when the Destroyer created his own race of creatures—demons—dear old Dad felt threatened. He convinced Gaia that their brother was plotting to create the world and everything in it in his image, and together they created a great spear that could kill a god. Only, neither of their creations could wield it without being completely destroyed."

"So, they made you," Charlie said. It pleased him that she was able to keep up so well.

"A soldier with one purpose. To drive the spear through their brother's heart and rid the world of Darkness and Destruction. To be fair, Gaia had little to do with what came of me. Always the neutral party, once she had given God the sacred wood for the handle, she went back to her own realm."

He noticed Charlie looking him over a little more closely, and said nothing to interrupt her thoughts. The light continued in the distance like a growing lightning storm building up to wash over them, but it made no move to get closer.

"So," she said finally, "I take it you won? Seeing as you're here talking to me, making my life one big cluster-fuck."

He gave a thin-lipped smile, something passing behind his eyes. "Yes. Yes, I won," he said, though it sounded nothing like an accomplishment.

A dark shadow sprouted behind them and Charlie turned sharply on her heel. Lucifer wrapped his hands around her shoulders, holding her back against his chest as they watched the shadow take the vague form of a giant man. The light that had been crackling in the distance shot down to the non-existent ground in front of the shadow giant with a sharp crack that echoed all around them. From the strike, a smaller figure ran towards its foe, a smaller dark shadow swirling around in his chest where his heart should be.

"I gave up everything for my mission. Life. Love. Happiness. My father's call pulled me from what could have been a life of peaceful contentment and called up to arms."

"Love? You?" Charlie said, sounding skeptical.

Wow, this woman could kill the mood. He lowered his face beside hers, taking in a slow breath before continuing. "Yes, Charlie. I have loved. And I loved well. But can we please focus? I'm revealing my big dramatic heartbreak, and you are kind of ruining the build-up."

He didn't have to see her face to know her eyes were rolling at him. He smiled. Whether or not he liked to admit it, he was rather fond of that particular mannerism of hers. It was so... human. No, it was *her*.

"Moving on. I took up arms, just as I was made to do. You see, with both the light and the dark inside of me, I could get closest to him while still holding the spear. And I did. Right through his heart."

The light stretched at the small figure's hand until the form included a long spindle-like spear. They watched together, Lucifer quietly drinking in the way her body moved as she drew in one excited breath after another. Even if her mouth didn't distract him, the smell of her hair was doing a fantastic job of it all on its own. The figure jumped and flipped before them like a leaf tumbling on the wind until the spear pierced the shadow giant's heart.

"Bullseye," Lucifer whispered in her ear.

"So, you killed the Destroyer. You did what no being could," Charlie said. If only it was so simple.

"Shhhh," Lucifer shushed, gently grabbing her chin to turn her attention back to the scene. "You'll miss the encore. My favorite part."

The chest of the shadow man began to glow around the tip of the spear, the glow spreading larger within the center of him. As the light seemed to pour into it, it seeped away from the smaller figure. From an outside viewpoint, it was as though the shadow were siphoning the light from the other being, while the small shadow within its chest started filling in the rest of it. It tried to pull free, but the giant imploded in on itself, taking with it the last drop of light from the small figure, who fell to his knees on the ground.

Charlie was so still and quiet beside him, that Lucifer dared not make a move to even look at her. His heartbeat pounded heavily in his chest as he wondered what her exact thoughts were watching everything unfold. Though he knew, she'd not yet seen everything.

The kneeling figure thrashed back, then forward, his fists beating into the ground in front of him. They could see his back rise and fall in heavy breaths before he threw himself back again, his hands shooting to the top of his head as two large spikes shot up and out of his skull.

The figure exploded into a fine mist, swirling darkly against the white void until it came upon a new giant—this time made of near-blinding light. It reformed into the horned shape of the man, kneeling at the giant's feet, begging. The giant turned its back on him, and from the center of its chest a new light being, the same size as the shadow, charged out and attacked.

The two beings swirled about one another, light and dark, fighting and dodging until, with a mighty blow from the light one's sword, the shadow being shot violently downward to the ground. Around him, the white void melted into dark masses and peaks, until one lifted the shadow-being so that he sat upon it in a circle of shadow.

When Lucifer risked a glance at his companion again, he found her covering her mouth with her hand, a look of pure disbelief shining in her hazel eyes. He licked his lip, dislodging her from his grip and taking a step away to give her a moment to process all of it.

"He... blocked you out?" she finally asked.

Lucifer didn't answer, the words still paining him deep down. The intuitive little detective saw his silence for what it was, and her face contorted from a look of pity to a look of disgust.

"You did exactly what was expected of you," she said, staring at the figure on the throne, "and he tossed you aside like garbage."

"As will always be the *love* of God. You are special to him until your use has run its course."

"What happened when you killed the Destroyer? I saw... but I don't think I understand what I saw. You went from light to shadow. Was it your light that killed him?"

Lucifer shrugged softly. "Yes... and no. It was my light that helped me fight against him but when I reigned victorious..." he scratched his neck, not wanting to look at the little show anymore. With a violent wave of his arm, it all disappeared and they were again surrounded by nothingness. "My light left me. Devoured by the Darkness and leaving me with nothing but the part of me that's formed of shadow."

"Can you get it back?"

"Doubtful. No, I imagine it's still with him in whatever box he's landed in."

Charlie looked even more confused at that. "Box? I thought he was dead."

"Oh, you precious woman," he laughed, sliding a hand across her shoulders to start her walking with him again. "The thing about gods is it's incredibly, *unfathomably* difficult to kill them in the permanent sense. I'm sure my father and Gaia both believed the spear would be it, as that's what it was crafted for, but the world cannot exist without darkness. It's as much a necessity as air or water. You cannot have creation without destruction. Something

I think my wily aunt knows full well. Of course... that's just speculation on my part." He grinned wide, thinking about all the years of careful pondering he'd enjoyed.

"No, the Destroyer was imprisoned on another plane of existence, safely tucked away from this realm, Gaia's realm... all of it. And he has my light to keep him company. To answer your question. I did not kill him; he's just locked away."

"Do you *want* it back? If it was possible, I mean."

He thought about that for a few moments, amused at the question. "Now, Charlie. Why would you think I would want that after ruling over Hell? After having all this power?"

Charlie stopped mid-step, forcing him to halt with her. She stared up at him with the most earnest look he'd ever seen given to him. "Because I saw your pain when God turned his back on you."

Lucifer's good-humored smile fell slowly. Yes, it had hurt. Quite deeply in fact. To him, there was no greater betrayal than what his father had done to him, but the last thing he wanted was for anyone—even the spectacular Ms. Brant—to pity him. An exaggerated sigh escaped him and he looked away from her, shaking his head.

"I think that's enough revelation for today. Sleep well, Ms. Brant." With a wave of his hand, Charlie's form was swept away like so much dust in the wind, leaving him to stand alone in his own mind.

"Yes, that's quite enough."

The smell of flowers filled his nostrils the moment his eyes began to open. Rich, fragrant, and full of the essence of life. When he finally opened his eyes, he found he was cuddled up against Charlie's side. She was still sleeping peacefully, her face relaxed more than he'd ever been allowed to see. She was beautiful when she wasn't busting his balls.

No, she was captivating even then.

Lucifer could watch her sleep all day, and probably would have if given half the chance, but knew she'd wake soon. Knowing she would probably be less than ecstatic to wake up with the Devil spooning her, he lifted up to give her some space and immediately took notice of the fresh growth of flowers that surrounded them. No, surrounded *her*. Impossible. Only he could change this realm how he saw fit. Yet, the truth was staring him right in the face.

Like some sort of fairytale princess, lost to a night of deep sleep and awaiting true love's first kiss, Charlie was laying in the middle of a colorful blanket of flora that he had not had any part in creating. As if she weren't already enchanting in her own right.

"What are you?" His words were a mere breath of a whisper. No, not a princess. Not a fairytale one anyway...

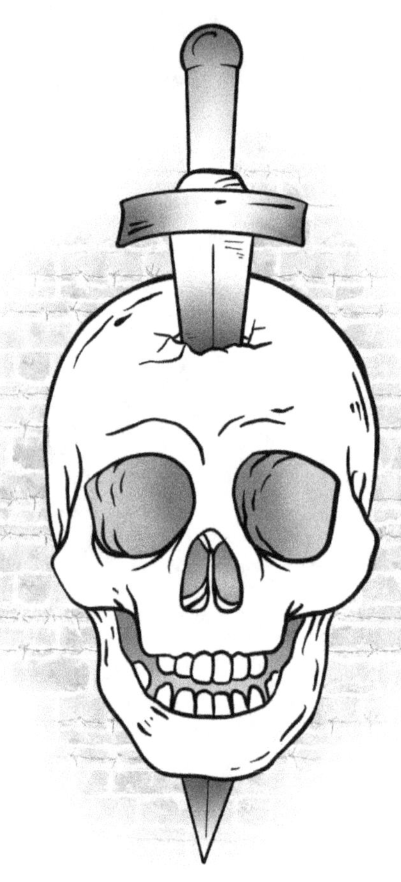

Chapter 16

BRIAN HADN'T FOUND ANY trace of Charlie since her little disappearing act. Since *he* had taken her. It was highly unlikely he would be able to track down Lucifer. Even if he did, it wasn't like the Devil would actually tell him anything.

The only other person that might know where else to look was Carmen. Surely, Charlie had told her best friend everything that was going on. Given her some clues he could use to find where Lucifer might be keeping her.

Trying to convince Carmen to help would be difficult, considering how much the woman hated him.

She'd be running through the park, as she did almost every night. Vega lived her life to the tick of the clock, a habit from her military career. She carried that discipline and drive through her time with Evairlast and into her new civilian way of life. It had no small part in getting her where she was today.

The steady rhythm of feet hitting pavement put him on the ready. Any moment now she'd round the curve that cut through the trees and into his line of sight.

Within moments, she appeared, her dark ponytail swinging behind her like a metronome. She paced herself well, not quite falling to a brisk jog, not pushing herself too hard and fast. He could see the sweat darkening the neck of her tank top. She had been going for a while now, which was good for him should things take a turn for the worse.

Brian caught up to her easily, pulling up to run beside her. The dark glove fit like a second skin, covering her from her fingertips to just above her bicep. A wide strap sprouted from the top hem and wrapped around her chest, attaching to the glove again on the opposite side of her arm. He hadn't been privy to Evairlast's file on Vega, but Jarred had told him about the I.E.D. that had nearly killed her. Vendettas aside, he had to give her respect for pulling herself up and pushing forward.

She slid a look at him as they ran side by side, her skin glistening with sweat. He flashed a smile at her, and she rolled her eyes, slowing to a stop.

"What the hell are you doing here, Brian?" Carmen said between each breath as she pulled out her earbuds.

"Where's Charlie?" Brian kept his grin frozen in place while shoving his hands into his pocket. He was trying to act like the boy scout people claimed he was.

"Do I look like her handler?" She snorted and shook her head.

"Aren't you?" he asked.

Vega hadn't seemed amused at that.

With a shrug, he glanced around at their surroundings. A seemingly idle movement, but in reality, every glance and observation had its purpose. The park seemed to be emptying for the night, leaving them alone.

"I just mean, I know you watch her back. And I appreciate that you do that for her. I know how hard-headed she can be, especially when she's on a job."

She looked at him with a raised eyebrow, trying to decide what he wanted from her no doubt. "Yeah, I mean someone has to look out for her. Her deadbeat ex-husband really did a number on her when he left her, you know."

Her words should have hurt him, but their deadly edge glanced off him. "We had lunch together the other day," he said, still trying to stay on her good side. "Hashed things out. It was a long time coming, but I think we're going to be okay."

She rolled her eyes at him, moving to put her earbud back into her ear. "That's great for you. Always nice to see assholes escape their consequences."

She turned to continue her run and he grabbed her gloved arm, keeping her in place. Vega stopped mid-step and looked at his hand on her arm, then up at him with a look that was anything but friendly.

His grin was gone. "Where... is... Charlie?"

That was the only thing that mattered in this moment. Not pleasantries, not old friendships. His orders from Michael took priority over keeping things friendly.

Vega looked him over, but he just stared down at her.

"What the hell did they do to you?" she asked, softly.

With a shake of her head, she held her hands up as though to say she didn't want to know. "Like I said, I'm not her handler. She can do whatever the hell she pleases. For all I know she could be in Vegas right now and I wouldn't give a damn," her eyes narrowed in on his face, "as long as it gets her away from you."

"She's in danger and I need to find her."

Vega was still looking him over, sizing him up. "Charlie is a big girl. She can handle herself."

He saw the subtle twitch in her eyebrow. She was a good soldier once, but clearly, civilian life had made her rusty, she wasn't able to keep that stoic facade up. Brian could tell there was a hint of worry in her tone. That was what he needed in hopes of making her crack.

"See, that's where you're wrong. I need to protect her. I'm the only one who can."

Vega laughed at that. "The hell you do. Look, you lost the right to protect her when you tossed her aside like garbage. She's better off without your help." She yanked her arm free before crossing them over her chest. "Now if you're done, I need to finish my run."

Brian stared at her for a few moments, holding her gaze. She was a fierce woman, he'd give her that.

Finally, he stepped aside and held an arm out as if to say, "after you." When Vega finally broke eye contact, she jogged off ready to leave him behind. He'd let her believe she'd won this particular fight.

She was about ten yards out when Brian called out, "Does Jarred know about Camilla?"

Vega stopped so abruptly, she nearly stumbled over her own feet. She stood with her back to Brian while he watched her shoulders rise and fall a little more animatedly. The contortion of pure hatred on her face when she turned around was as clear as if she were standing right in front of him.

"Evairlast is good about keeping what's theirs safe," he added as she stormed closer to him. "I could keep her safe."

"Is that a threat, Hart? Because if it is, I would think long and hard on what it is you're about to say next." Vega stared up at him like a snake about to strike.

He simply smiled down at her, his dimples belying the mania surging within him. "Not a threat. A promise."

Her gloved hand shot out at him, fingers wrapping around his throat with an unrelenting grasp. His feet left the earth as she lifted him up by his neck, her eyes wild.

There wasn't even a hint of struggle from lifting a man twice her size.

"I have a promise of my own. If you so much as look at my daughter, breath in her general direction, I will fucking end you. And anyone else your bosses might send in your place. Do you hear me?"

He wrapped his hands around her wrist, but gave no other indication that was moved by the situation he found himself in.

In fact, his smile only seemed to widen as he added, "Even Jarred?"

Her fingers dug even harder into his throat and his hands tightened.

"Anyone," she hissed out, her eyes shining around the edges.

That struck a nerve. The faintest of tremors shook under his hands and he knew he had an opening. He kicked off her, using her as a springboard to leap back, and land in a ready stance for what was yet to come.

"That I'd be dying to see," he said, raising his fists.

Brian hadn't put too much force into the kick, so he wasn't surprised when she recovered quickly.

"You won't be around long enough to," she said.

"Come on, Vega. Just tell me where Charlie is," he offered again. "We really don't have to get your family involved. You can walk away and go live your little mommy fantasy. Just tell me where to find her."

She kicked upward but he blocked it easy with both hands, redirecting the kick away from him. As she spun, she brought her elbow up and used the momentum to drive it back into his sternum. He stumbled back a few steps while she reset herself in a defensive stance.

"She *is* my family, you piece of shit."

A deep laugh escaped Brian and he idly rubbed the spot her elbow had struck.

"Family. Right." He lunged at her, swinging his left fist at her but missing as she dodged. His right was already in motion by the time she'd moved and he caught her in the ribs, nearly knocking her off her feet. "You abandoned her, too, Vega. Or don't you remember?"

Vega swung her gloved fist at him, but it glanced off his shoulder, giving him an opening to drive his own elbow down onto her back, dropping her to her knees. Groaning, she dug her fingers into the ground.

"Weren't you there, too?" he continued, circling her as she breathed through the pain. "Didn't she save your ass? And what did you do to repay her? Snagged yourself a shiny promotion while she got fired. *I* saved her. *I* sacrificed everything for her! You were the one who called them. You separated her from her real family."

Vega forced herself back up as he swung, blocking with her gloved arm, and responded with an uppercut to his chin. It connected, but with little effect.

"Tell me something, Chief. Have you told her yet?" he asked as he brushed his chin, slowly circling.

He could see his words soaking in. Something more than just the anger she had towards him.

"Oh..." he said "You haven't. This whole time she's been feeling like she's losing her mind, and you have the answer right there." He started to laugh, "Jesus, and you think *I'm* a sick son of a bitch?"

Vega screamed wordlessly, lunging for him again. He straight-armed her, shoving her to the side as he pulled a thin black cylinder from his belt.

"What would she do if she knew? You think she would just laugh it off?"

Vega lunged a second time, clearly winded. With a flick of his wrist, he extended the ASP in his hand and brought it sharply across her face. She was still far enough out of reach that it only sliced her cheek open with its small tip. It could have been much worse.

And it still might be. He was getting tired of this shit, and extra tired of her mouth every time he came around. She was the one that dripped poison in Charlie's mind. Turned her against him. If it wasn't for Vega, none of this would have happened. The urge to shut her up for good was strong. It would remove an obstacle. The plan could still work.

Unsurprisingly, the ex-Marine did not stop. Blood poured down her cheek, but he had given her more than enough reason to try to put him down. She kicked out and swept at his feet. Rooting his stance, he let the hit connect. Dropping his knee down on her leg, holding her in place, he whipped the ASP across her face.

"Come on, Vega. Don't make your kid an orphan," he said, hovering over her.

Laying on her back, covered in dirt and blood. "Fuck you." A fat glob of bloody spit ejected from her busted lips onto his face, and he wiped it away in disgust.

His boot connected full-force into her ribs and she curled into herself with a painful cry. Strike after strike, Brian hit her with fist and baton, feeling a steady urge to snuff her out rising within him. As he made to bring the ASP down again, her gloved hand reached out and stopped its descent, her fist wrapping around the thin metal and crumbling it like a soda can. He let go and punched her in the back of the head before standing to his full height.

"A freak like the rest of us." A wild grin spread across his face. "They made modifications to me, too. Brought me to my fullest potential. Too bad they just dumped you off before they were done with you. I guess they realized what a waste of time you'd be after you gave them what they needed."

He wiped his mouth with the back of his arm as he stared down at her, moving to stand next to her head. "Maybe I will make Camilla an orphan after all."

He lifted his boot, ready to bring it down on her face when he heard a whisper on the breeze. *"That'll be all."*

Dazed and confused, Carmen's battered face appeared under Brian's foot, and he reeled back, nearly losing his balance. He blinked at her still body as though it were the first time seeing it, his stomach lurching with each newly discovered cut and bruise. At first, he was in shock at the state of her, not knowing how she had ended up like that.

Then it all began to flood back in.

Waiting for her in the dark. The awful things he had said. The complete lack of humanity as he beat the crap out of someone he once broke bread with. It was all disconnected. As if he'd watched the whole thing through a screen of static.

He looked down at his hands and couldn't decide whether he was shivering from the adrenaline or the guilt. His jaw clenched as he squeezed his bloodied knuckles, letting them fall to his side. Glancing behind him, he found Michael standing calm and patient.

"You asshole," he hissed through gritted teeth.

"What's done is done, Brian. I had no time. You were going to ruin everything if we continued to do it your way. You left me with no choice."

Brian could still feel traces of the command echoing in his ear. The need to find Charlie slowly coming down. Damn Michael — He used the command to trigger that part of Brian's psyche to go hunt like it was nothing. It sickened him. The fact that he was used like a fucking puppet. He never liked it then, and he sure as hell hated it now.

It was one of many fail-safes that Evairlast implemented for all their soldiers to make sure that the mission always went smoothly. The perfect soldier—one who suppressed their very being. Their emotions... No empathy, no compassion, none of those pesky feelings to hinder the mission. It was clear that Evairlast wanted more than soldiers. They were forging weapons to go up against creatures that looked just like them.

Michael walked closer as Brian pointed to Carmen's prone figure. "And this is what happens when you don't proceed with caution. She didn't deserve this."

"There will be a lot more undeserving souls suffering if we fail. I dislike this part of the job as much as you, but it is necessary. If it was someone you did not know, and the choice was between them and the end of all, would you still feel the same?"

"Then why stop me? Why not have me finish the job?"

"Because her death means nothing to the cause," Michael snapped. "I am more than ready to accept that deaths will be inevitable in this war, but only when necessary. We are not the monsters, Brian. If you had killed her, it would do nothing to stop what is coming. In fact, her death may only serve to drive your Charlie to him faster. But this," he waved a hand at Carmen, "may be a good message for Charlie to come to our side."

Brian cursed as he turned away abruptly. "She'll never forgive me."

He spoke softly and not to anyone in particular. He was grateful that Michael didn't speak. This was not what he signed up for. At least he didn't think so.

He hated lectures, hated being controlled. He got enough of that from his time in the military and still had issues with Evairlast. But, as much as it angered him to admit, Michael had made some valid points. Did he want Carmen dead? No. Not really. In the heat of the moment, maybe. Losing that moral instinct, that concern for your fellow man was easy. After all, that was what he was trained to do. It made life easier to not care.

This wasn't normal. Something had taken hold of him while he'd hurt her, something he hadn't realized he had inside him. All the times his superiors used the trigger, not once did he like it. This time?

He recalled the sound of his own laughter as he taunted Vega. His voice had sounded so distant, but there was no denying it was his. It should have scared him, but it didn't.

That should have scared him more.

"So now what?" Brian asked.

"I suppose you are right. We want Charlie on our side."

Michael looked down at the woman for a few moments and sighed, nudging her shoulder with the toe of his boot before moving it and letting her drop back into place. He leaned down, his hand hovered over her head as a white glow pulsed. Before Brian could ask what he was doing, Michael stepped away from her. "Call an ambulance for this one. Get her to a healer. She won't remember much;

that's all I can do. We will find another way to get to Charlie."

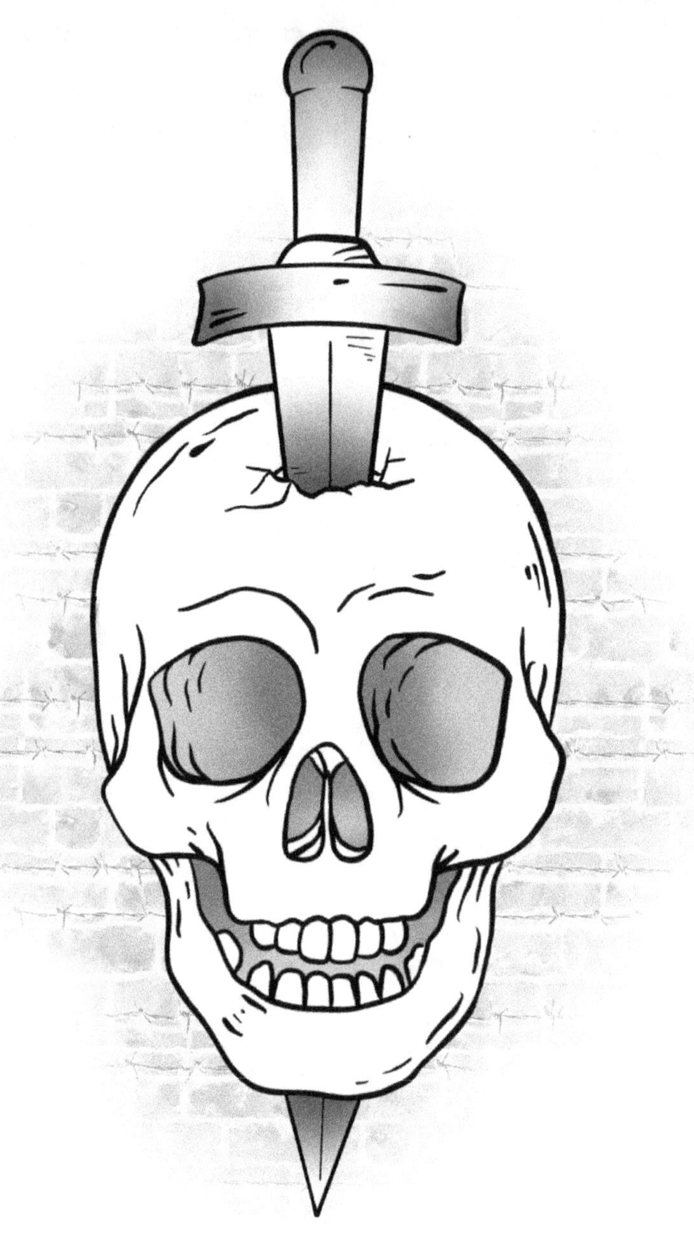

Chapter 17

AMONG THE OSTENSIBLY ENDLESS sea of his angelic siblings, Gabriel had to be one of the few Lucifer could tolerate. While the majority seemed to have little else going for them outside of an impenetrable sense of duty to the vague missives bestowed upon them by Michael or their father, Gabriel was different.

This particular Archangel was known as the Messenger of the Heavens. Which, if you ask Lucifer, was just another way of saying he had a flair for gossip.

While Gabriel was the angel responsible for bringing proclamations unto man, it didn't come without its price. Their father's holy book, for example, credits Gabriel with telling the Virgin Mary of her blessing. Lucifer, however, knew the truth of what really happened and how Gabriel—after several glasses of honey wine—had spread word of her condition.

The punishment for his continued gossiping had been great: banishment from their home to live among the humans on the earthly plane. Not that it stopped Gabriel from collecting useful information from behind the pearly gates. It was quite impressive, really. Lucifer had never riddled out how he was still able to possess such juicy tidbits of intel when he couldn't so much as set a single feather in paradise. That fact alone made him give Gabriel respect—even if the angel's heart was still a little too pure for his liking.

With all that said, when Lucifer needed answers his other brothers would not provide, going to Gabriel made the most sense. It also didn't hurt that his good natured spirit made him easier to manipulate.

It had taken a little more time than he'd expected, but eventually Lucifer spied his quarry in a booth at the back of a diner. The place was depressingly empty for the time of day. A foreboding sign for the proprietor, but a welcome detail for Lucifer.

Gabriel may be more meek than Michael, but he was still an Archangel. Letting one's guard down would be foolish. And dealing with the unexpected in the midst of humans was a headache Lucifer did not care to endure right then.

"Not today, Lucifer," Gabriel said as his brother approached his table. His eyes never left the plate of steaming waffles in front of him. "I wish for my appetite to remain intact."

Ignoring him, Lucifer slid into the booth and draped an arm over the back, his smile growing wide on his lips. Gabriel let out an exaggerated sigh before setting his fork down and tossing an agitated glance at Lucifer.

"Oh, it's lovely to see you again as well, brother," Lucifer said, with only a slight tease in the words. "I'll be brief. Give me the answers I seek, then you can have all the waffles you want in total peace."

"I'm in no mood to talk, so," he waved his hand dismissively before picking up his fork and returning his attention to the sweet confection in front of him, "begone, Beast."

Lucifer waved his hand and the waffles disappeared just as Gabriel brought a bite to his lips. His lips curled triumphantly as Gabriel's teeth clenched loudly on the fork.

"That hurt, Gabriel."

Gabriel's eyes closed, his shoulders and head falling with clear annoyance. "Lucifer, give me back my damned waffles."

Mild-mannered as Gabriel may have appeared to the casual passerby, Lucifer knew quite well that his words weren't so much as a plea, but a thinly-veiled warning. He glanced up at Lucifer, his nose flaring and eyes glowing with ethereal light.

The King of Hell recognized the impatience. The anger.

Not that he felt threatened by it.

"Nope," he said, unperturbed. "I need answers first."

"Well then I must extend my deepest sympathies," yet there was nothing sympathetic in Gabriel's tone. "I am not a textbook or a tome. Perhaps the library can help... or the local newspaper? I hear there is a columnist there who reports all sorts of answers for their desperate readers. As for myself, I keep my ears closed and my lips sealed."

"This from the angel who nearly got a young girl killed because he couldn't hold his wine or stop gossiping about the—how did you put it, again? 'Miraculous circumstances surrounding her condition in her husband's absence.'"

Lucifer didn't miss the flash of ire cutting towards him from across the table.

"It worked out in the end," Gabriel seethed.

"Ah, yes. I suppose it did, didn't it?" Lucifer conceded. "For *everyone* involved. A whisper from a holy messenger, a little divine damage control. Mary was suddenly blessed instead of spoiled and dear old Dad had more of his heavenly propaganda for the masses."

It was truly the least any of them could do for the poor girl, as far as Lucifer was concerned. She'd narrowly escaped being stoned to death and instead became a renowned figurehead for his followers. Lucifer could never blame her for following her heart in the impossible world she lived in. Free will being his thing and all that. Truth-be-told, her son had been a decent fellow whom Lucifer respected.

Unfortunately for Gabriel, his loose lips continued to become an increasing liability for the holy-than-thou ones and, after a few millennia, he found himself banned from Heaven.

He grinned as Gabriel seemed to be void of any sort of argument against his words. There would have been no point in arguing, and he knew it. Regardless of how much the reminder ruffled his feathers.

"I am in no mood, Lucifer," he grumped.

Lucifer didn't give a damn if this was pissing Gabriel off or not. It was those loose lips that he needed now, and he was determined to not leave the angel in peace until he gave him what he sought.

"Why is our dear brother here?"

Gabriel leveled Lucifer with a dead stare.

"You'll have to be more specific... There are so many-"

"Michael," Lucifer interjected, each syllable sliding past his tongue with grave finality.

Gabriel's face shifted from annoyance to the unmistakably empty stare of concealment. "I don't know."

Lucifer leaned forward on the table, scrutinizing every muscle twitch and bead of sweat on Gabriel's face. It was good to know some things never changed.

"You're lying," he whispered. "You've never been good at it."

"Yes, my purse remembers our little card games quite well."

Gabriel stared at Lucifer head on. Each moment that ticked on in silence pulled at another thread within the angel, one after the other. While Lucifer held strong, his face unreadable, Gabriel slowly came undone before him until, finally, he threw himself back heavily in his seat.

"Look," he said, finally, "the last I knew, he was still in Heaven trying to decipher some portents that had come up."

"Portents?" Lucifer felt a squeeze on his heart. For the first time since interrupting his brother's breakfast, his smile had faded away to nothingness. "Are you sure?"

Gabriel shrugged. "Michael's sure. Do we need much else?"

It was Lucifer's turn to fall heavily into his seat, his eyes vacant as thoughts danced around his head. Here he'd foolishly thought this was just another little game of hide and seek with Michael. Just him being hunted down and dragged back to his palace in the underworld, which in turn would make him all the more motivated to leave again. And so, the wheel would continue to turn.

For once, Lucifer realized, this was not about him.

That couldn't be right.

"You didn't know?"

Gabriel's voice pulled Lucifer back from his thoughts and the pair stared at each other without mockery or rancor. Finally, a nervous laugh escaped Gabriel. Lucifer drummed his fingers on the table before letting out a deep rush of air from his mouth.

"No, Gabriel. I didn't know." Lucifer huffed. "How long, how many?"

"Oh... well–" Gabriel paused, and Lucifer watched him count them up on his hand.

When his tenth finger lifted, and he returned to counting in his head, Lucifer clenched his jaw.

Finally, the angel answered. "Thirty-something last I heard. There has been a fair few in the last five years. Like that bleeding bible they found encased in ice somewhere in the desert."

Lucifer stared slack-jawed at his brother. If that were true, it was no wonder Michael was lowering himself to walk this realm. Shit was truly hitting the apocalyptic fan.

"There has also been an influx of demons coming topside. More specifically," Gabriel's eyes slid suspiciously to Lucifer before saying, "some Princes have been spotted."

Lucifer's eyes narrowed. "Bullshit. I've been keeping them in check."

"Eh," Gabriel said dismissively. "Have you, though?"

"What are you implying, brother?" Lucifer spoke through clenched teeth.

"Look, I know you've been elsewhere lately," Gabriel leaned forward, dropping his voice to a conspiratory whisper, as though concerned the empty walls were listening. "Whether in your head or in your... pants... you've clearly been distracted as of late."

"Is that right?" He asked. "And what could you possibly know of where I've been?"

"Demons talk. A lot." Gabriel warned. "Shocking as it might be, not many are fond of you."

Lucifer responded with a half-hearted laugh. He couldn't understand why it was so shocking to them that demons would be disloyal or appear to switch sides when it served them. Of course, they would talk if it meant saving their own leathery skin. It was what they did.

Really, he was no fan of theirs either.

What was actually shocking was the demons thinking they could do anything to convince the angels to leave them be. That was the true head scratcher.

"I am failing to see the point of any of this."

"The point is, you get distracted, and a few demons slip out. That's all I'm saying."

"But that isn't all you are trying to say," Lucifer prodded further.

Gabriel sighed deeply, resigning to the fact that he had been cornered. "There's been talk that this girl who's had your eye... that she's not exactly what she appears to be."

"If you mean to say she's an even bigger pain in the ass than she seems I'd be inclined to agree–"

"You don't think she's a pain in the ass," Gabriel cut in. His lips were actually curled in the barest of smiles as he looked at Lucifer. "Or maybe you do, but there's more to it. And it's that 'more' that has our brother's wings in a knot."

Lucifer stood, trying to keep his face blank. What he wasn't about to do was feed the celestial gossip anymore tidbits, especially about Ms. Brant. If Michael were truly vexed by her, and thought she had anything to do with the portents he'd been chasing down, Lucifer wasn't going to give him anything else to feed his delusion.

"I'm sorry, Lucifer."

"For what?"

Gabriel shrugged his shoulders. "For whatever it is that's coming. I don't think we are in for a good time. Any of us."

Neither did Lucifer. He must have truly been distracted to have missed thirty omens.

"Can I have my waffles back now?"

Lucifer shook his head and laughed. A snap of his fingers brought back a mound of hot, delicious Belgian waffles. The look of relief that ran across his brother's face elicited another chuckle before he turned to leave him to his meal.

"Hey Lucifer..."

"Hmm?" Lucifer shoved his hands into his pockets as he glanced back at Gabriel.

"I know you won't just walk away from her, especially if Michael is involved. Hell, his dislike of the idea is probably just going to encourage you to get even closer to the lady."

Lucifer squirmed at just how insightful Gabriel was on that one.

"Just be careful. Something is brewing. The portents... the demons... hell, even Michael being here? Something decidedly not-good is on the horizon." Gabriel let out a sigh as he appeared to be searching for his next words. "Be cautious of him. We both know he's delusional. If he truly believes something... he..."

"I know." Lucifer said softly. "Thank you. I'll try not to kill him."

He started to walk away but spun back around as a thought came to him. "Oh, Gabriel. Do me a favor. Have him call me. I have a gut feeling you're going to see him soon."

He placed a business card on the table. Lucifer's earthly contact information shone in gold lettering.

Gabriel grinned and shook his head and he pulled the card off the table and held it up, the card vanishing in a flash of gold and white. "I'll pass him the message."

Chapter 18

Charlie

ANOTHER DAY SEEMINGLY PASSED by. It went much smoother than the day before, but Charlie was still in a bit of shock after what she had learned about Lucifer. About all of it. She sat in front of a vanity brushing her long hair with the soft bristle brush, staring at the note that was left behind after she had awakened in the garden.

Dearest Charlie,

Someone will soon collect you from the garden. Please enjoy the rest of your day until then. I ask kindly that you stay in your quarters until further notice.

~ Lucifer

Part of her had hoped that he would have been there when she came to but instead, an aged old paper folded neatly on top of a silver plate was beside her. Maybe it wasn't a great idea to get emotionally invested with the Devil.

Getting bored with brushing her hair, she tossed the brush down on the table. What the hell was she doing? This was beyond ridiculous. She didn't even brush her hair this much at home. Her attention shifted to her painstakingly boring room. There was no real form of entertainment. No TV. Hardly any books that she would ever read. The last thing she wanted to do was sleep. What did he expect her to do? Sit here? Well she wasn't going to do that.

Throwing her hands up in the air, she stormed to the French doors. Instead of throwing them open like she normally would have elsewhere, her hand hovered over the doorknob. For once she was actually thinking about what could happen beyond the doors. He didn't exactly warn her, but he spiked her curious nature. It annoyed her to no end that it he was toying with her, yet again. Lucifer and his mind games.

She chewed on the bottom of her lip. What could go wrong? Death. Dismemberment. Hellish nightmares of biblical proportions. It gnawed in the back of her brain. That should have been enough to keep her sitting in her room like the good little girl she was...

A little adventure couldn't hurt, right?

Charlie pulled the door open. No alarm, no boo-by-trap, no impending death. So far so good. Honestly, beyond her door was much more mundane than her imagination would have thought up. Still, no reason to let her guard completely down. She was in Hell after all.

She peeked her head out, looking from left to right. Silent as the grave. Eerily quiet and unmoving, as if even the atoms around her were frozen in time. For a moment, she held her ground at the door. When nobody came running to force her back into her room, she made a break for it.

If that had been a test, well... she failed. The woman made a living snooping around, checking things out. The phrase *curiosity killed the cat* should be tattooed across her damn forehead.

Her heart was going a million miles a minute as she moved down the corridor. Finally sure she wasn't being followed, she let her feet slow to a leisurely pace. Charlie grew fascinated by her surroundings. For one, everything was freakishly clean with the white flooring and walls and curtains. Even the paintings and tapestries were muted and easy for her eyes to skim past unnoticed. It felt wrong when paired with the owner of this place.

Lucifer didn't exactly give clean and sterile vibes.

The further Charlie wandered, the older the decor became. About twenty minutes down one wing, the white changed to deep woods and burgundy tones. Another turn down a darker hallway found Charlie moving past rows of old doors; each one more unique than the last. Itty bitty doors that would barely fit a cat...ones so large she didn't even realize how wide they were. As she swept her gaze up a particularly tall and narrow door, she realized that above her there was no ceiling. Instead a cloud hovered above her or a thick fog.

The hall of doors seemed to go on forever, and Charlie considered turning back and returning to her room before Lucifer discovered her gone and got his tighty-whities in a twist.

Did the Devil wear tighty-whities? He seemed more like a boxer guy. Or more likely, commando. Realizing she was now entertaining herself with the mystery of Lucifer's underwear, Charlie stopped and dragged a hand sharply down her face.

"What is *wrong* with you?" she asked herself.

She resolved herself to go back, but as she readied to turn around, a door further down the hall caught her eye. Her feet pulled her forward, abandoning all ideas of going back in favor of checking out this new find.

When she reached the door, she felt the strangest pull to it. Like a lingering presence that reminded her of home. She couldn't quite place it, but she found her hand reaching. It's just a door, she thought to herself, but her hand didn't agree. It slid delicately over it.

The craftsmanship of the door was insane. Rather than a simple smooth slab of black and gray marble, it had been painstakingly carved into impossible detail. Whoever made it really had a deep passion for sculpting, much like all the other doors that lined the hall. But this one. Something about it, besides the craft of it, drew her in. It felt familiar. The doorknob was equally beautiful–shining gold with delicate filigree carved all over. She reached to grab the doorknob but stopped as she felt a tapping on her shoulder.

"Excuse me."

Out of fright, Charlie whirled around and swatted at whoever touched her. However, her hand went through the figure that was standing there.

"I'm sorry I didn't mean to frighten you..." The frail old woman stepped back with her head lowered. She looked afraid of Charlie. The notion softened her heart in a way that only old little ladies could do to you.

"It's alright, I just didn't hear you and this is kind of a scary place." Her sheepish grin told all how she felt about being down here.

More or less, the fact she was caught red handed doing something she ought not have been doing. Maybe she should be grateful for the interruption.

The old woman's face lifted back up and smiled gently at Charlie, but an awkward silence fell between them. She noticed the woman was not entirely there. Not mentally... physically. As though she were looking at a mere *thought* of the woman. A slight glimmer rippled across her very pale appearance, giving quick peeks of the door behind her. *Through* her. Only one thing came to mind: she was looking at a ghost. Or a spirit. Was there a difference?

"Was there something I could help you with?" Charlie found herself asking.

"Wondering if you wouldn't mind helping me. I'm afraid I cannot open that door, and my family is on the other side of it."

Charlie glanced over her shoulder at the door then back at the old woman. She contemplated her request and wasn't entirely sure if she should do that.

"Couldn't you just–" she waved her hands in a gesture of passing through each other. "*Move* through it?"

"I'm afraid not, dear." Her soft smile never faulted on her face.

She lifted her hand up. Moving it side to side to show how transparent she was. There was a soft chuckle before she moved her hand back down to her side. Hadn't the woman touched her? She found it odd but not enough to care too much. The door did look heavy.

"Umm, sure. I can try." Charlie offered with a shaky tone.

There was this gut feeling she shoved down. One that warned her that this might not be a good idea. But the woman was just an old lady. Should be no harm letting one spirit reside with her family, right? Charlie went ahead and grabbed the doorknob and pulled with all her might. The door felt stuck as it fought against her. She pulled and pulled until a bead of sweat slid down the base of her neck. After taking a moment's pause, she pulled one last time then the door finally cracked open.

"Thank you so much!" The lady clasped her hands in front of her from pure joy as she faded to the other side.

"No problem."

With that, she quickly shut the door.

"What... did you *do*?"

Charlie glanced over her shoulder and back at the woman that was definitely very solid. Her eyes were green like emeralds as she looked between Charlie and the door, her expression less than pleased with whatever she was seeing.

"I, um... who are you?" Charlie asked, taking a step away from her to put a little distance between them.

The woman stared at her with intense annoyance painting her delicate features. Her hair framed her face in tight caramel-colored curls, bouncing playfully as her head moved–though their host seemed anything but playful. She was young and lovely, with a soft round face, glittering green eyes, and smooth, perfect dark skin. The polar opposite of the spirit that Charlie had just helped.

"I asked you a question," the woman snapped, ignoring Charlie's. "Did you seriously just let a spirit pass through? Is that what I saw?"

Charlie shook her head softly but stopped as she realized that it had probably been *exactly* what she'd done. Not that she knew what that meant. Her mouth opened, no sound coming from it as of yet, but she was interrupted by another voice behind her.

"Abbyyyyyyy... No need to be such a cunt, darling. Is that any way to treat Luci's guest?"

Charlie turned around to find a male joining them. He towered over her, standing even taller than Lucifer and twice as wide in the shoulders, with long wild hair flowing past his shoulders and a wild beard to match. The first word that sprang to mind as she took him in was "lumberjack." Like someone you saw in an Old Spice commercial, or the cover of some smut novel with his shirt unbuttoned and hair blowing in the wind.

It was a striking contrast to the light and airy texture of his voice, or the cutting playfulness of his words. It *definitely* did not match the pink floral blouse barely holding it together across his chest.

"She just opened a door for one of his spirits. The old woman," the woman, Abby, explained.

A soft gasp erupted from the big man, and he glanced down at Charlie with a huge smile. "You did not!"

"I... did? Was that bad?"

His meaty arm draped over her shoulder, pulling her in against his side. She wasn't too comfortable with the touchy-feelies of it, but what exactly was she going to do? Shake him off?

"Child, that little old bitty played you like a harp. Don't you know she slaughtered her entire village? Poisoned the stew served up one night and by the next morning they were all lying dead in pools of their own feces," he said, his voice sounding absolutely amused at the recollection, while Charlie looked mortified.

Abby groaned. "Asmo, can you maybe take it down a couple *hundred* notches? Ugh, how can anyone take you seriously when you talk and look like... that?"

"Bitch," he said, blowing her a kiss before returning his full attention to Charlie.

"I... I didn't know."

"Well of course you didn't. Who would expect you to?"

"Lucifer isn't going to be happy that he lost one. Especially the old one," Abby reminded him. Looking at the door the spirit had passed through, her expression bored. She added, "She was one of his favorites."

He waved her off, not even bothering to look at her, "He'll live. I have a feeling Luci has far more pressing matters on his mind."

"Luci..." Charlie said to herself. "You're um... Asmodeus? Right?"

Asmo's Cheshire grin widened further. "Oooooh, he talks about me. Color me flattered."

"I think we both know there was nothing flattering about it," Abby snipped.

"Go eat a dick," he said, his grin still firmly in place. "Yes, I am Asmodeus, and that tramp over there—who is in desperate need of getting laid—is Abaddon, or Abby as I like to call her."

"Nice to... meet you?" Charlie said. This felt like a fever dream.

Abby rolled her eyes and crossed her arms over her chest. It was clear she was used to this sort of behavior. Charlie looked between the two and finally decided she needed to go. She ducked under Asmo's arm and put more distance between herself and them.

"I should really get back to my room." She gave a sheepish grin while holding her hand up in defense.

Both Asmodeus and Abby stared at each other and smiled before both tucked each of her arms in theirs. "It's too late now."

"We should give you the grand tour."

She should have stayed in her room.

Damn it, she should have just listened to Lucifer.

All three started walking in unison, Charlie feeling completely uncomfortable about her current situation. On one side, a demon who seemed indifferent about her presence. On the other, a hulk of a man who appeared as if he could break her in two without breaking a sweat. As if he could feel her discomfort, Asmodeus patted the hand that rested on his forearm.

"Grand tour?" Charlie repeated as she looked over her shoulder, longing to go back to the moment where she should have minded her own business and left the old woman alone...

Her stomach flipped around inside, queasy at the growing unease with every step they took. Briefly, she remembered the mark on her arm—the one Lucifer said allowed him to feel what she felt—and tried to shove those feelings down through her arm. She'd hoped it would broadcast that she was very much in need of some rescuing from her host, but instead she got the strangest feeling that he was laughing at her.

Bastard.

"Don't worry little human. We aren't here to hurt you. We were sent to collect you." Abaddon's voice was soft as if to comfort Charlie, but the sickly-sweet grin was anything but comforting. In fact, she seemed to get some sick enjoyment out of Charlie's discomfort.

"I'm honestly shocked that you got this far down here on your own. I mean, really. Anything could have happened. This is Hell after all, honey."

Asmodeus reached across with his Charlie-free arm to twirl a lock of her hair in his thick fingers. Seemingly satisfied with whatever it was he'd been checking out, he dropped her hair and smiled warmly at her.

"I'm not," he countered. "Something tells me our guest is a little spicier than you give her credit for."

He winked at Charlie before returning his sight to the hall ahead of them, placing his hand gently on top of her seized arm. "But yes, the cow to your left is correct. You've been invited to dinner, and though the whole sleep deprived cop look works for you, it's not quite what I'd consider dinner appropriate. Especially for our King's special guest of honor."

Abby glared at Asmo, apparently not amused at being referred to as a cow. "Calling the kettle black darling? Last I checked I'm not the one carrying around giant udders."

Asmo's lips pursed in a catty smile as he stared at Abby over Charlie's head. His eyes gave a very pointed sweep from her face to her chest then back again. "You don't, do you? I hate that for you."

It was actually hard not to be at least a little amused at the pair's jabbing between one another, even if they were currently preventing her from leaving their company. There was a sense of sibling rivalry to their bickering that reminded her of herself and Jenna. Even Ben got in on it sometimes.

Though the party was usually over once their mom overheard the things flying out of their mouths.

Charlie had the impression that Abaddon might actually stab her if she even thought she was laughing at her, so amusing as it may have all been, she made a point to not let the smile surface. Instead, she attempted to divert the conversation back to something a little less threatening.

"I don't know how 'special' I am. I'm just a girl with a badge," she said, and she found herself actually having to resist using air quotes as she said it... Catching herself, she added, "Or... was. Honestly, I'm just your normal, run-of-the-mill, fuck up of a human."

Abby's smile returned, amused at the comment. "Oh no no, *cher*. As much as I detest agreeing with Asmodeus, he's right. You are far from normal. No run-of-the-mill human, as you say, can open the doors down here." She gestured to the doors they were passing by.

Charlie carefully considered each door they passed, so much so that she didn't even notice the pair releasing their hold on her arms. She had been walking alongside them on her own, but for how long?

"They look like regular doors to me. Maybe designed by someone with more money than sense, but still..."

"Let me paint a picture for you," Abby said, folding her arms curtly in front of her. "We have been in and out of this place since... well... basically the beginning of time. Asmodeus and I are both Princes of Hell, meaning we literally control our own domains and have powers that I won't even try to get your little mundane brain to understand. Very few beings are on our level, and yet even *we* cannot open those doors."

Charlie risked a glance up at the demon, but Abby seemed determined to keep her eyes straight ahead as they continued on. Regardless, Charlie couldn't help but wonder if she was seeing just a hint of something flash behind those cool eyes. Jealousy?

That wasn't a question Charlie was willing to ask. She liked her skin where it was, thank you very much.

Jealous demons aside, Charlie thought about the implications of what she'd just been told. Powerful demons, Princes of Hell—whatever that meant—couldn't do what she had done. Couldn't open a simple wooden door. What did that mean, though?

Charlotte Brant, amazing door-opener extraordinaire! Bah.

Charlie's curiosity was once again piqued but considering it had caused her to free a mass-murdering spirit moments ago, she decided to pocket this particular one for another time. And possibly another audience. Perhaps

Lucifer would take her questions a little more to heart than these two.

Now that was a laugh.

Clearing her throat, she went back a few steps in the conversation. "You mentioned something about dinner?"

"Yes, dinner," Asmo answered quickly. Perhaps he was also eager to move past the subject before Abby imploded. "You do eat, right? Please tell me you aren't one of those sad little coffee and cigarette meal plan girls?" He eyed her a little before seemingly deciding that wasn't the case. "No, you aren't. You look far too healthy.

"So, yes, Lucifer has ordered quite a spread in your honor. We've been enlisted to get you dressed. Didn't realize we'd have to hunt you down in these dark halls, but I should have. Who could resist scoping out actual Hell? So how did you meet our beloved King?"

At the mention of dark halls, Charlie glanced over her shoulder taking in the million square footage of pale marble flooring and gauzy white curtains billowing from high arched windows. It was actually brighter than her own apartment. The only hint of color came from some of the unique doors that lined the walls. Maybe they had a different perspective than what she saw. Maybe.

"Of course I eat." She tried not to sound offended. "I figured I was only gonna be here for a couple of days? I guess I wasn't expecting much of a fuss."

Asmo quirked a brow at Charlie. "Are you saying you don't eat every day? Well, that saves on the grocery bill for sure."

Technically, Charlie did have a habit of forgetting to eat. It really depended on how busy she was. Not easy to stop chasing the bad guy just to slide into a drive thru for a cheeseburger, but if she went too long Carmen was pretty good and stuffing her face—against her will or not. So yeah, she ate almost like a normal person.

Yet for some reason she really expected Lucifer to throw some water, cheese, and bread her way until he let her go home. If she was being honest with herself, it didn't even make sense to her. He had actually been an almost-gentleman the entire time.

Of course, it didn't help that she was beginning to feel that "prisoner" and "guest" were loosely interchangeable for these guys.

"Anyway," Asmo said suddenly, cutting through her little thought-spiral, "back to the important part. Are you going to tell us about your meet-cute with our Luci?"

"He... just walked into my office one day."

Abby and Asmo both turned their full attention to her, expectant.

"And... asked me to help him find his lost dog."

The demons exchanged a look for a brief moment, before laughter burst out of both of them. At first, Charlie wanted to be annoyed at them laughing at her but the more it settled into her head, the more she began to recognize how ridiculous it sounded. The King of Hell traipses into some human's office asking to find his puppy. Reluctantly, a smile crept up on her own face and she joined them in their amusement.

"Well, as far as pickup lines go that is something else," Asmo said, leading the group around a corner.

Abby shook her head, still laughing softly. "Did he drive up in a white van, too?"

The trio turned another corner and Charlie realized they had made it back to the hall where her room was. A black garment bag hung on her door, a plain black box sitting neatly beneath it in sharp contrast to the pale marble floor.

"Perfect timing," Asmo said. "Now you can get dressed and we can inquire more about your first meeting with Lucifer over a delicious meal."

No doubt Lucifer would love to have *that* conversation.

"What's wrong with what I'm wearing?" Charlie asked, looking down at her dark slacks and burgundy button up.

She thought she looked pretty presentable. It was better than her favorite band tee and ratty jeans. Then again, she was sort of wishing she had had a moment to change into exactly that before Lucifer popped her away from her apartment.

Abby gave a silent—albeit judgy—once over before she responded. "Everything."

"What Abby means is, while it's very you, you might find yourself...uncomfortable... compared to the rest of us. Lucifer truly spared no expense and it's always good to humor his flights of fancy."

"Are you implying Lucifer is an overgrown manchild who throws a fit when he doesn't get his way?" Charlie asked as Asmodeus opened her door.

Abby choked back a laugh, trying to suppress it with the back of her hand.

"Side-stepping that one because I do enjoy my head—" Asmo said in a rush of words. "If not him, then humor me? Beauty and the Beast is my favorite human movie, and I can't pass up such a set up."

"Why should I humor *any* of you?" she asked, making her way into her room.

Abby cut her off, leaning against the doorframe as she smiled down on Charlie. "Because it's either this or we find other means to entertain ourselves. I do like a good old-fashioned torture."

As her grin spread wider, Charlie took notice of the sharp teeth that had taken the place of that perfect smile.

She stepped back, bumping into Asmo, his hands curling gently around her biceps. His soft chuckling vibrated against her back. "Trust me, sugar. You'd much prefer dinner. Now Abby, put those away. We're supposed to make her feel welcome."

Abby chuckled and returned her face back to normal. Charlie was grateful that at least one of the demons seemed to have a little more tact, and that he was keeping the other in check. She'd come face to face with her share of criminal types over the years, looked down the barrel of more than one gun, yet she understood those were humans and human things. She had no idea what limits these demons had.

Abby was terrifying.

"Right, dinner it is."

The moment they walked back into her room, Charlie groaned. She hated being in there. It felt like a prison; albeit a gorgeously decorated one.

Asmo let Charlie go and plucked the garment bag from the door, following behind the women. Once inside, he immediately opened the bag, letting deep red fabric spill out of it like a rush of silken blood from a wound. He fished the gown out of the bag and held the hanger up with one hand while the full skirt draped beautifully over the other forearm.

Her heart skipped a beat when she saw the full effect of it.

"Wow." Her mouth dropped as she slowly stepped forward. "It's beautiful."

Abby scoffed behind her, the sound of her heels echoing in the room as she retreated to a chair by the fireplace. Charlie grabbed a bit of the skirt, examining the smooth fabric as it slid across her fingers.

"What kind of dinner is this?" She found herself asking.

A sea of smooth crimson, full skirt, tight bodice with straps barely thick enough to bear the weight of the gown. The dress had been a labor of love for whatever seamstress created it. It was a dress Charlie would probably never have reason to see again in her life.

While she was leaning over inspecting it, Asmo leaned forward enough for his rumbling whisper to catch her ear. "Be our guest..."

The idea that a demon—especially a demon of lust—had such an appreciation for fairytales was hard to wrap her head around, but the more she thought about it the more sense it made. There had been more than enough people joking over the years about how a certain world-famous cartoonist with a passion for humanoid mice had to have sold his soul to the Devil for all his success.

Maybe it wasn't so far off target.

Slipping the satin through her hands, Asmo laid the dress out on the bed behind her, then retrieved the box, opening it to reveal a pair of simple but elegant black pumps. Lifting them out, Asmo let one dangle from his index finger and leered at Abaddon with a cheshire grin.

"Oh my... aren't these the exact heels you've been salivating over all week, Abby?"

Charlie shifted her attention between Asmo and Abaddon. Abby looked as though she might kill Asmo right then. The demon didn't say a word, though. Instead, she crossed her arms and looked as far away from the shoes as she could manage.

"So, when is dinner?" Maybe changing the subject would help.

Asmo seemed much too pleased with having silenced the other demon. It was obvious this was a long-played game of chess between the pair. Charlie wasn't sure how she liked being in the middle of their games.

Setting the shoes on the bed, Asmo returned his attention to their human guest and crossed his arms. "Less than an hour. So, you really should get a move on. Come on, let's shed those street clothes." He moved to grab the hem of her shirt. "We still have to get ourselves good and ready, too."

Charlie swatted at his hands. "I can dress myself. Thank you..."

She quickly put distance between herself and Asmodeus, using one hand to swat away while she grabbed the dress with the other. Spying a carved wood dressing screen, she backed away until she could disappear behind it, out of sight.

With a little more privacy, she made quick work of slipping out of her clothes, keeping her ears open for where the demons were on the other side of the screen. The red was striking compared to the light surroundings that it felt almost unreal, even as it weighed heavily in her hands. She stepped into the center of the skirt and shimmied it up her body, sliding her arms through each strap before reaching behind her to try to zip it up.

It was a valiant effort on her part, but eventually she had to concede that she would actually need a little help.

Groaning, she closed her eyes and shook her head to herself.

"Could I get some help zipping this thing up?"

Heels clicked across the smooth floor approaching behind her. The dress pulled at her back, and she straightened up, pressing the bodice in against her stomach to make it a little easier to zip. Any tighter and she would need a crowbar to wedge into it. Once the zipper was up, and her breathing sufficiently restricted, she relaxed her shoulders.

"Let's see you, sugar," a female voice purred at her.

Turning around expecting to see Abby, Charlie was surprised to come face to face with another woman she'd yet to meet.

She was shorter than herself, with a face that had been carved by the gods. Warm tan skin, heart-shaped face with a luscious pout, waist-length hair in shades of gold and brown. But what really caught Charlie by surprise was the almost caricature-like curves on the woman.

The word "pillowy" sprang to mind. If pillows could be made of sin.

"Who are you?" Charlie blurted out, trying to recover from her moment of surprise.

The woman smiled wickedly, crossing an arm under her massive chest and tapping a finger to her lips. "It's me, gorgeous. Asmodeus."

"Right," her eyes cut to Abby who was still lounging bored in her chair, picking at her nails. "Is it always games with you two?"

"Yes," Abby said simply, not even bothering to look up.

Charlie rolled her eyes. "Whatever. Where'd Asmo go?"

It was strange, but she actually felt a little less comfortable without him there to be a semi-friendly barrier between her and the other demons.

The woman laughed behind her hand and the sound was warm and sensual. Charlie squirmed at the sudden heat flashing through her, and she put a little extra space between them with a step back.

"Child," the woman purred again, placing her hands on her hips, "It's me."

Leaning forward just a little, her face shifted into the visage of the lumberjack.

"Boo."

Charlie jumped back, crashing into the partition. Only Abby's sudden presence managed to keep it from clattering to the ground while Charlie tried to control herself.

"This is centuries old African Blackwood!" Abby hissed, inspecting the partition for damage.

The woman—Asmo—was busy laughing, reaching out to grab Charlie's hand and guide her back in front of her. Charlie simply stared down at her, at the face that had gone back to its beautiful, bare-chinned, feminine beauty.

"What... the... fuck." Charlie's jaw was hanging slack as she tried to wrap her head around the fact that this was the large, burly man that had just been there.

"I get that a lot." "They get that a lot."

Asmo and Abby's voices rang out in near-perfect unison as they said it.

"Oh. Well–" Charlie fought to keep her eyes forward and not look at the cleavage staring at her.

"Wow," Asmo said, ignoring Charlie's obvious discomfort. "You really do look amazing. Luci has no idea of the treat he's in for. Wouldn't you say Abby?"

"*Jolie*," Abby said in effortless French, though she barely seemed to be looking.

Charlie glanced at the shoes still on the bed and then back down to her feet. Honestly, she rather go barefoot than shove her feet into those uncomfortable looking things, but she already knew that wasn't how this was going to go.

She honestly was debating on giving them to Abby, but something told her the Prince of Pride wouldn't appreciate the gesture.

"I'll put those on later. They look like torture."

She fought a smile, wondering if there was a spot in Hell where people were made to walk endless laps in 4-inch stilettos. She would put money on that being where she'd be put if she ended up here.

That one, or the room where you had to push a grocery cart behind oblivious people blocking your way at every turn.

Chapter 19

LUCIFER CHECKED HIS WATCH again—a meaningless habit in this realm. By earthly standards, it had been a little over an hour since he sent the demon idiots to collect Charlie and the tie he'd barely managed to decide on was getting excruciatingly tighter with every passing moment she didn't enter.

Had he pushed too hard? Knowing Ms. Brant, it was very likely. She was a hard read most days, but one thing he already knew about her was she was not a woman who liked to be pushed. Which made pushing her all the more fun.

Hearing footsteps from across the room, Lucifer quickly stood from his seat at the head of the table, holding a hand against the knot forming in his stomach. They'd met many times in many settings over the years, but those had been dreams. In a world where Charlie wasn't trapped by the confines of human reality. In a world where anything could happen and she was free to explore pieces of herself she was too afraid to show.

Lucifer was honored to be allowed to be a part of those moments.

He had never imagined he would finally get to spend an evening with her like this in real life.

The massive double doors pushed open, light spilling into the dimly lit room as they parted. The demons walked through, and the swell of excitement ebbed. Where was she? Had she rejected his invitation? Did she not like the dress?

Maybe blue was more her color.

His heart actually started to ache as he waited for her to enter.

Certain the demons had done something to offend her, his eyes hardened and he opened his mouth, ready to chew their heads off when the third figure emerged from behind, stepping between them. Whatever cutting words he was ramping up died in his throat at the sight of her in that dress.

Not a morsel on the table looked quite as delectable as her.

"Yes, we are late. Your pet hussy over here tried to make her look like a clown," Abby drawled. "Had to practically hose her off to fix it."

"You just have no eye for art," Asmo said, flipping her long hair over her shoulder.

"Your *art* made her look like she escaped the circus."

They moved away from Charlie, leaving her standing alone at the entrance of the dining hall while they found their seats on either side of the table. Even as she stood there, painfully awkward and twisting her fingers, Lucifer couldn't think of a more beautiful sight.

"You look sensational," he whispered, though the room carried it easily for all of them to hear it clear as a bell.

Even though she didn't speak—a strange occurrence in and of itself—the expression of tender gratitude and soft, rosy flush that claimed Charlie's features spoke clearly to him.

His slack-mouthed awe slid into a whimsical grin and he shook himself out of his stupor. "Don't listen to Abaddon. There is nothing clownish about you, my dear. Nothing at all. Please, sit. I wasn't sure what you enjoyed so I sort of chose a bit of everything."

Was he babbling on? Surely the King of Hell does not babble.

A half chuckle left her, and she moved to the end of the table opposite Lucifer. "It looks amazing. Thank you. So much better than cheese and water."

Lucifer gave Charlie a confused look. "I'm sorry, cheese and water?"

"Don't worry about it," she said, but he looked from her to the demons to see if they knew what she was talking about.

Abby shook her head as she slid into the chair she claimed as hers. Asmo only seemed to have eyes for the food before them. He'd get no help from them.

While the demons both settled into their seats, Lucifer moved quickly to the chair in front of Charlie and pulled it out. He helped her into her seat, and at the risk of life and limb, gently grabbed her hand, lifting it so he could place a light press of lips to her knuckles. He watched her as he did so, smiling behind her hand as her cheeks pinkened a touch more.

Deciding to give her a chance to collect herself rather than tease her, he released her hand back to her and made his way back to his own chair, touching his lips while his back was turned to her. He could still feel the warmth from her skin caressing them.

Claiming his seat at the head of the table, he gestured to the food stretching between all of them. "Please, help yourself to whatever you like. It is all yours for the tasting."

It was a wonder the table held up the weight of all of the dishes that had been prepared. He truly had spared no detail, making sure to include foods from every corner of the earth and even some hidden delicacies very few were privy to from remote tribes across her globe. Steamed, baked, fried, boiled, fire-roasted... meat, vegetable, pastry... and libations for every tongue. There was a little something for any palate and he would be lying to himself if he said he wasn't excited to see what she picked out for herself.

He watched closely as Charlie looked over the plates and bowls within her immediate reach. Her face was a joy to watch as she considered it all—serious and discerning at first, then deliberating over a choice or two, then finally lighting up with a real sparkle in her eyes as she noticed something in a pan he could not quite see from where he sat.

Eagerly, she reached out and freed a fist-sized piece of bread from the pan, still steaming with its warm freshness. He realized as she plopped it on the plate in front of her and started to lick icing from her fingers that she had chosen a soft cinnamon roll. It took her a few moments before she looked up to catch him watching her, all but freezing with a finger in her mouth.

Now that was an unexpected choice.

"Sorry," she said, seemingly unable to hide her smile. "I love cinnamon rolls. I usually have one every morning from this little bakery downstairs from my office," her eyes flashed up at Lucifer with a mischievous gleam, "but some jerk interrupted my last one and I haven't seemed to have a moment of peace since."

Now Lucifer hated to admit that the name-calling was a tiny hit to his ego, but the sheer playfulness of it helped to soothe the burn a bit. "Well I'll have to find this jerk and kill him if he robbed you of such an obvious pleasure."

She grinned at him and his heart leapt. He quite enjoyed this side of her. He'd caught glimpses of it in her dreams, but the real thing was so much better. Like the difference between looking at a postcard from Greece versus swimming in their crystal-clear waters.

"It's really a shame we didn't invite the whole family tonight," Abby said suddenly, and loudly, reminding him that she and her brother were still in the room. "I'm sure they'd get a kick out of your guest." Her eyes glowed a little as she spoke.

Lucifer cast her an annoyed glance. "And why do you think that is, Abaddon? Hmm?"

He waved a hand in the air beside him. Servers moved from the walls, having barely registered as existing in the space until that moment, and began pouring drinks and setting plates.

"Speaking for myself, I am pleased you chose to join us tonight," he said to Charlie, dismissing the demon. "I was certain we'd catch you scaling the palace walls trying to escape my company."

Charlie opened her mouth, but before she could say a word Abby cut her off.

"Well, it's not everyday a human can open the doors to the afterlife. I'm sure the others would be thrilled to meet such a talented human. Besides, you know Beelzebub loves a good feast."

"Is that right?" he asked, his eyes sliding cooly from Abaddon to Charlie before he grabbed his wine glass and settled back in his seat.

Now *that* bit of information was truly unexpected.

"He's the Prince of Gluttony," Asmo said, answering the silent question on Charlie's face between bites of lamb. "Sort of a touchy topic for Luci. He's always tricking humans into thinking he's Lucifer."

Lucifer sipped his wine, mulling the implications of what Abby had revealed around in his head, adding it to the increasingly long list of things he found interesting about the detective. Finally, he looked at Charlie and gave her his warm smile once more.

"Well," he said finally, "one must sate their sense of curiosity before it swallows them whole. For someone as inquisitive as you are, I should have expected you would go checking out your surroundings."

Charlie looked between all of them before turning her eyes to lucifer. "I uh, apparently let the old lady go..."

His smile faltered only slightly at her confession. "Oh."

"I'm sorry... I really had no idea."

Now that was a little more disappointing to hear. He'd grown quite fond of her.

"Never mind about that," he offered Charlie with a sparkle in his eyes. "What's done is done. I'll figure out a way for you to repay me later."

"You know there is a saying about curiosity and the cat..." Abby piped up again with a wicked grin. Lucifer's annoyance was beginning to shift into a hostile displeasure every time she opened her damned mouth. "You are rather lucky, pet. You could have been dismembered."

Abby's eyes bore into Lucifer's as she said it. The demon's boldness made even Asmo slow on her eating, looking back and forth between Abby and their King.

"She is no one's pet," Lucifer's voice cut sharply across the table, staring coldly into Abby's unmoving stare. "With all the unfortunate souls trapped here, you have more than enough toys to play with, Abaddon. Charlotte is our guest, not one of the damned deserving of eternal torment. Unsink your claws. Or seeing as you're so keen on dismemberment at the moment, I will have no choice but to declaw you. Do you understand?"

Rather than cowering at his unspoken threat, Abby's smile widened from ear to ear. She plucked a piece of fruit off a serving plate near her and tossed it into her mouth, letting her gaze slide from Lucifer to Asmodeus. She lightly winked his way before finally heeding Lucifer's warning and going silent.

For now.

He was sure she was far from finished with whatever it was she was trying to accomplish. She was baiting him, he knew this already. To what end, he was still unclear on, but Abaddon rarely did anything without some end in mind. Realizing how close he had come to falling for her bait, he cleared his throat softly and let his posture soften once again.

"We are here to have a lovely dinner. So let it be so." The plea came out with more of a tone of finality than suggestion.

Shooting one last warning glare at the demon, Lucifer almost visibly shed the skin of irritation and cast it aside. "To her credit, Charlotte, she isn't wrong. It's quite a curiosity that you were even able to open one of those doors. Must be why she can't seem to drop the subject. That being said, it's not something I am too concerned about. The old woman's stories were starting to get repetitive. A consequence of having eternity with no new material, I guess."

A wave of empathy washed over him, and he realized it was coming to him through the mark. Charlie was feeling sorry for him?

What could she possibly be feeling that way for?

"I see." she said softly. "So, I did you a favor. Debt paid."

He smiled at Charlie, giving a soft shake of his head. "Not quite. But that's a matter for another time. Doors and demons aside, how are you liking your visit so far? Has anything caught your eye during your little unchaperoned exploration?"

Lucifer sipped his soup, watching her intently. She seemed to be easing into her surroundings more. A fact that warmed his heart more than any soup could manage.

"Honestly? It's been interesting to say the least." She glanced between the two demons before turning back to Lucifer. "But aside from a few moments of what-the-fuckery, it's been pretty pleasant. Asmodeus has been especially friendly. As weird as it feels to say, they both have managed to make me feel... welcome."

Lucifer's eyes were only for Charlie as she spoke. It was as though everything else in the room had melted away. He smiled genuinely as she spoke of her time with the demons, glad to hear they had mostly behaved themselves without his supervision.

He might have had to kill them otherwise.

"I'm thrilled you have been treated well. You are indeed very welcome here."

"I'm honestly just surprised this place isn't full of brimstone and fire and all that. Didn't expect it to be so... light and airy."

Lucifer chuckled.

"Tell me, Charlotte. Would you feel a sense of comfort, of *home*, surrounded by hellfire with the stench of sulfur thick in your nostrils? This is my home. And I, like any man, enjoy the comforts of such."

"Well, no." She paused for a second before adding, "I didn't mean to offend."

Lucifer took another spoonful of his soup before adding. "The fire and brimstone is in the dungeons below."

He met her gaze, smiling at her. She rewarded him with another smile of her own.

"So, I'm not too far off."

"Look, I might be the King of Hell, but I do have other things to do than woo you. I have a job to do here, as unpleasant as it may be. But trust me when I say I would much rather spend my days bothering you and deepening that little wrinkle between your eyebrows."

Silence stretched between them for a moment, but this one didn't feel awkward or tense like other times before. This silence was warm. Pleasant.

"What's with that ugly scar?" Abby blurted out, destroying the moment.

Charlie's face slid from cheerful, to embarrassed, to hostile.

"What's with that ugly face?" she sniped back at Abby.

The demon shifted in her seat, her eyes flashing dangerously, but before she could even stand, Lucifer waved his hand. The gold inlays decorating Abby's chair unfurled and wrapped around her stomach, pulling her back into the seat. More grabbed her forearms and kept them bound to the arms of the chair.

Asmodeus had her face in her hand, sighing. "What did you expect, Abby? Really."

"This is your last warning, Abaddon," Lucifer growled, having jumped to his feet. "I will not tolerate mistreatment of my guest and if I have to flay the skin from your muscles to make my point then I will. And I will hang your pelt in my gallery should you need a reminder of my lack of patience."

The demon stilled in her prison, and when Lucifer was certain his message had been well-received, he sat back down and released his magic on her chair. The gold bindings slid away from her, leaving her sitting rigidly as they redecorated her chair.

The silence remained. Good.

Sliding eyes to Charlie, Lucifer was afraid that he might find her ready to leave, bereft of all the good feelings he'd managed to provide her. She wasn't leaving, which was a plus, but she was staring down at her plate, rubbing a hand over the scarring on top of her shoulder.

The scars were never there in the dreams. A fact that broke his heart.

"Charlotte," he whispered, afraid to spook her further.

"It's kind of funny actually," she said quietly. He didn't dare interrupt her by asking what was funny. It was obvious that words she was dying to say were building up in her throat. "This was the most horrific injury of my life. I nearly lost my arm, and that was the better outcome that could have happened. Twenty-two months of rehabilitation just to get back to normal. I'm not complaining—I know I'm lucky that it was even possible after something like that. I still have my arm... and it's almost 100% back to good... nothing but these ugly scars to remind me that it almost wasn't."

Lucifer slid a warning glare at Abaddon, who was smartly being quiet.

"But these aren't the scars that hurt the most. Those are in here," Charlier pointed to her head before dropping her hand down again and looking up at Lucifer finally.

"The most difficult wounds to heal are those whose scars go unseen to the eye. They are marks upon the soul that you carry through existence until it becomes your master... or you become theirs," Lucifer said.

She didn't argue.

"What happened?" Asmodeus asked.

Lucifer shot the other demon a warning glare to match the one he'd given Abby.

"You don't have to talk about it, Charlotte."

She smiled at him, though it was sadder than all the other smiles she'd given him that night. "I know."

She turned to Asmo, grabbing her wine glass and taking a deep drink. When she was done, she loosed a soul-deep sigh. "I was working one night, getting ready to raid some warehouse. Back when I was a real cop. Carmen—my partner—and I were getting in position outside of one of the entrances and some wild animal came out of nowhere and jumped us."

"That must have been terrifying," Lucifer said.

"Actually, not really," Charlie said.

It surprised him how matter of fact it was. She wasn't trying to save face, or be brave. It's just how it was.

"It was behind Carmen, and I just jumped between them," she elaborated. "She has a little girl. Just the two of them. So it really wasn't a question. I knew that I had to keep it off her and dove in."

"Like some sort of superhero," Lucifer said with a smile.

"Hardly." She waved him off. "Just impulsive. Anyway, they never found the thing, so I hope it didn't continue its rampage around town. Never heard of any other attacks so it must have taken off into the bayou or something."

"Did you get an award or something?" Asmo asked, finishing a fruit tart. "I mean, you saved another cop's life. You humans seem to be all about your police officer's lives. They must have put you in the paper at least. I hope they used a good picture of you. Nothing worse than being immortalized with a shitty picture in the paper."

Lucifer chuckled, but as he looked from Asmo back to Charlie and saw the lost look in her eyes, his humor drained away.

"Try being immortalized as the crazy bitch who saw a monster no one else did," she said simply.

Asmo's smile dropped, and she cast a glance at Lucifer. She gave him an almost apologetic look, as if silently begging for him not to punish her for upsetting Charlie. Lucifer rolled his eyes at the demon, returning his full attention to Charlie instead.

"What did you see?" he asked.

Charlie shook her head. "Doesn't matter. It's not real. It only existed long enough to destroy every facet of my life. My job, gone. Psychologist deemed me unfit to carry the badge. Husband—"

Lucifer's spine stiffened as she brought up the soldier. He wasn't sure what it was about this particular subject that caught his breath in his chest, but he sat there watching her carefully. Waiting for something he couldn't even put into words himself.

"Well, who wants to be married to a crazy chick, am I right? I don't really blame him for skipping out on me, but damn was the timing something else. He could have at least waited until I was discharged from the hospital. Not too keen on the whole sickness and health part I guess."

Something beyond sympathy passed through him at that. Something burning hot and thirsting for reparation. The fury he thought he could only feel towards the two demons living in his home—or his self-righteous brother—ignited hot and violent in his belly.

Brian had created an injury that far surpassed what the beast had done to her. His betrayal had ripped her heart open, leaving her to bleed her heartbreak each and every day. The pain had lessened over time but had not stopped completely.

How did he know this? It was such a surety, as though thinking back on his own painful memories.

Memories of losing *her*.

He wasn't sure what words of comfort he was about to offer to her, because no sooner than he opened his mouth to do so, Charlie grabbed her wine glass and threw it at the wall behind Asmo. A fire of rage similar to his own contorted her features as the glass exploded, and he realized exactly how he knew how much Brian's departure destroyed her.

It was the same reason that she was feeling his ire towards the soldier now.

The connection between them was growing stronger. Perhaps dangerously so.

Hoping to ease the no-doubt stifling emotions raging inside of her, Lucifer threw up those impenetrable psychic walls, blocking the mark between them. Almost immediately, he saw the tension in her body ease.

"Noted," Asmodeus said softly, picking tiny pieces of glass out of her hair. "Touchy subject."

Charlie took a deep breath, closing her eyes as she blew it back out through her lips. Lucifer watched her closely, feeling responsible for making her get so worked up. He couldn't even blame it on the demon bringing the subject up. This one was his mess.

When she opened her eyes again, they stared at one another, both unsure of what to say. It was Charlie who broke the silence first.

"I'm sorry. I don't know what came over me."

"Nothing to apologize for, my dear," Lucifer said. "Just some jerk getting you all worked up."

He smiled at her.

"Yeah," she said, the word blowing out on another rush of breath. "Yeah, the jerk is really something isn't he?"

It was hard to gauge the intent behind her words. But then she smiled at him and it made the room feel a touch lighter again.

"So is the crazy bitch," he said with a smirk.

Charlie's mouth dropped open in disbelief, a huff of a laugh escaping her. She ran her tongue across the inside of her mouth, crossing her arms in front of her and leaning back in her chair. Lucifer simply took another bite of soup, smiling down into his bowl.

Feeling way too pleased with himself and his ability to return the mood to something slightly lighter, Lucifer chuckled to himself. When he risked a glance back up at Charlie, he was met with a face full of mashed potatoes. It clung heavily to his cheek, sliding off to splash into the soup below, splattering his shirt.

He was stunned. Speechless even as he sat there processing what had just happened. The unusual sound of pure genuine laughter erupted from Charlie and Lucifer used the back of his hand to wipe some of the mess off his face.

The next sound of laughter, though a bit nervous, came from the demons. He glanced at them, scaring them into silence with a shake of his head before taking note of some red gelatin sitting perfectly on a silver platter. Without second thought he scooped out a handful and returned the favor. Her eyes widened, but before she could save herself, she wore it.

An all-out war broke out at the table. The beautiful display of food flying from one end to another, splattering everywhere in a collage of color and texture.

Abby squealed sharply, "My hair!" before vanishing from her seat.

Not a moment later Asmo was gone too, crying about her expensive designer dress.

It was just Charlie and him in the room.

He moved around the table, using the platter as a shield to block her assault. She was absolutely relentless as she continued volleying things his way. The woman had a damn good arm, her aim spot on. A playful growl rolled from his throat as he thrust his shield to the floor and vanished, reappearing behind her.

"That's cheating!" she exclaimed as she whirled around to meet him.

He wiggled his eyebrows at her before trying to wrap her up in his arms. She was quick, dodging the move with such ease that he actually found himself even more impressed. As he whirled around, he was met with her own wicked smirk. Lucifer dropped his gaze to her hand, spying a glass filled with ice water.

"I wouldn't do that if I were you," he warned playfully.

"Oh, is that so?" She challenged, matching his energy.

In moments like these, he knew it was common practice to tell the threatening party that they "wouldn't" follow through. However, Lucifer had some first-hand experience in just how much Miss Brant *would*. Ice water was nothing compared to a bullet, and she had already wasted one of those on him.

He had no intention of making that same mistake twice.

"I'm telling you," Lucifer said, stalking toward her with a menacing smile that somehow wasn't dulled by the slop clinging to his face and clothes. She matched every step of his with a backward retreat, though the glass held steadfast in her grip. "You will regret it if you try."

Her eyebrow twitched up and she looked for the briefest of moments as though she might be considering lowering her weapon. Stubbornness won out, though, and she lurched the contents of the glass towards him.

A flick of his hand and the icy water slowed inches away from its target, only to reverse momentum and cascade over Charlie in a bone-chilling wave. A shriek erupted from her, and she stood, dripping and cold, in absolute shock.

"I did warn you," Lucifer said with a tsk of his tongue, finally stopping in front of her.

He grinned down at her, victorious.

"Yeah. Yeah, you did," she conceded, wiping the water from her eyes. "You do that often."

"It's not my fault you don't listen." His breathing slowed as the excitement of the moment started to calm again.

Even dripping wet and covered in food, she looked absolutely charming. She turned those beautiful hazel eyes up at him and for just a moment he forgot to breathe. Twisting her lips, she looked to be deep in thought before she closed that last final step between them so that they were invitingly close to one another.

Was this a trap?

Trap or not, Lucifer was caught up in the very air of her. He reached up and gently moved aside a strand of hair from her face. She repaid it by placing a hand against his chest and he thought his heart might claw its way from his chest just to let her touch it.

"You're right about that," she whispered, looking at her hand as her fingers lightly played with his shirt. "And I'm not about to start now."

He had a breath of a moment to give her a quizzical look, before he felt an icy rake of pain slide down his spine. He cried out, his back arching and twisting to find an empty glass in her other hand, its contents soaking the back of his shirt and pants.

"Ohhh, you wicked woman!" he cried out in the midst of belly-deep laughter.

Looking far too pleased with herself, Charlie set the glass on the ruin of the table. She started walking backwards towards the door, trying to hide her grin behind her hand before turning around.

"Good night, Lucifer," she called behind her.

Lucifer watched her disappear through the doors and found himself smiling in a way he hadn't smiled for eons. Every fiber of his soul felt alive and ready to take over the world. Charlotte was every bit the beautiful, amazing, and frustratingly complex woman he'd grown to care for.

The thought stilled him instantly.

He hadn't thought of it like that. It was true he'd been intrigued by her for some time, even enjoyed her whiplash-inducing mood swings where he was con-cerned... but for the first time he realized it had become something much more dangerous.

The Devil was in love.

Chapter 20

∽ Charlie ∽

CHARLIE BROUGHT THE BACK of her hand up to her mouth, trying to hold back the cackling laughter that wanted to escape as she left Lucifer in the dining hall. No doubt that she'd pay for her ill-won victory later, knowing him. Somehow, the thought didn't worry her.

This was the most fun she'd had in days. It was a nice break from all the chaos, even if most of that chaos was caused by Lucifer. She couldn't be mad at him. Not at that moment anyways.

Using the wall to steady herself, she slipped out of her heels, unable to walk another painful step. Her feet touched the cool marble flooring and a sigh of relief blew over her lips. The freedom felt amazing on her feet. Collecting the shoes, she noticed the mess they'd become, which only made her continue her examination onto herself.

A hot bath was in order.

Once she was hidden in her room, Charlie leaned against the door and realized her face was beginning to ache from the smile that had yet to leave. The evening had been full of highs and lows. Between a catty demon, rehashing one of the worst times of her life, and her feet screaming in pain from the tortuous heels, there was plenty to be upset about.

Yet... she wasn't upset. About any of it.

Images of Lucifer played through her head, over and over, fighting off any icky feeling she might have had. His face when she walked into the dining hall. His chivalrous defense of her to his demon—though her witness to his more dangerous side, however brief, definitely reminded her that he was more than a just charming annoyance. Even the sight of him covered in mashed potatoes and puddings, stalking toward her with the dangerous but playful look in his eyes had made her feel things she couldn't deny.

Pushing away from the door, she walked further into her bedroom. She needed to get out of the dress. There was almost a sense of sadness at the ruin of such a beautiful gown, but she had zero regrets about the events that had caused it.

Strolling up to the large stand-up mirror next to her window, Charlie took in the absolutely ridiculous way she looked. She looked like the floor of an all-you-can-eat buffet.

Probably smelled like it, too.

The moonlight streaming in through the window only enhanced the mess she'd become, shadows dancing over every chunk of food clinging to her. A bath was out of the question. With all the food on her, she'd basically be making a Charlie-stew.

Shower it was, then. Though she imagined it would still not be great to rinse it down the drain, it was at least better than soaking in it. She could only imagine clogging Hell's plumbing with bits of roast and Jell-O.

A soft, almost hesitant knock sounded from the door behind her and she chuckled to herself before inviting them in. Asmodeus was probably coming in to have "girl-talk" about what had happened. Strangely enough, Charlie wasn't against the idea.

"Charlotte," Lucifer's voice whispered through the darkness.

Looking over the shoulder of her reflection, she watched as he emerged from the shadows of her room. His face was clean. His tie was gone, as was his dinner jacket, leaving him in only his partially-unbuttoned—definitely stained—white dress shirt and dark slacks.

"I'm surprised you didn't just magic yourself completely clean," she said with a smirk before flicking her eyes back to her own reflection. She grabbed the skirts of her dress and fluffed at them. "I know if I had the ability to, I would save this thing."

Lucifer smiled over her shoulder as he approached her. "Yes, well. I can always buy you a new one. Besides, I just... didn't want to waste another minute."

They locked eyes in the reflection of the mirror, and her pulse sped at the longing look on his face. The air around them felt electric, like static prickling her skin.

"Another minute for what?" she asked, her throat tight.

He stepped into her, her shoulders bumping his chest as he moved his head beside hers. "What are you doing to me, Ms. Brant?"

"I'm not doing anything." But, oh, he was doing things to her being this close.

He chuckled and it tickled against the side of her face. His hand moved to her shoulder, fingers tracing delicately over the curve of it, though his eyes remained locked onto hers. It brought a shiver through her spine.

"That's where you're wrong," he said. "I haven't been able to get you out of my head for days. Every waking moment, you're there. When I'm talking to someone else, it's only your voice I'm longing to hear. When I eat…"

The devilish grin that followed made her heart skip.

"It could all just go away if you let me go home." But she didn't want to go home. God help her, but she wanted to be right here.

"I think we both know that I'm not going to let you go until I have to."

She turned around at that, the challenge of his words igniting that extremely pig-headed side of her that didn't like being told what she could and couldn't do. Even if she wanted to stay with him, if he thought she wouldn't leave because he said so then she would make sure he was very aware that he had no control over her.

Even if it was a pretty little lie.

"You said you'd take me back in a day or two," she reminded him. "I guess you aren't as much of a man of word as you claim to be."

A hand was suddenly against her chest, pushing her back against the mirror. Lucifer stepped into the last bit of space and looked down at her as a low growl trickled from his lips. His jaw worked, muscles moving as they tensed.

Finally, he said, "I told you. I never break my promises. I will take you back in a day or two."

Charlie opened her mouth, but he cut her off with a press of a finger to her lips.

"Time is such a strange concept. What amounts to an hour where you are from, can be an entire day in other planes of existence. Why, I do believe as far as your ex-husband is concerned it's barely been a handful of hours since he watched you run away with me."

She smacked his hand away from her mouth and he smiled at her, taking a step back and giving her a little more space. Good. Space was good.

Her finger waved threateningly in his face as if a loaded gun before jabbing sharply into his chest. "I did *not* run away with you, Lucifer. If anything, you kidnapped me. *Again.*"

He gave a shrug of shoulders that was far too unbothered for her taste.

"You have to admit, though," he started. She was pretty damn certain she would *not* admit to whatever he was about to say. "As far as kidnappings go, this has been quite fun."

That little wrinkle between her eyebrows he claimed to love so much must have been the deepest it had ever been, judging by the grin on his face. And people said women had intense mood swings. Lucifer slipped from joyful, to despondent, to full of rage, and back to playful with such ease, she was beginning to wonder if he was okay. In a mental sort of way.

And she absolutely wasn't going to admit he was right. Even though he was.

"Whatever, the point is you tricked me. I don't appreciate the games. Never have, and I won't start now."

They stared at each other again, both looking as though they had much to say on the subject but neither wanting to be the first to speak it. Just when Charlie felt she may have finally won this round, Lucifer released a breath of a growl and shook his head.

"You're right. So, in the spirit of dropping all the little games," he said, looking up at her with such heat in his eyes that it actually startled her for a moment.

His hands found her arms and he stepped into her, forcing her to crane her neck to look him in the eyes. He walked her back against the mirror. The air hitched in her throat.

"I have lived since the beginning of time. I have borne witness to miracles and tragedies beyond any mortal's comprehension. Have seen destruction on a global scale wipe out every living breathing creature so that the Creator could start anew. Watched family dynasties grow strong like the Sequoia and Redwood for generations only to be obliterated by the hubris of a single fool.

"When I say that I have seen all there is for this universe to offer, I say so without hyperbole. With that said, out of all I have endured, all I have seen, there is but one single thing that continues to escape my understanding in ways that no other thing on this plane of existence and every other has managed—*you*."

Charlie stared up at him as he spoke, each word extinguishing the flame of her anger a little more fully. The fierce intensity in which he spoke captivated her, but his confession ignited parts of her she hadn't known she could feel until that moment.

Her lips parted, preparing to respond in some way to his outburst, but she couldn't get the gears in her brain to function. It felt as much an accusation as an admission, but what was he accusing her of?

"You getting soft on me, Morningstar?" The words slipped out on a shaky whisper.

She couldn't decide if his face was one of stunned amusement or if she had actually broken something in him. For all the aggressive bluster surrounding his words, there was something intimately vulnerable in them. Perhaps this was not the moment to poke fun at the Devil.

Yet, she apparently could not help herself. Ever.

His finger found her chin, curling around it so that she had no choice but to stare up at him while he considered her. "Charlotte... Where you are concerned, you will find there is nothing soft about me."

Charlie couldn't ignore the way her stomach tightened as he said that. However much she wanted to argue or taunt him—something that was becoming a favorite pastime of hers—the look of wild hunger in his eyes told her she would not win. Not this time.

Not when he said things like that.

How could he say those things and look at her like that and still hold onto such an air of control. As aggravating as he could be, his complexity was fascinating to her. The part of her who had loved being a detective wanted to pick him apart and lay him out on a table so she could get a better understanding of him. To peel away each layer and leave him bare.

Her lips twitched as she fought off a wicked grin at the thought of that. A bare Lucifer. Now that idea had some merit.

The silence was agonizing. For probably the first time since he walked into her life, Charlie wished he would speak, but he just stared down at her, so incredibly close but not closing those last few inches and putting her out of her misery.

Fuck it.

Grabbing his shirt, she yanked him down to meet her lips, not giving him one more second to tease her. He stiffened against her, caught off guard by her sudden change in attitude no doubt, but eventually relaxed and pulled her tighter against him.

There'd been dreams, some more vivid than others, where she'd tasted Lucifer's hungry kiss. Where his tongue danced against hers—when it wasn't busy with more wicked things. Even as the memories of those dreams started to linger longer in her waking hours, they were nothing like the real thing.

Lucifer growled against her lips and she was jerked around, forcibly spun to face away from him. He gazed at their reflection over her shoulder, his breath coming in deep but steady beats that rocked her with each draw and release. Her skin, what parts of it weren't still caked in whatever food had hit her, had become flushed with heat. Her parted lips pulled into an amused grin as she took in the sight of them.

"We look ridiculous," she whispered through the tightness in her throat.

He rewarded her with a warm chuckle beside her ear. "I think you look like dessert."

Another thrill rushed through her and she watched his hand snake around her waist, slithering through the folds of her skirts like a serpent seeking refuge. Fingertips found the top of the slit that had been cut in the soft fabric and her heart jumped into her throat.

"What are you doing?" she whispered again.

"Getting a taste."

As he contended with her gown, his other hand moved up her arm, dragging his nails lightly up her bicep until he found the thin strap on her shoulder. He let the strap guide him down to the neckline, pulling it down as he slid his hand between her bodice and breast, cupping the warm flesh gently.

Charlie let her head fall back against him and arched her back slightly as though offering him more of her flesh.

Her entire body trembled for him, eager and ravenous. He toyed with her nipple, letting his thumb run over it in teasing circles before pushing the front of her dress down and exposing her bare breasts with his own shudder of satisfaction.

Slipping beneath the opening of the dress, his other scheming fingers found their prize and slid between her legs. Charlie gasped softly but before she could find another ill-timed comment or half-hearted argument, Lucifer's free hand covered her mouth. His eyes sparkled in the mirror glittering with sinful intentions as he took in the sight of her standing against him, half-exposed, flushed, and wanting more.

"Let's not ruin this moment with reason, Ms. Brant," he teased, grazing her ear with his teeth, one hand still holding over her lips and the other tucked inside her panties. "Just... watch. Watch me unravel you."

Charlie held his gaze for a moment, before sliding her hazel eyes to her own image. There was something darkly delicious about the way he held her, and it tightened things low in her body, things that were screaming to be released. Begging for him to make all of those wet dreams real.

His fingers started to move again, sliding over and through her in a dance that could only be the result of a millennia of experience. The weight in her grew heavier with each twist and tease, and she struggled to breathe through the limits of his hand but even that only made the sensations heighten that much faster.

A low shuddering breath tickled across the side of her face as he quickened his touch, sliding two fingers inside of her and curling them in deep, pulsing flicks that maddened her. Her muffled moan encouraged him to move faster, to push deeper, harder as they both watched her body react in the reflection. Her breasts swayed softly with each deep thrust of his fingers, her skin glistened with sweat, and her knees nearly buckled. Only Lucifer held her up it seemed.

Unable to resist any longer, Charlie slipped a hand behind her, finding Lucifer hard and thick and wanting. The unexpected touch brought a deep moan from him and she reveled in the sound, thrilled that she could produce such a reaction from him. Her smug victory was short-celebrated, though.

Not one to lose in this battle, Lucifer slipped a third digit into her, and Charlie thought her pleasure might burst out of her skin. He released the hand on her mouth and she drew in a sharp breath as he claimed her breast, holding it while he quickened his pace inside her. Unable to hold back even a second longer, Charlie reached up for him, grabbing the side of his head as the orgasm took her and she erupted against him.

The room felt eerily silent once her cries of passion subsided, and they stood together in a trembling, sweaty mess. Lucifer turned his face into her neck, breathing deeply and loosing a soft chuckle as they regained their wits. When Charlie was finally able to refocus, she looked at him in the mirror and he met her eyes with a boyish grin she wasn't sure she'd ever really seen on him before.

"See?" he said finally, his own voice strained. "Wonderous things can happen if you just... shut... up."

She wanted to bite back at him, but who was she kidding. She still wasn't sure where she left her voice. Instead, she turned her head to look at him and gifted him with a shuddering laugh of her own, then nearly cried out again as he pulled his fingers from her and slid them into his mouth.

He drew them out slowly, staring into her eyes as he savored the taste of her orgasm.

"Mmm."

The sound slithered over her and she found herself chewing on her lip again, fighting to not groan at the sight of that. All sorts of naughty ideas presented themselves, each one better than the one before. There was the bed. Then again, a shower was definitely still needed.

"Shower?" was all she managed to say to him.

With that devilish grin firmly in place, Lucifer nodded. "Yes... you definitely could use one."

Her excitement quickly died away as he turned on his heel and walked, not to the bathroom, but to her bedroom door. As he grabbed the handle, she released a disgruntled sound.

"Are you kidding me?"

Not even bothering to look back at her, he walked through the doors and called behind him, "Dessert was delicious, thank you."

"Lucifer!" she called out, but the doors severed them from one another like a wooden curtain drawing at the end of a great performance.

What a son of a bitch. She had half a mind to chase after him and give a piece of her mind. Letting out an exaggerated sigh, she turned on her heel ready to head for the shower, but with only one step out a wave of intense energy shot through her, nearly making her knees buckle.

When she was sure she could stand again, she glanced down at the mark. "Really?" she said through clenched teeth. "Cold shower it is, then."

Chapter 21

AFTER THE PREVIOUS NIGHT'S adventures, Charlie was not even remotely ready to wake up. She held onto the cusp of her deep sleep as long as possible. Her arms were wrapped up in pillows, she was snug deep inside the giant comforter, and it was still relatively dark in her quarters.

Yet, there were unusual sounds that stirred her awake. At first she thought they were part of her dream, but as the moments ticked on, it was becoming clear that was not the case. Unwilling to surrender, she flipped over and tried to block it all out, covering her eyes and ears with her pillow. It nearly worked, until something landed solidly on her causing her to sit up with a start.

"This is blasphemy!" A very pissed off pride demon pointed to the object on her lap.

It took a moment for Charlie's tired eyes to focus on the black heels—well the not-so-black-anymore heels. They were covered in all sorts of things from last night.

"And the dress!"

Charlie glanced over to the dress hanging up by the mirror. A grin started across her face, but she stopped it before it took hold.

Truthfully, Charlie didn't feel the need to apologize for her evening.

"I agree," she finally said.

The sentiment seemed to be enough to ease Abby's ire, and she lowered the second shoe she had been preparing to throw at her. Her shoulders relaxed, arms crossing over, and she started shaking her head.

"Weren't you the first one to throw something? Whatever, get up. Eat breakfast. And if you get any on me I will skin you alive. I don't care what Lucifer says."

Charlie's eyes grew wide to that threat, "Noted."

Slipping out of bed, Charlie headed to a table that held all sorts of little goodies. She scanned the array, in search of one particular item. When a cinnamon roll did not appear, she felt just the tiniest bit disappointed.

Ah well.

Grabbing a piece of pineapple, she placed it in her mouth and poured herself a cup of coffee. Her stomach growled loudly, drawing a derisive look from Abby. Now that she thought about it, she didn't exactly eat the food last night as much as declare war with it.

Charlie paused for a moment as and thought struck her, and she turned to look at Abby. "Why are you in my room?"

"Ugh," Abby rolled her eyes, huffed, and moved from where she stood and plopped down in the seat across from Charlie. "I got babysitting duty today. Can't have you releasing anymore souls."

"Oh?" Charlie raised a brow. Her heart ached a little, but she ignored it. "Lucifer's doing?" She asked with a grin across her face, already feeling as thought she knew that answer before even asking.

Abby flashed her eyes up at her, "Well, I wouldn't be here otherwise. I have other things to do."

"I can imagine," Charlie said.

"What happened to that one?" She still wasn't sure what *that one* was. A horse? The size of the kennel was right but didn't horses stay in barns and stables?

Abby opened a large box, releasing a few flies from inside it while a sly grin spread across her face, "That one? Well, that one ran away from home."

The smile faded and her whole demeanor shifted a little too quickly for Charlie. Abby gave a dramatic sigh, pretending to sound sad as she continued, "Lucifer was quite torn up. He wouldn't shut up for months about that beast."

"Wait," Charlie said, holding her hand up as she recalled their first meeting. "You mean he really was looking for his dog? That wasn't just some bullshit line?"

A growl rolled from the cage next to Abby as if the beast inside understood her words. Charlie's heart beat fiercely in her chest as bright red eyes began glowing from within the shadows. She took an involuntary step back and Abby's face split victoriously.

"I wouldn't do that if I were you. They do like to chase."

The beasts slowly emerged from their cages looking up at the demoness before turning their eyes toward Charlie. A scream caught in her chest as the creature of her nightmares flooded her mind.

Their fur was as black as night. They had docked ears, like a Doberman's, but their tails were as long and fluid as a cat's, whipping around their bodies as if they were ready to pounce. They might be Lucifer's sweet pet "doggies" as he called them, but they were nearly as big as a horse. When they looked at Charlie, their eyes seemed to soften as if they recognized an old friend.

Charlie on the other hand, was abuzz as puzzle pieces started to click into place, one by one. Pure and utter rage formed at the base of her gut when she realized she'd seen their missing sibling once before.

"How long has the other been gone?"

"I want to say... about five years?" Abby said with a matter of fact tone and Charlie felt the air leave her lungs.

The heads hung low as they came forward, shoulders hunched in. Charlie could hear the soft whines as they drew closer. She was frozen. Every molecule in her body screamed to run. Run hard and fast away from the deadly creatures who would turn her into so much meat and sinew, but she was rooted to the spot. Abby looked at the hounds in wonder.

"Peculiar. How are you doing that?" Abby chimed in as her eyes darted up toward Charlie.

"Doing what?" Her hands trembled as she looked at one and then the other.

One of the hounds pushed closer and lowered their head for Charlie to pet them like a cat needing that praise and affection. By no means was she wanting to do that. When the beast realized this, it took the choice out of Charlie's hands and nuzzled her anyway. She flinched, afraid it would finish what its brother started and rip her arm off, until a loud rumbling purr rolled out of the creature's throat. The other circled around Charlie before plopping down on its stomach by her feet.

"Wow." Abby's eyes were wide as she stared at Charlie. "No, seriously. Who the fuck are you?"

"Nobody." Charlie answered a little too quickly.

As she stood there, she started feeling a sort of strange inner peace by patting the head of the large hound.

The second animal whined, growing impatient for its turn. She glanced down just as it stretched and yawned. Rows of teeth lined the inside of its mouth, teeth that looked as though they could rend flesh from bone with ease. Teeth that were long and sharp and familiar. She winced as her scar twinged.

She knew what those teeth could do. Intimately.

Her feet were moving before she could even register it, taking off in a sprint out of the kennel room and through the twisting corridors that Abby had led her through. She didn't know where she was going, only that she needed to get away. Far away.

Her chest wanted to implode inwards, with how tight it was feeling. Pure and undeniable rage swirled with panic, and she found herself hoping Lucifer could feel every sharp stab of it.

How long had he been toying with her? The last five years had been nothing but one lie after another. *His* beast had attacked her that night, not some wild dog. *His* creature had set into motion a domino effect of complete and utter bullshit. Bullshit that had destroyed her entire life.

Charlie burst through a random door. She had no clue where it would lead but hoped it took her somewhere away from the palace. Anywhere but here. On the other side of the door, a bridge stretched on to a field of green with bursts of wildflowers.

It looked inviting. It looked *safe*.

She didn't get the chance to step further before a hand gripped her shoulder and ripped her back inside.

"Have you lost your damn mind?!"

Charlie stumbled backward until she was facing Lucifer. Concern and anger waged a war over his face, each emotion fighting for reign.

"You bastard..." Her words came out in a low hiss as she tried to catch her breath.

"I'm not sure what's happening but–"

"You've been lying to me!" Charlie cut him off before he could finish. He paused and blinked before he spoke again.

"I have never lied to you."

"Explain your missing *'doggie'* to me then."

Understanding wiped his face clean.

"Yeah. Didn't think I'd meet them? I mean honestly..."

"Charlie, let me explain."

"My life has been ruined because of you!"

Tears welled up behind her eyes, and she swatted them away, violently scrubbing the heel of her palm across her eyes as if to dare those tears to fall right now. Feeling safe from the threat of being so vulnerable in front of him, Charlie dropped her hands heavily to her sides and shook her head. "What did I ever do to you?"

"I never released the hellhound on you, if that's what you're implying. He was taken from me and had apparently escaped in the process." He stepped towards her and she stepped back. Nonetheless, he persisted. "Hellhounds are like cats. They drift between different realms with no particular master. It usually goes to a king, or queen, for comfort and food. They just so happen to fall under my care this time."

"What does that have to do with me?" She bumped into furniture trying to keep away from him.

"The hound was afraid. It was hurt and went to the closest thing that felt like home." He sighed softly. "Charlie, I don't think you're entirely human."

Laughter erupted from her, despite the tears that started falling–traitorous assholes. She was going insane.

He *was* insane. In fact, he drove her across that particular bridge with everything that had happened in the last few days.

"You never once noticed anything abnormal happening around you?"

"You're crazy." Charlie may have said the words but her mind wandered to different events through her life that were a bit odd and hard to explain. Still didn't believe it. She couldn't. "I'm just a woman. A stupid woman who let herself get sucked into all this."

"Fate is a fickle bitch." His face lost all emotion right then. Charlie flinched at his words, aware of just how much fate had fucked with him.

"I..." She started to say before Lucifer grabbed her hand and pulled her to the nearby conservatory.

In one swift movement, he shoved her hand deep into a pot of soil. Charlie tried to fight and tug her hand away from him, but he barely budged. It was like resisting a mountain of iron.

With all the pent up anger inside of her, she watched as things erupted to life in the pot. Flowers, upon flowers, as it seeped over the ceramic spreading all over. Finally, Charlie jerked her hand back to herself. Looking at it as if it were not her own. What the fuck was all that?

"You are so much more than you think, Charlie."

"Fuck you." Charlie said seething with anger as she turned and walked away.

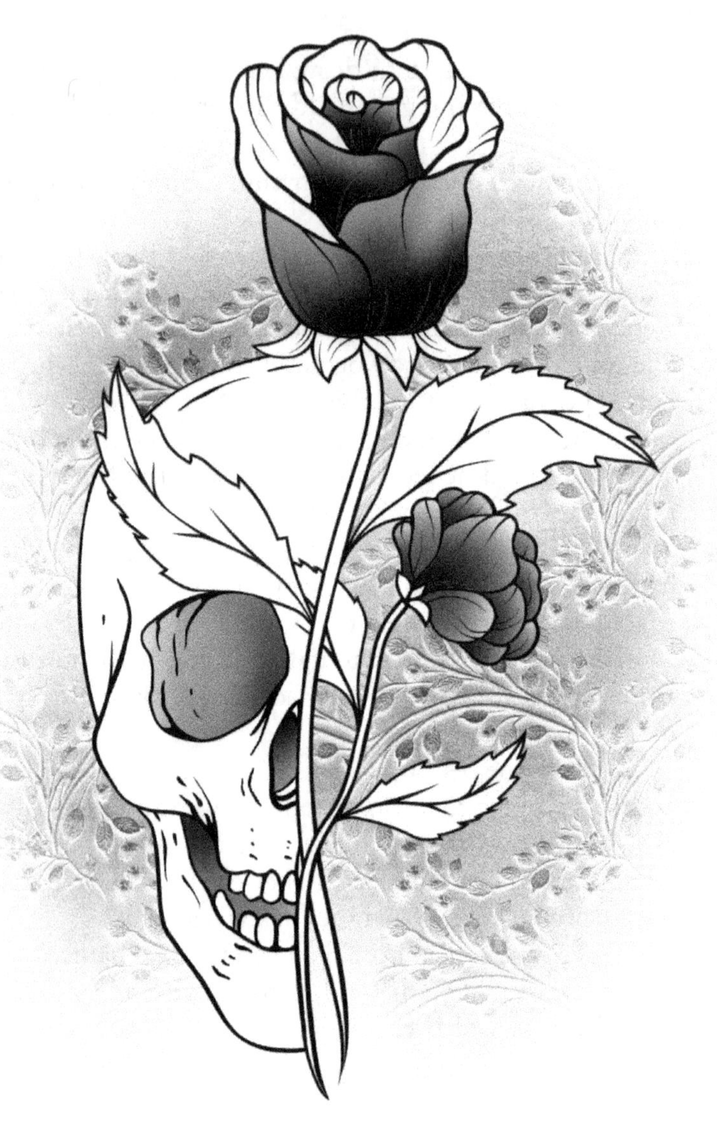

Chapter 22

NOTHING HAD BEEN THE same after that day. Discovering the hellhounds, realizing Lucifer had been lying to her, making flowers like some sort of discount comic book supervillain... Charlie lost it. She couldn't remember exactly how she got back to this room, or when, only that she'd been laying in the same spot for hours.

That and freaking out like a crazed animal, chucking priceless nicknacks at Lucifer when he attempted to comfort her. She remembered that part vividly.

At least he gave up after the third try.

Her life didn't make sense anymore. How could she be anything but human? She'd lived a fairly mundane life. Boring even. Aside from getting attacked by some hellbeast and being labeled as batshit crazy by everyone around her.

She was just a human. A lowly bondsman for fuck sakes. No, she was a human being. Even with her mother's whole witch thing, with all her beliefs and eccentricities, it was still a human existence. Herbs and candles and crystals coming out of her wazoo. She'd never seen the woman turn a man into a toad, or any of that other mythical nonsense. C.J. Brant was a human woman and Charlie had come out of her human womb.

Maybe she should call her mom.

Oh, wait. She couldn't.

Charlie buried her head in the pillows, screaming into them hoping to wake herself up from this never-ending nightmare. The crackling sound of broken glass crunching under shoes alerted her to company and she grabbed her pillow, throwing it hard towards the door. She still wasn't ready to see *him*.

"Whoa!"

That was not the voice of Lucifer. Her eyes strained to see a very masculine Asmodeus standing in the pile of broken vases. He was holding the pillow that was tossed at him, looking hesitant.

"Spying on me for your King?" she said, dryly.

"Actually, no." His eyes turned up to her, but she wasn't quite sure how to read the look on his face as he stepped into her room all the way. He glanced down again as his shoes kicked the glass on the floor. "Redecorating, are we?"

Charlie rolled her eyes, hugging her knees to her chest, "Your *master* doesn't know how to take a hint. So I had to be a little more aggressive." She said "master" with venom, pouring every ounce of her anger at him into the word.

"I can see that. Well... they were hideous anyway," he said with a smile. Asmo appeared to be trying to lighten the mood. It wasn't going to work. Tossing her pillow to the bed and sitting beside her, he looked her over a little more closely than he had before.

"Can I help you?" she snapped.

His lips curled into a smile. "You need a facial."

"Fuck you too, demon bitch."

Asmodeus' eyes widened a bit, but his smile only stretched wider. "You know, I see why he likes you."

Charlie had nothing to say to that. Nothing nice, anyway, so she said nothing. As mother used to say, and all that shit.

"Seriously though," he continued, "you look stressed. A facial can help loosen you up a bit. Not be so wound up."

"Jack Daniels works better," Charlie grumbled under breath. "If you guys are so worried about me being wound up, then tell Lucifer to send me the fuck home."

"Well, you and I both know that just isn't going to happen any time soon. Not after what he saw you do."

"Two days. He said he would take me back home in two days. I just want him to keep his word," she said, sounding as exhausted as she felt.

But it was more than that. In fact, if she were being fully honest with herself, she would admit she actually enjoyed her time there with him. Enjoyed *him*. She was in Hell. It should have been an awful, terrifying experience. Yet every moment had been the exact opposite.

She could breathe here. Breathe in a way she hadn't been able to for a long time.

So why was she angry that she'd been here longer than promised? That she hadn't been taken back to her menial existence. To the empty apartment and unfulfilling job.

The mere shadow of the life she had thought she'd have.

And with that thought, the truth struck her. The truth that was more awful and terrible than Hell itself:

Her anger had nothing to do with being tricked into staying longer. Charlie was angry because the man whose company she had grown to enjoy, whose presence was becoming less annoying with each passing day, and whose kiss still burned on her lips, had been the reason her life had completely shattered.

Asmo shrugged in response. Charlie knew it wasn't up to the demon whether she could leave or not, and having no opinion on it was probably a survival method for him.

She sighed, dropping her forehead to her knees with a long-suffering groan. "I just wanted to be a cop."

"What does that have to do with any of this?" Asmo asked, clearly confused.

Ah. Right. He wasn't privy to the runaway train of thought in her brain. "Just trying to understand what exactly I've done to deserve this shit hand that was dealt to me. That's all. I just wanted to be a cop. A good cop. I had a partner, I was good at my job, and I came home every night to a beautiful soldier who fucking loved me.

"Then your master's little dog gets loose and in one fucking moment everything is taken from me. My mental health, my job, my husband, my sense of identity. Gone!" Another long groan erupted from her. "But no worries! I can grow fucking daisies from my god damn hands! All is fucking good in the hood!! Let's not forget that the literal fucking Devil is keeping me prisoner!"

A hand moved over the back of her hair, making her jump in surprise before she realized Asmo was petting it. For some reason, it made her feel incredibly uncomfortable. Maybe it was the whole lust demon thing. Having the ruler of all things naughty—who happened to look like a fucking Fabio knockoff—petting your hair was one of the weirdest fucking things to date and there was a *lot* of weird going on.

As though he could sense her discomfort, he stopped. "Oh. Right. I forgot what I was wearing. Let me fix it."

When she looked up from her knees again, she saw....
Huge freaking tits. She jumped back a bit, putting some
space between her and Asmo's new curvaceous form.

"That is *not* better," Charlie said, trying to keep her
eyes averted.

"Why not?" Asmo asked, amusement clear in her voice
and a wide, knowing grin splitting her face. "Oh my. Charlie. You're not *attracted* to this form, are you?"

Charlie balked at the accusation. "No! I mean... It's
not that it's... well... You're beautiful, of course, but how
would *that*," she made an absentminded gesture at her
chest, "help? "

Asmo tapped their chin, looking innocently in
thought. Of course, doing so only seemed to squish their
chest even closer together, drawing even more attention to
it. An effect Charlie was certain the demon was fully aware
of.

"I mean, I don't know." Asmo looked down at the
shelf of flesh all but bursting from the top of her shirt and
giggled softly. "It seems to help a lot of people."

"Can I ask?" Charlie started, trying to go for firm eye
contact. "How do you do that?"

"Do what? Change forms?"

Charlie nodded, fighting the slight pinking in her
cheeks.

Asmo smirked, her full lips curling in an impish smile.
"Oh, that's easy. As a Prince, I can control how I appear on
the outside. It makes it easy to blend in when we're up top.
It's not like the lesser little demons who have to possess a
human to do so."

Charlie went green at the thought. So demon posses-
sions were real. Of course, they were. "So, Abby can do it
too?"

Asmo nodded.

"Lucifer?"

The demon played with their hair as they thought about the answer. "He's a little more difficult to explain. He wasn't made as we were, nor was he made as the angels were. The image he puts on now is the same as it was when he took to the battlefield before he was forced onto the throne of Hell." Asmo paused for a moment. "Well I guess it's not that hard to explain."

Charlie blinked at that, focusing on the part at the end. "Wait... *forced* onto the throne?"

She tried to remember what he had shown her days before, the whole scene played out for her in light and shadows. She hadn't thought of it at the time, whether or not the throne that he had sat upon was his choice or not.

"Yeah," Asmo said with a sigh. "Poor soul. When he imprisoned my father, the crown demanded a head to rest on. You can't just leave Hell without a ruler, you know. Can you imagine? With the Destroyer gone, the crown was forced onto the one who defeated him. Our Lucifer.

"He had no choice but to take the throne and this was why God turned his back on him. Or at least that's the schtick the angel boys are sticking to. It's a complicated mess honestly." Asmo rolled her eyes at that. "But make no mistake, God knew exactly what would happen when his brother was imprisoned. He had to."

Charlie's eyes fixated on a spot on the floor in front of them, taking in this new information. It was even worse than she'd realized. "I didn't know..."

"Of course you didn't. Not many do. Even the demons and the angels know very little of the truth, but only the demons are willing to call it what it was. The heavenly assholes would prefer to twist it into some tale of traitorous intent rather than admit the faults of their father."

Charlie shook her head. "Jesus. Knowing all of this, you guys almost sound like the good guys."

"Nononono, do not get it twisted, honey," Asmodeus said with a laugh. "There is nothing good about us or the Destroyer. Some might surprise you and can be pretty decent on a good day. But most of us work with an agenda in mind."

"And what's your agenda?" Charlie asked, genuinely curious.

Asmo smiled again, wagging her finger back and forth. "A lady never reveals her secrets."

Charlie shifted uncomfortably, but Asmodeus simply laughed, patting her knee lightly. "Oh sweetie, you don't have anything to worry about from me. You aren't my type. Besides, I am not about to be the dumbshit demon that goes after Lucifer's boo thang."

"I am *not* his... 'boo thang'," Charlie said quickly, shaking her head furiously.

Asmodeus' smile remained unshaken at her protesting. She leaned back on one hand, crossing a leg over her knee. "Maybe not to you, but you can't speak for the Devil. You should see how he reacts at the mere mention of your name. Excited. Frustrated. Longing. Intrigued. I may not be the angel of love, but I know when something is more than just lust."

Charlie stared at Asmodeus as though she'd grown a second head. Maybe she could.

"You know, I don't even know if he realizes how he feels yet. It'll be fun to watch it all unfold. I'm more curious how you'll unfold." Asmo's eyebrows wiggled.

Heat crept up Charlie's neck. Oh... he realized it. What "it" was, she had no idea, but at least one thing was certain: Lucifer had some sort of feelings for her. Guilt chased the flush away from her cheeks.

She'd felt something, too.

Damn him.

"I think you're reading way too much into it," Charlie said, standing up and walking towards the door. She swept her foot across the marble, pushing the shards of glass aside. "And I really need to leave this place."

Asmo chewed on her lower lip for a moment, contemplating something as she stared sharply at Charlie. Finally, after a few moments of awkward silence, she stood. "Fine! I can help get you home."

Charlie turned to look at the demon, unsure if she was being serious or just fooling around some more. The longer she talked to Asmo, the more Charlie realized there wasn't much that she seemed to take seriously.

"Seriously?"

"Yeah, it will be a piece of cake." Asmo flipped her hair over her shoulder and sauntered towards her. Charlie stepped back with a hand up.

"Won't Lucifer be pissed?"

"Aw, don't worry about little ol' me." She flashed a smile as she stopped in front of Charlie, invading her personal space. "He's like a grumpy cat. Eventually, he'll get over it. Besides, I like you. I can't stand seeing you like this."

Charlie wasn't exactly buying that, but she didn't press the situation any further, so she just nodded. From what she knew of the demon, she seemed to enjoy riling Lucifer up. If Asmo were to take her, Charlie was almost certain this was just another way to get under her King's skin.

Right now, she didn't give two shits about how he felt.

Asmo stepped beside Charlie and wrapped her lean arm around hers. "Can you tell me where home is, hun? I can't read minds after all."

Her words were like a purr in Charlie's ear which gave her an uneasy feeling. She may have been helping, but Charlie didn't forget what she'd said about demons and their agendas.

She half-smiled at her, "New Orleans. You can take me to the St. Louis Cathedral."

A chuckle escaped her lips, "Smart girl."

The all too familiar dark wall surrounded them. She didn't think she'd ever get used to the feeling as light seeped away and shadows melted around them. When the darkness receded, they were no longer in that damned room, but standing in the alleyway separating the Cathedral and Presbytère. The Père Antoine Alley was dark with the sun setting off in the distance. There was hardly anyone around. At least not anyone sober from what Charlie could tell.

Asmodeus was giddy with glee as she let go of Charlie's arm to stand in front of her. "This is where we part, sugar. I'm gonna go round me up some fresh meat. Ta ta for now."

Charlie didn't really want, or need, to know what Asmo planned to get up to. She groaned to herself as she watched the figure made for sin saunter off towards the bar. Her shoulders fell forward as she turned her body towards the other way. She needed to get the hell out of here.

Instead of going straight home, she decided to take a detour to the Cafe Du Monde off the square. She passed a news stand along the way, eyeing the most recent paper. Thursday. Lucifer had taken her on a Tuesday. Four days in Hell actually had only been two days here. It was just as Lucifer had said.

Apparently, he had kept his promise after all. Or was it Asmo who kept his promise?

Before she even reached the Cafe, the smell of fresh ground chicory coffee tickled her nose. It was real. You could smell it, touch it, taste it. Anything was more real than this whole week she just had.

As always, the place was packed shoulder-to-shoulder with locals and tourists alike. It was one of the most famous eateries in the city, with its name stirring recognition easily no matter where it was uttered. She always found it funny that so many people raved about it like it was literal Nirvana.

Especially because—in her opinion—Morning Call beignets were far superior.

Were the Cafe any other eatery in any other part of the country, she was sure the rushed service and powder-coated tables, chairs, and floors would receive relentless criticism. She could practically breathe in the powder sugar hanging in the air as children giggled, blowing the generous heaps from the fried dough as they bit down. But since the Cafe Du Monde had secured its fame in decades of travel blogs and pop culture, 1-star ratings gave way to words like "charming" and "authentic."

Even with the sun bowing out for the evening, the heat barely let up. The fans in the awning side of the building did very little to keep up, and Charlie couldn't bring herself to slide through the maze of bodies shuffling into the covered patio. Instead, she slipped further into the building, passing the line for the bathroom, and taking a table by one of the windows, taking advantage of the air conditioner.

At least there were less people there. It gave her a chance to take a breath and get her head on straight. She ordered a Cafe Au Lait and a small plate of Beignets, knowing she needed to put something in her stomach, though it was a half-hearted attempt.

What was she going to do? Everything that happened in Lucifer's palace played about in her head over and over, and she still couldn't make sense of it. What she could make sense of, she wanted to forget.

The parts she didn't want to forget, she should.

The waitress set her order down without even a word before heading off to return to the food line for the next order. They were efficient. Charlie had to give them that. She could even appreciate the lack of small talk.

The talk she needed was far from small, and definitely something the wait staff did not get paid enough to deal with. She could only imagine trapping some poor soul as they rushed about trying to keep the hungry masses at bay, telling them all about the Devil and how he'd locked her away for four days... or a few hours.

Yeah, she was so not about to extend the whispers of her crumbling sanity further beyond the walls of the police department.

The soft *clickity-clack* of typing drew her attention to a woman sitting close by, working furiously on her laptop. Next to her computer, her phone sat clean and bright blue and somehow managed to escape the thin layer of powdered sugar that assaulted every object in the place. Lucifer never did return her phone. Shit.

Leaning over, Charlie cleared her throat trying to catch the woman's attention. "Excuse me. Hi. May I borrow your phone?"

The woman's eyebrow rose high and Charlie realized that there were probably a hundred petty thieves stalking the tourist spots asking very similar questions. The woman's reaction read very clearly two things: she was a local, and she was not about to be that fool.

"I'll sit right here the whole time. I lost mine somewhere and I just need to call someone."

The woman hesitated then nodded her head, seeming to have judged that Charlie was a trustworthy soul. Charlie let out a sigh of relief as the woman handed her the phone.

Her fingers punched in numbers on the device automatically. She needed to talk to someone she trusted. Someone who wouldn't think she was crazy. The person least likely to think that was Carmen. And even if she did think she was nuts, she would be able to help her through it. Like she did before.

The ringing continued in her ear, much too long. Finally, it clicked over to voicemail. Carmen's voice instructed her to leave a message. Charlie's foot was anxiously tapping on the ground as she tried to reach Carmen again. Perhaps she was away from her phone. That was the hope, but the phone went straight to voicemail the second time.

Before Carmen's voice could finish the instructions, she hung up. A low, frustrated growl rolled through her teeth and she cradled the phone in her hand, thinking.

Everything she'd done, everything she'd learned, it was just too much to riddle out herself. She needed a soundboard. Someone to listen while she hurled thought and theory at them until reason came to the surface. Thinking long and hard she raised the phone again.

Her family was an option, but the idea of bringing them into this chaos felt like a knife in the gut. She just couldn't do it. Or wouldn't. Whether her motives were protecting them or dodging uncomfortable conversations, that could be figured out later. Bottom line, she was not about to open that can of worms.

Just as she was about to give up and return the phone, an idea struck her that surprised even herself.

Charlie punched in another number that she knew by heart. She held her breath, waiting as it rang in her ear. When it clicked over and that rich familiar voice greeted her, she released a breath.

"Hey Brian..."

Chapter 23

THE GATE CLOSED ONCE the last tour finished their wanderings around the famous cemetery. Michael found the whole thing strange and incredibly macabre. Thousands of people throwing good money away just to walk through the crumbling tombs and snap pictures of the famous resting place of one Marie Laveau.

It had gotten so bad in recent years, with foolish people taking pieces of the voodoo queen's tomb, that the caretaker and owners of the cemetery not only stopped tours in the early afternoons, but also stopped all free-wandering exploration without a tour group. It was probably the second smartest thing they did, right behind having not one but two decoys they comically called "the faux-Laveau".

She may have been a godless heathen, but Michael still had to have respect for her memory. It was disgusting to vandalize the resting place of any human, no matter their beliefs.

The changes also happened to work to his benefit. With the cemetery cleared out, he would have ample time to talk to his estranged brother outside of wandering eyes.

He stood outside the structure for the Italian Benevolent Society, staring up at its beautiful architecture with great appreciation. They didn't make structures of such magnificence much more these days, so he always took a few moments to soak them in as he came upon them. A fitting housing for those that loved his father.

"So how long do we have to wait for this clown?"

Brian's voice cut through Michael's silent reverie, bringing him back to the unsavory business at hand. He turned ethereal blue eyes on his current partner-in-crime and leveled him with a look of pure... boredom.

"This clown is my brother. And he could easily set every cell within your body on fire and make it last for an eternity."

The soldier looked unimpressed by Michael's warning, which told Michael everything he needed to know about him. Brian was not only wholly unprepared to fight against Lucifer, but his arrogance at his own ability—enhanced as it may be—could prove deadly if he wasn't careful. Still, he wasn't about to try to make a mortal understand the severity of all of this. Not if they weren't open to the truth.

"He reached out several hours ago, and asked to negotiate," he said again, having told Brian this already. "We are lucky he approached us first. Now we just wait for him to show."

"Is it normal for you to just give him the upper hand? Let him make all the rules?"

"Lucifer doesn't play by rules, least of all those made for him. Even if I'd set the time or place, he would have twisted it to his liking some way or another." A ghost of a smile graced the angel's lips, as though a fond memory from years past had popped into mind. "Letting him think he has control just proves to be more efficient in the end. He's a child like that."

"Me, a child?" Lucifer's playful tone whispered through the air around them, sending both men on alert.

They looked around the tombs surrounding them, trying to pinpoint a location, but could not see the Devil anywhere. That is until Michael glanced up to one of the statues gracing the Mausoleum. Lucifer sat on her lap with one arm wrapped around her shoulders, smiling down at the both of them.

"Well, to that I can only say.... I know you are, but what am I?"

Michael sighed, pulling his gaze from his brother to look over at Brian. "See?" he said with an air of long-suffering exhaustion. "Late as always, Lucifer."

"What can I say? I like to make an entrance almost as much as I love watching your head implode." Lucifer, patted the neck stump of the headless woman he sat on, still grinning down at them.

"Where is she?" Brian asked through clenched teeth. His chest heaving up and down, taking a step forward.

Lucifer wasted no time leaping from the tomb to land inches in front of the detective, his eyes glowing with a molten intensity.

"Ohhh, you brought the ex? How delightful." The smile still plastered on his face did not quite match the antagonistic nature of his words. "So are you two screwing now? Getting a little action while you're earthside? I know how it feels to need to scratch an itch but can I just say, I assumed you had better taste."

Brian lunged at Lucifer, only to be stopped by Michael's arm across his chest. Seeing him rise to the occasion, Lucifer couldn't help but laugh.

"Ooooooh, here I pegged you for a bottom, but that was top energy if I ever saw it."

"Lucifer!" Michael barked, cutting off his brother's taunting.

If he had been anything less than an angel, he was sure Brian would have gone right through him to get to his brother. Humans and their emotions. It was going to get him killed one day.

"We are not here to discuss anyone's sex life. You wanted this meeting, so... what is it you want?"

"I don't know, *brother*, what could I possibly want? You tell me," Lucifer said, clasping his hands behind his back and giving Brian one last amused glance before pacing away. "You're the one cramping my style, after all. Chasing after me like I'm some lost cat."

Lucifer was trying to play ignorant. A turn of events Michael hadn't expected but also didn't appreciate. He had to know more of the truth than he was letting on. Gabriel had been the one to give him Lucifer's little message after all, and he could only imagine what Lucifer had managed to pull out of their brother before that.

"You know I can't just leave you to do... whatever it is you want to do," Michael countered. If Lucifer could play ignorant, so could he.

"Never stopped you before," Lucifer retorted. "All the many times you've been sent after me, and yet you send your lap dogs to do your dirty work." He eyed Brian as he said it, watching the man visibly stiffen. "You don't come personally unless there is something big on the horizon so... again... you tell me. What is dear old Dad so afraid of this time that he sends you on such a futile errand?"

He leaned back against the iron fence, arms crossed as he waited for Michael's answer. Michael simply stared at him with a deadpan expression.

"Oh, it must be bad," Lucifer said, though he sounded more like he was on the verge of laughter than any sort of real empathy.

"You can't go down this path. Stop while you're ahead, before people get hurt," Michael replied, finally cutting out the bullshit.

"Mmm, you're going to have to be a bit more clear. Which path? I do tend to take quite a few, you know."

Michael's glare steadied on Lucifer, holding his gaze for more than a few heartbeats before Lucifer's humor drained from his face.

"Oh. You mean..." His eyes flicked to Brian standing behind Michael, then back to his brother as another grin curled his lips. "I'll have to give a hard pass on that one, brother. I've taken quite a shine to the lady you see."

"It doesn't matter. You will stop before things progress," Michael commanded.

"Or what?" Lucifer chaffed. "You'll sick your love-sick pup on me?"

"I'm just waiting for the chance," Brian spoke through clenched teeth, encouraging a groan from Michael.

"Excuse me while I tinkle in fear," Lucifer said blandly.

"Shut up, Brian!" Michael shouted. As though his lips were glued shut, Brian stopped whatever he was getting ready to say.

A soft electronic melody erupted from Brian's pocket.

"Going to get that?" Lucifer grinned at Brian who was glaring at him. Michael shook his head, before seeing Brian stormed off from them.

"Finally alone, Loverboy," Lucifer said with a wink to Michael.

"Can you take anything seriously!" Michael said.

The jokester facade slipped away instantly, leaving Lucifer looking not only completely serious, but completely pissed.

"As you wish," he said before he was on Michael, grabbing him by his shirt and pushing him back against a tomb. Plaster and dust crumbled from the impact.

"How about this for serious: I am *seriously* done with your threats and your shit. Now tell me, what does Charlotte have to do with any of this?"

Michael didn't even flinch from Lucifer's outburst. He was used to these erratic behaviors, even if he was the one to cause them. To say the Archangel was relieved that he was taking things more seriously was an understatement. His eyes looked down at the hands before flicking back at Lucifer.

"You need to be the bigger person and walk away. Or you will both be the reason why the Destroyer escapes his prison."

"Hm," Lucifer said, "And why would the Destroyer be interested in who I hook up with?" His eyes slid cooly to Brian, looking almost disappointed when he realized Brian was too wrapped up in his call to hear him.

"He doesn't," Michael corrected. "Honestly, not a single soul cares who you talk into sharing the most boring three minutes of their life, but you do need to step away from her before you unwittingly guide her down the wrong path."

Lucifer snorted at his insult, but truthfully Michael didn't really care who won this little battle of barbs. There were much more pressing matters to worry about.

"Are you worried about her salvation, brother?" Lucifer said, intrigued. More mocking than anything else. It pissed Michael off.

"I'm worried about the salvation of us all."

Lucifer's eyes narrowed, not in anger but in concentration. He stared at Michael as though he were trying to figure him out, to find out if he was being forthright.

"What aren't you telling me, Michael?"

Movement in the distance caught Michael's attention. Brian wiggled his phone in his hand, then pointed with his thumb to the entrance behind him before turning on his heel. Michael wondered for a moment what he had found out, but would have to wait until later to ask him.

Lucifer's question hung in the air for a while, allowing the sounds of the city to seep in from outside the cemetery walls. The sounds of people laughing, of cars moving over damp pavement, of the ferry in the far distance. The sounds of life being lived. Life that would be threatened if the Destroyer found a way out of his cell.

Lucifer turned his body to him, arms crossing as he waited for an answer. Would he heed Michael's warning if he told him? Or would he use this opportunity as just another way to stick it to their old man? It was hard to ever predict his reactions, but even Lucifer had a sense of self-preservation. Especially if he truly was developing some sort of attachment to the human woman.

With a sigh, Michael went for honesty. "If you do not step away from her, if she gets too close to you and your kingdom of damnation, you will set off a chain of events that will end in the death of all. You, me... and Charlotte included."

"Well if that isn't the most convenient thing I've heard—"

"It's the truth. On our father, you know I am not lying to you."

Lucifer waved a hand at Michael, turning away from him.

"Father this, father that. It's always the same tune with you. Such a loyal son to some asshole who can't be fucked to care for the millions of people begging for his aide. If *father* cares so much about the well-being of the world then why doesn't he come down here himself and snap his almighty fingers and make all the evil go away. Oh, right, I know the truth to that..."

"It doesn't matter what you feel towards us, Lucifer. It doesn't change what will happen if you don't see reason and leave her alone. He will use her against you, Lucifer. There is only one thing the Destroyer wants more than to destroy God, and that's the crown that sits on your pretty little head. Do not give him the leverage to win."

"I tell you what," Lucifer said, clasping his hands together, pointer fingers extended and pressed against his lip. He stepped up to Michael and tilted his head softly, thinking. Finally, he poked him with his fingers before dropping his hands.

"You tell me exactly what dear old Dad saw when he looked into his divine crystal ball, and I will heed your warning."

They stared at each other in silence, Michael's breathing getting deeper as Lucifer's smile grew.

"Ah. Well, that's his *modus operandi* isn't it? Blind. Faith."

"I am a servant and a warrior of the Lord," Michael began, but Lucifer cut him off.

"Yeah, yeah, yeah. We all know. The perfect son, fighting the good fight, all that melodramatic crap. It doesn't change the fact that you don't know anything about what is coming. Not really. And, I am sorry, but as the only one here who has experienced exactly what blind faith gets you, I think I am going to take my chances with the girl."

Michael's jaw clenched, his hands flexing at his sides.

"Why must you be so selfish, Lucifer? Can't you for once think about the fate of the lesser beings, of your siblings?"

"I did once," Lucifer snapped, his eyes glowing, "and look where it got me; deep in the bowels of the inferno and hated by those I protected! I will not let him move me around the chessboard again!"

Black smoke exploded around them, and by the time the wind carried it away, Lucifer was long gone.

"Damn it, Lucifer," Michael whispered.

He paced around for a few moments, trying to figure out his next move, but his anger swelled inside him and he found his fist thrusting through the side of a nearby tomb. As quickly as the anger had exploded out of him, it ebbed away, leaving him in a quiet state of calm once more.

He hated how easily Lucifer got under his skin.

Lucifer obviously would not listen to reason—he was stupid to think the man even knew the definition of the word. He was far too wrapped up in his hurt to see the bigger picture. Still wounded, after how many millennia? Michael would not allow the world to burn over the selfish actions of one single entity.

Perhaps he should try a new angle. Lucifer may be okay with the world being destroyed, but he was fairly certain the woman would see things differently. He'd make certain of that.

Chapter 24

THE COFFEE IN CHARLIE'S cup had gone cold long ago, and there were few things worse than cold chicory. Only the men who had recently decided to screw her world up could top that feeling.

She should have been able to call her brother for advice. Ben had always been good for a bitch fest, always laughing at her romantic misfortunes—not that he had any romance in his life to compare to. It was always in that loving sibling way though, and he did come off with some pearls every so often.

Of course, he had been M.I.A. lately, which meant when she needed him most he was not accessible. Go figure.

Then there was Lucifer. For the briefest of moments, she thought he might actually be able to trust him. Then she realized just how stupid that was. He'd shared such an intimate moment with her, something beyond sex and lusty feelings. He had cut his heart open and let her stare into the very lifeblood of him.

He had gotten past the walls she'd put up after Brian.

Slick as he was, a part of her couldn't help but wonder if all of that had just been a show. Something to feed her ego and make her lower her guard so he could do... whatever it was he had planned to do. He was the Devil.

Master of sin. Now she knew what kind of creature he was. If it wasn't for him, she'd still have the life she loved. She doubted that she could ever forgive him. She hated him for that.

And hated how much she had burned for him, even now. That part made her feel the most foolish.

Then there was Brian; the jerk who she couldn't help but still love. They'd shared most of their life together until Lucifer's hellhound ruined everything. Or maybe it had just opened her eyes. Maybe what it had truly done was force Brian to show his true nature. What sort of man up and leaves his sick wife?

Of course, that was apparently a lie too. That wasn't who Brian was afterall. She'd always thought herself a good judge of character. Even with her anxiety making her question everyone's motives, she couldn't help but feel like she was wrong about everything.

Maybe he did have his reasons to leave, just like he'd said. After seeing his James Bond secret hideout, it really made her think more about how things ended. He still wanted her safe.

And that was why she'd called him tonight.

She'd been staring out of the window for about twenty minutes, watching the people passing by, going on with their normal lives, and leaving her coffee and beignets untouched. She hadn't even noticed Brian making his way toward the Cafe. When he dropped his helmet on the table, she swept her gaze from the window and up to meet his face, feeling... numb.

Brian slid into the seat across from her, not daring to take his eyes off her. "Where were you? What's wrong?"

The words were forming in her mouth, ready to unload everything onto him, but all that came out were tears.

It was just a single tear at first, then two, and then the water flowed freely. Metal scraped against the hard floor and arms slipped around her, lifting her up off the chair. Brian picked her up and sat down in her chair, letting her settle in his lap the way he'd done a thousand times before in the past.

His hand stroked her hair as she cried silently against his neck, "Jesus, Charlie. What happened? I don't think I've ever seen you like this."

A bitter laugh erupted against his neck and she sat up, wiping at her eyes. "Yeah, you wouldn't have, would you? Being gone and all." She could feel him stiffen under her and instantly regretted saying it.

"I'm sorry, Charlie. I really thought I was doing what was best. A little pain now to save a world of it later," he explained. "But it wasn't just a little pain. And for that, I can never be sorry enough."

Charlie looked at him for a few moments then let out a small puff of air, shaking her head. "No, I'm sorry. I shouldn't keep hitting you with the same thing every time I see you. It's not fair."

He smiled at her, and it was genuine. "So, again, I ask: What happened?"

"Where do I even begin?" She sniffled as she used the back of her hand to wipe tears away. Sitting up, she looked down at Brian's face; he had quite the passive look on it. "I found them."

"Found who?"

Charlie let loose a deep sigh, sliding off his lap finally and moving back to her own seat. She fidgeted with her coffee, slowly stirring it as she tried to figure out how to explain it to him.

"The thing that attacked me that night."

Brian's eyes widened just a touch before returning to normal. He leaned back in his seat heavily, rubbing his hand over his chin. "Really? How? What was it?"

She mirrored his posture, leaning back in her chair and combing her fingers through her hair as it hung next to her face. What harm could it cause to tell Brian?

"It was a hellhound. Some weird beastie type thing that Lucifer owns. When he took me that night, he brought me to his home," she explained. She risked a glance at him and saw a look she'd never seen before on him.

Jealousy?

"In Hell," she continued.

The jealousy shifted into shock at that. He blinked a few times, processing what she was telling him. "Hell. Wow..."

"It was an experience." Her words trailed off as her eyes looked off to the side. "Either way, I can't help but feel that everything is Lucifer's fault." Every bit of what she said had way more feelings than she anticipated. Charlie glared off in the distance before Brian's hand moved up her back.

"I can only imagine."

"Brian, I just... I am so sorry." As much as she felt betrayed by Brian in the past, she felt just as betrayed by Lucifer now. For someone who hated betrayal, he really pulled one on her. "If it wasn't for him, I would've never gotten hurt. I wouldn't have lost my job...You..."

Everything was so screwed up.

"You couldn't have known," he said. "It's not your fault."

She appreciated his attempt to comfort her but she still couldn't help that nagging feeling.

"The Devil's a monster. Why was I surprised by that?" she asked. "I mean, how stupid do you have to be to not realize what he is?"

"Nah," Brian said, trying to give her a friendly smile. "I mean that's what the Devil does, isn't it? He lies, he cheats, he betrays. He's the ultimate villain, Charlie. He's going to do villainous things."

She groaned, leaning forward to put her head in her hands. His hand moved in soft circles against her back. The words were honest, but somewhere deep in her gut she felt... gross.

As much as she hated the things she'd learned, there was still a part of her that didn't want to believe it. It *hurt* to believe it. The pain moved up to her heart, and it ached for Lucifer.

"But the thing about evil," he continued. "It doesn't have to win."

She lifted her head a touch, looking at him through her fingers. "Win? Against fucking Lucifer?"

"It wouldn't be the first time in history. Not if you have the right people on your side."

"Yeah," she snorted. "Like who? The Archangel Michael?" The name dripped off her tongue with heavy sarcasm. Even though she knew that Michael existed and was, in fact, a rival of Lucifer's, Brian wouldn't get the truth behind the joke.

"Exactly," he said, completely serious.

She blinked at him a moment then rolled her eyes, "Yeah. Right. Let's just give him a ring and see if he'll answer."

"Michael will help, I know he will."

"That sounds extra cheesy, Brian."

"No, I'm serious. I can take you to him."

Charlie stared at Brian long and hard. "What do you mean?"

"You think you can hang out with the Devil, but we can't call on an angel?" He countered and she narrowed her eyes at him.

"So you just happen to have his number in your pocket?"

"Well, kind of. You could say that."

"What haven't you been telling me Brian?" She glared at him, "Beyond just the super-secret agent bullshit–"

"Yeah, well you can't tell everything when you're a James Bond monster hunter, now can you?" A soft chuckle erupted from him but Charlie wasn't having it. She pointed a finger towards him, still giving him the stink eye.

"We are *so* not done with this conversation. After all this bullshit, you and I are going to sit down and talk. Real talk."

"Fair. That's fair." His cheesy grin all but faded at that.

Going to Michael of all beings didn't sound like a good idea, given everything Lucifer had told her. But she was running out of options. Guilt weighed heavy in her gut at the thought of going to the one person Lucifer had been warning about, but the whole lying to her thing... the fact that he knew all the answers she'd been looking for and never said a word to her.

"He can help. I promise."

Her brow quirked at his persistence. "Sure."

Brian smiled and patted her hand before standing up and tossing some cash on the table. "Come on, then. Let's go meet him."

"What, now?"

He grabbed his helmet off the table as she stood and slid it over her head, giving it a playful knock on top when her hazel eyes narrowed at him through the visor. "Yes. No reason to drag it out, is there? Unless you got a hot date?"

There was something in the way he said it that caught her off guard. Almost sad. Why he felt he had any right to be jealous of whatever imaginary guy she may or may not be dating, was beyond her. As far as she was concerned, he forfeited that right the day he filed those papers.

"Yeah," she found herself saying. "So let's not take all night."

Of course, she was lying. The only guy she'd had any sort of interlude with was the guy she was getting ready to give up. Not that she'd been expecting anything to come of it.

A hand lightly touched her elbow, and Brian's smiled down at her pointing towards the direction of his bike. "This way."

He'd tucked it away off the road, hidden behind a bit of fencing and some trees. Not exactly legal parking for a cop. It made her smile, but she chose to say nothing. Now was not the time to tease him. They got situated on the Harley and were soon off, barreling down the road and dodging the occasional drunk pedestrian that wandered off the curb.

"Where are we meeting him?" Charlie asked when they finally reached a red light.

He glanced over his shoulder, his dimple taunting her before turning forward again. "Off the beaten path. Do you still not believe in ghosts?"

"What? Of course not," she said a little too sharply.

It wasn't as honest as the many other times those words left her mouth. Not since that day at Lucifer's. But that wasn't a ghost, was it? She was in literal Hell, so where else would the souls of the departed be? But hanging around on earth?

"Good," he said, just before the bike sped forward again.

Charlie's head buried into his back as her arms held tightly around his waist. She used to love riding with Brian, but after he left she hadn't so much as looked at a bike. Her heart raced in her chest as they picked up speed. Even under the current circumstances, she couldn't fight off the bubble of laughter spilling out of her.

For just a moment, she could pretend things were the way they had been years ago. Just her and Brian, barreling down the streets of New Orleans. She knew how dangerous it was to get sucked into how things used to be, but damn it she could use a little escape. A little comfort from the familiar.

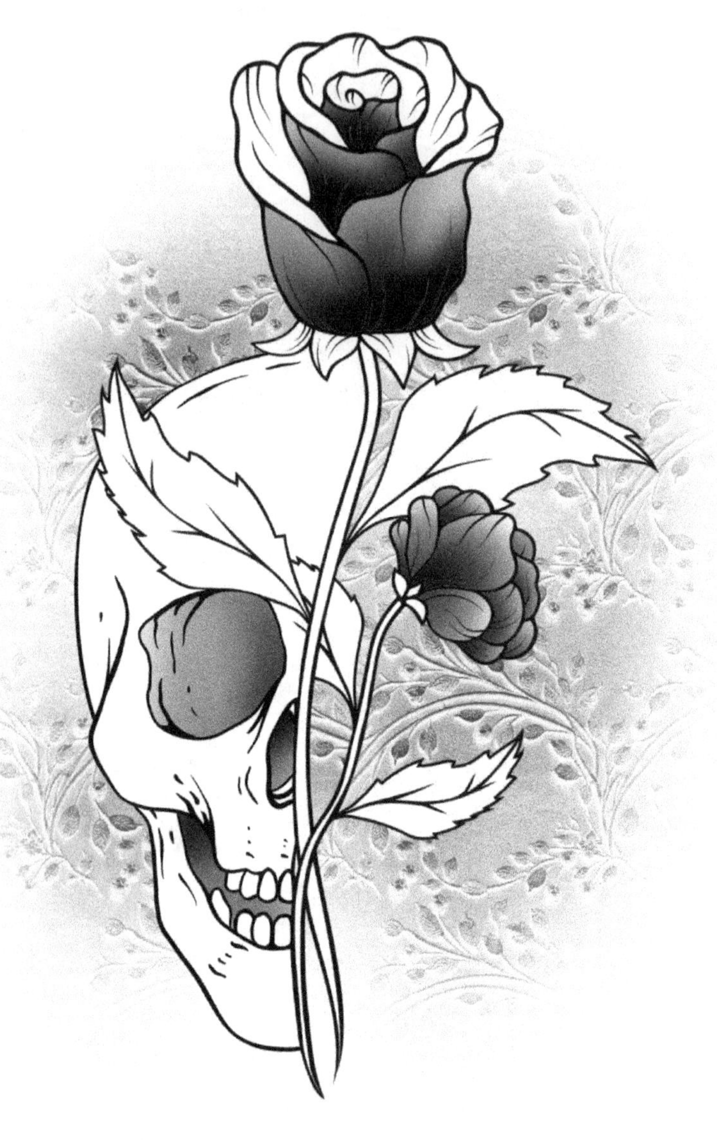

Chapter 25

Charlie

ABOUT TWENTY MINUTES AFTER agreeing to meet with Michael, they were driving around Behrman Memorial Park. It wasn't until they pulled onto General Meyer Avenue that she realized where he was taking them. When they neared the center of the property, Brian shifted his bike on a narrow concrete path that cut through the lawn. The path ended at a line of overgrown trees, which was where Brian decided to park.

"No fucking way," Charlie said as the crumbling entrance of the Touro-Shakespeare Home came into view.

The place had been long abandoned after the flooding from Hurricane Katrina, and it had been slowly falling to pieces since. She remembered hearing rumors of it being haunted in school, but then again it was New Orleans. Everything from lavish hotels to bus stops was supposedly haunted.

Whatever brings the tourists, she supposed. It was one of the biggest reasons she was so skeptical about ghosts and spirits. It had just become so trendy.

During her time on the force, she had been called here more than a few times. Sometimes it was to bust up a crack den, sometimes it was chasing the bad guy in there. But never was there a specter floating in the wings, waiting to scare her.

"Michael should be in the chapel. I know, it's a little on-the-nose," Brian said with a smile.

"You're telling me." She pulled the helmet off and handed it to him.

"I'll be in shortly."

Charlie looked at him wildly. "Aren't you coming?"

"Yeah, but I'm gonna pull the bike behind the trees so no one sees it. Don't want anyone calling cops out here thinking some suspicious activity is going down." His smile remained firmly in place. "You go first. I'll catch up."

Charlie stared at the back of his head as he pushed the bike into the trees.

The grounds were way overgrown, suffering from years of neglect. This property was beautiful once, like so many city treasures beaten by Katrina's wrath. The closer she got, the more she had to admit that there was still a sort of beauty to it, even in this state. But that beauty was easy to miss when she thought of how many crackheads and miscreants crawled in and out of the grounds. With that thought, her hand instinctively went to her hip.

"Shit," she hissed.

So much for the comfort and security of cold, loaded steel. She never did get a chance to grab her gun from her car, what with all the kidnapping and other bullshit. This was probably the longest she'd been without her firearm since she'd entered the force.

Not a mistake she'd be making in the future.

Cussing to herself, she pushed forward. He was an angel. They were supposed to be the good guys, right? She would just go in there, tell him what she knew about Lucifer, and ask him to help her right the wrongs he'd caused her in exchange. Simple.

Navigating the destruction of the building was a little more difficult than expected, but she managed to cross over shattered floor tiles and busted furniture thrown about the place with little trouble. He'd be in the chapel. Of course he would.

The chapel looked hollowed out. Pews were torn out from the floor and taken to God knows where. Graffiti decorated the walls and ceilings and floors, only able to be seen by the large number of candles filling the room. Even the pulpit wasn't untouched.

Beautiful graffiti art of Monarch butterflies surrounded the podium on the center of the pulpit, and high above it were Old English letters spelling out the word "Shame." The word glared down at her as though it knew exactly what she was preparing to do, and it shone its judgment over her head.

She was about to betray the Devil. Most stories would call her a hero for such a thing. So why did the heavy weight of guilt slow her footsteps now?

"Detective Brant," a familiar voice called out from her right.

He sat it in one of the broken windows, half-hidden in the shadows. Her eyes narrowed trying to force her eyes to adjust to the dim lighting. She'd heard that voice before.

"Glad you decided to come."

She frowned as he sat forward, allowing her to see his full face.

"I know you," she said softly. "You're the detective asking about Lucifer. Brian's partner."

The last revelation hit her like a ton of bricks. Why hadn't Brian mentioned this detail before now?

"One and the same, but you can call me Michael instead," he said as he slid off the window and calmly walked toward her. He kept a respectable distance, unlike the last time they'd met.

"I apologize for all the Cloak and Dagger rubbish, but I'm sure you understand. We're dealing with some pretty unearthly circumstances here. Not really something that can be openly discussed in a busy restaurant."

"Point taken."

It made sense. Charlie could barely wrap her head around all of this and she had been shoved violently in the middle of it. What would the unsuspecting bystanders going about their day do if they overheard talk of the Devil walking among them? It made perfect sense.

So why did she still feel that little itch between her shoulder blades?

"So Brian tells me you're finally willing to help me with Lucifer," Michael said as he locked his hands in front of him.

He was staring at her intently, the blue of his eyes somehow still visible in the shadows, but all she could think was when exactly did Brian tell him that? They'd jumped straight on the bike from the cafe and made a straight shot here. Maybe he shot him a text when he was parking the bike?

"I–" The sound of crackling debris caught her attention and she turned to see Brian walking into the room.

He gave her a small smile before he leaned on a wall by the entrance. Feeling just a little more secure with him at her back, Charlie turned her eyes back to Michael who was still waiting ever so patiently. Almost pleasant.

"Before I help, what will you do? Are you going to hurt him?"

It surprised even her, but she didn't want anything horrific to happen to Lucifer. She may have been pissed at him, he'd earned that without question, but he didn't deserve to be hurt. She just wanted him to leave her alone.

When she glanced at Brian, she found his smile had disappeared and he was looking rather put off at her concern for Lucifer. She rolled her eyes before focusing back on Michael.

"Don't tell me you have feelings for my brother," the angel said, and though his smile stayed she swore she could hear the ghostly traces of distaste in his words.

Her hand shot up, shaking it side to side. "No-no-no. Don't confuse my concern for anything more than passing curiosity."

Even she didn't believe the words as they fell out of her mouth.

Michael's eyes darkened, the first layer of pleasantness falling away.

"Look, I just want him to leave me alone. He clearly has an agenda and I don't like being part of these games."

"Mmm, games are something he likes to do." Michael moved around her, stopping at the doorway she'd come in and inspecting the stone threshold. "I don't want to see anyone hurt. That is the whole point of all this."

"And what exactly is 'all this'?"

A new smile curled his lips, one that shifted from friendly to contemptuous. "There is something coming. Something that is greater than you and I. Greater than Lucifer. He thinks he can just do what he wants and ignore the consequences—"

"He's the Devil," Charlie interrupted. "Does that surprise you?"

Michael leveled her with a look she couldn't fully read but continued. "Even the Devil knows when to yield when it comes to protecting his own skin. Yet, this time, he's struggling to understand the weight of the matter."

She noticed a silvery figure walk out from the corner of her eye, distracting her from Michael for just a moment. Cold shivered down her spine rubbed her arm to get rid of the chill.

"So, he's willful. We all know this. I still don't see how any of this has anything to do with me."

"You're a key player to someone else's game, I'm afraid. And your involvement serves as nothing more than a distraction for my brother. One that others will take great advantage of, I'm afraid." His words were anything but sympathetic.

"I don't want to be a part of anyone's game. I don't want to be a distraction, a player... I just want to go back to living my shitty little life in peace. What part of that don't you assholes understand?"

"That is not your call to make, but I *am* trying to help you. I'm not your enemy."

Charlie snorted, rolling her eyes again. As she did, she noticed another silvery figure hanging around the corner of the pulpit before disappearing through the walls.

"He just wants to help, Charlie." The words drew her attention away from the figures and towards Brian before looking back to Michael who was studying her much more intently than before.

"What do you see, Ms. Brant?" There was hardly any emotion to his words.

She didn't answer him at first. Her eyes drifted past him seeing yet another figure sitting on the windowsill where Michael had been moments before. Only this one was staring straight at her. Charlie's arms dropped to her side.

She felt, more than saw, Michael turn towards what she was looking at. "You can see it too."

"I'm an Archangel, Ms. Brant." He turned to her, his ethereal blue eyes piercing right into her soul. "Of course, I can."

Brian pushed himself off the wall and moved to stand next to Charlie. "See what?"

"Grab her."

Charlie looked between Brian and Michael. "What?"

Brian grabbed her forearm, but his grip was loose. Uncertain. Charlie shook him off and started for the exit. "Keep your hands off me!"

"*You will comply,*" she heard Michael whisper.

The fuck she would.

Iron-like hands wrapped around her arm and she twisted around, pushing against Brian with her free hand. He didn't so much as sway from her struggles. When she looked into his eyes, she saw... nothing. He was empty, as if everything that was Brian had leaked away leaving him hollow.

"Brian, what the hell are you doing!? Let me go!"

Charlie turned to find Michael towering over her before snatching her hand and pulling it towards him. She didn't even see the knife before it swiped across her palm.

Blood pooled from the cut, filling her palm quickly until it spilled over the edges of her hand and dropping like heavy raindrops onto the floor. Roses began to bloom from the small puddle.

Everyone stilled as they watched. Even Charlie was frozen in awe.

That was something new to add to the ever-growing list of what-the-fuckery.

"It's too late," Michael slowly tore his eyes away from the miraculous happenings at their feet to stare at her. "I truly am sorry, Ms. Brant. I had hoped I could intervene before it had gotten this far. I tried to give you both every chance to do the right thing, but now it's far too late."

"What do you mean it's too late? You haven't even told me what's happening! I hardly call that giving me a chance at anything, buddy!"

Heavy silence filled the air as he stared at her. Finally, he asked, "He took you to Hell, didn't he?"

"Yeah, so? Again, I repeat, what does that have to do with anything?"

A spirit lunged at them, grabbing hold of Charlie's arm. "P-please, miss. Please take me to the underworld? I want to see my family."

Charlie looked at the spirit, trying to ignore the frigid grip on her arm, but before she could answer, Michael shoved her backward out of Brian's grasp. She tumbled to the ground and had to lift her arm up to cover her eyes from a sudden blinding light. Charlie wasn't going to stick around to see what had happened. The second she reclaimed her bearings; she scurried to her feet and ran.

Getting out of there seemed like a good idea. Fight or flight had overtaken all other instincts, and though she was known to fight, she knew didn't stand a chance between a fucking angel and, apparently, Brian. She could figure out his newfound super strength later. Survival first.

Making her way through the crumbling maze, she stumbled out into an overgrown courtyard. The place was filled with small saplings and overgrown brush. Footsteps approached behind her, and she grit her teeth, pushing through the heavy foliage hoping it could give her enough cover to slip away.

"Trust that this is not the ideal end I had hoped for Ms. Brant," Michael's voice echoed around her, seeming to come from every direction. "All Lucifer would have had to do was leave you alone. Just as you'd asked."

She couldn't stay in one spot. Even with the echoes camouflaging his location, she knew not moving would leave her vulnerable. She continued to push through the brush and undergrowth, hoping that wherever she emerged, he wouldn't be standing there waiting for her.

"But he's too selfish for his own good. For anyone's good. He has great affection for you, of course, but he of all beings understands the seriousness of this matter. If he truly cared for you, would he have put you in the Destroyer's sights?"

Her heart seized and she stumbled to the ground, her hands tangled in the dried vines. That name. She remembered it from Lucifer's story. He was the being that Lucifer had been created to kill.

"The Destroyer is dead!" she found herself answering, immediately feeling foolish. But it was true. He was dead. So, all of this meant nothing. She prayed Michael saw the reasoning.

"You cannot kill Darkness, Ms. Brant. No sooner than you can kill Creation. As long as one lives, so will the other. It's the balance that allows this world to exist." His voice seemed a little more distant now, a little more focused to one direction. Charlie moved again, heading in the opposite direction of his voice.

Keep talking, bud, she thought as she pushed forward.

Every tree she brushed against thickened; sprouting buds of flowers and creating a floral curtain that made it way too hard to get through. Despite how fucking bizarre everything was, Charlie tried to push those thoughts down and use whatever element was on her side so she could get out of there. If the brush was slowing her down, it could slow them down too.

She'd take the win for now.

"But he *is* caged. For now. And it is my duty to ensure that does not change. It is not personal, Ms. Brant. I truly wish it did not have to come to this, but I cannot allow the Destroyer any leverage. For the sake of all life."

Hope pulsed through her as the plants started to thin up ahead, giving her a brief glance at freedom before a hand shot out and wrapped around her wrist. The overgrowth had wrapped thickly around them, but it was Brian's eyes that stared vacantly at her through the spaces between the stalks.

Her despair escaped her throat as she cried out, tugging violently against his grip. As she fought to pull herself away, vines wrapped around Brian's hand and forced him to let her go. With another small victory—if she could call it such—she continued onwards.

The weight of Brian's betrayal made the last stretch of brush all the more difficult to pull through, but finally she emerged onto a clear lawn. Having finally escaped the twisted maze, Charlie looked back to find a wall of green. Did she really do that? And more importantly, *how?*

The courtyard around her was empty. Wherever Michael had gone, he must have sent Brian the opposite way to cover more ground. Now she just needed to get out of there. Maybe she could find Brian's bike, take it back to the city.

She started toward the fence on the far side of the courtyard, taking one last glance over her shoulder at the plants that had become Brian's prison. What had happened to him? That was not the Brian she knew.

Later. She'd have to worry about that later, after she figured out how to keep this homicidal agent of God off her ass.

When she looked forward again, she walked into something solid. Michael's expressionless face looked down at Charlie.

"I'm sorry it had to come to this," he said, his voice almost solemn.

The blade in his hand stabbed towards Charlie. Even with the vines wrapping around his arms and torso, pulling against his forward movement, he was too strong.

Pain seared through her stomach, radiating through every inch of her. Charlie dropped to the ground as more vines wrapped around Michael, pulling him away from her, but it was done. Her eyes were glued to the knife sticking out of her.

She reached for the blade on instinct but winced the moment she put any pressure on the handle. It was good, though. She shouldn't pull the object from the wound. Leaving it would keep her from bleeding out. Right?

Fuck, she couldn't remember. Everything was fractured and jumbled, making it impossible for Charlie to think one simple cohesive thought.

Her head fell back, resting against the cool ground, and she closed her eyes to try and concentrate. Apply pressure. She slipped her hands carefully around the knife, pressing painfully against the wound but blood seeped through her fingers easily and dripped to the ground in a steady flow.

Tears streamed down the sides of her face as she lay there. The more she tried to relax the more the pain escalated. Eventually, the pain faded from excruciating to nothing at all. It just faded away like the world around her had begun to do.

She spiraled into numb darkness with only the fragrant aroma of fresh flowers to accompany her.

Chapter 26

Lucifer

THE MEETING WITH MICHAEL didn't exactly go the way he hoped it would have. Then again, there wasn't exactly any sort of plan when he had tried to arrange their meeting, other than to politely tell him to stick his feathers up his ass and leave them be.

If Michael had been willing to divulge a little more information about the portents Gabriel had mentioned, he'd have been thoroughly shocked. Not shocked that he would tell him, but surprised that their father had explained literally *anything*.

That Michael's assignment was less about him as it was about the dear Ms. Brant, that she specifically was part of whatever grand scheme was at play with their uncle... Now that was interesting.

And incredibly concerning for a number of reasons.

Lucifer ran a hand over his hair as he walked the lifeless halls of his palace. There was no destination in mind when he'd started. He was simply hoping to clear his mind.

Should he heed his brother's warning? Or do what he always did? Normally he would always go with option B, but learning the Destroyer was up to something had created an unease within him. The Destroyer's prison was locked tight in such an intricate puzzle that it would take eons to riddle out, if ever.

But what if he had? What if the Destroyer had finally found the key?

Charlie.

Lucifer knew there was something strange about the woman, knew that she wasn't as human as she appeared. He'd followed his curiosity over the last five years, watching her and taking in her extraordinary resilience. Despite what she thought, she had bounced back quite well considering everything that had happened to her. He'd gotten to know Charlie through her dreams, assured of the knowledge that as soon as she woke, she'd forget all about him.

At least that was how it had started. Lately, he was seeing that she was becoming more in control of herself on the dream plane. Remembering more—at least in a subconscious sort of way.

That was another indication of how unique Charlie was.

It was not easy seeing her unravel the way she had. She outright threw things at him to get him to leave and it had hurt something in him. She was like a... friend.

"Hmm, friend..." The word felt so new every time it popped up in his head. He hardly had any of those these days.

Allies, yes. Friends... he was genuinely pleased to call her such.

Even more complicated, however, were the feelings that had ventured beyond simple friendship. Feelings that he longed to explore but feared doing so. Feelings he had not had to endure since his first wife.

He banished the thought of her the moment she entered his mind. That was millennia ago. Charlie was now. It was extraordinary how a simple human was able to capture his eye not once, but twice. Though the first had become so much more in the years following their sordid end, this one he had every reason to believe was already... special.

He just needed to figure out why.

Lucifer quickly wondered how Charlie was doing. He'd had to sever the connection with her through the mark just so he could think. It was becoming difficult to work when pesky emotions like anger, sadness, and agony swarmed around him like mosquitos, courtesy of Ms. Brant's lovely temper. Giving some distance seemed to be the optimal solution in the matter.

The sound of broken glass under his shoes brought him back to reality. Somehow, through his brooding thoughts, he wound up outside Charlie's bedroom door. His foot pushed a few pieces aside, and he smiled just a touch.

She was passionate. That was certain. What wasn't certain, and what he'd hoped beyond all else, was whether she would ever forgive him.

With a sigh, he knocked on the door lightly, hoping he wouldn't provoke more of her ire. "Charlie..."

A long pause filled the air. There was no sound at all on the other side. Perhaps she was sleeping? He reached for the handle, hesitating.

"You are the goddamn King of Hell, Lucifer. She's just a woman. A tiny woman," he whispered to himself. "...A splendid, brilliant, terrifying but tiny woman."

Pushing the door open softly, he peeked into the room. His eyes landed on the bed first where he saw a figure that was much bigger than the woman he was looking for. Heat flared at the sides of his face, and he stalked dangerously toward Charlie's bed and its current inhabitant.

His hands grabbed the man on either side of the head and jerked him up.

The man's eyes were open with a blissful look upon his face, but he stared right through Lucifer, unbothered that his head was so dangerously close to separating from his spinal column. Nobody was home. Alive... but gone.

"Asmodeus..." the name came on the back of a dark growl.

Asmodeus walked into the room from the bathroom.

"Oh hey, Luci!" Her eyes were wide as she dried her long brown locks with a towel. "When did you get back? Playing with my leftovers?"

"Cut the shit Asmodeus. Where the hell is Charlie?" He released the man, letting him crumble to the bed to stare up at nothingness.

"Who?" Her brows perked up, feigning innocence.

A ball of black fire formed in Lucifer's hand, but Asmodeus simply threw her head back and laughed. "Oh, come now Luci. I'm just teasing, I know who you're talking about."

Asmodeus came further into the room, her open robe revealing all her best assets. Modesty was not a word in the demon's vocabulary. She sat in one of the chairs in front of the fireplace, one leg crossing over the other as she lounged about. "What do you want with her?"

"I don't have time to play these games. Where is she?"

She pushed her lower lip out in a sultry pout, dragging a fingernail along it. "Pity. You know how much I love games." Seeing that he obviously was not in the mood, Asmo released a puff of air. "She's back home. You had her all cooped up in this room while you were off doing whatever it is that you do these days. You know, you are a horrible host."

With a grunt, Lucifer chucked the ball of fire at Asmodeus, missing her by a hair as it exploded in the fireplace behind the chair. The heat of the fire was nowhere near as boiling as the waves of rage coming off of him.

"You stupid little demon! I was keeping her safe!"

Asmodeus didn't so much as bat an eyelash at his tantrum.

Realizing he would get nowhere with this one, he growled and turned away from her, thinking. Lucifer could easily track her, he just needed to reconnect through the mark. He closed his eyes and concentrated, murmuring Enochian words that had been lost so long ago.

The moment the mark reawakened, his entire being drowned in a violent wave of terror, anguish, and pain... and then it started to drain away into emptiness.

His eyes flashed to Asmodeus, "I will deal with you later."

A portal formed behind him, and he turned to step through. He knew exactly where Charlie was. He just hoped he'd be fast enough.

On the other side of the portal, he was met with a wall of flowers and lush greenery. He could see Michael entwined with thorny vines wrapped around his flesh, one particularly thorny vine wrapped around his throat. Even so, he didn't miss the smug look on his face. Not really giving a damn about him in his current state, Lucifer scanned the area for the person he was really here for.

When he finally spotted Charlie, every cell in his body went icy cold. He ran to her, falling to her side and pulling her into his lap. Her shirt was so wet with dark blood that he nearly missed the open wound in her belly. He quickly pressed his hand into her wound to try to stop the blood flow.

"Charlie! Charlie, you need to wake up! Wake up for me, darling. Open your eyes. Come on, stare daggers, roll them, glare at me like the idiot I am, just open your eyes."

For just a moment, she opened them. She stared at his face through thin slits, the faintest of smiles appearing as she saw him before she passed out again. She was paler than she usually was–how long had she been like this? How long had she lain here, dying, while Michael watched on happily?

He didn't know how to help her. The helplessness of it all drove him over the edge of reason. His hand started to glow softly over her wound, and he pulled it away from her, caught off guard. He watched as the glow started to fade away, and quickly knew what it was that he was doing.

His eyes turned back to Charlie, trying to focus more on her than the glow. "You're not going to die; do you hear me?"

"Lucifer, don't–"

Lucifer turned defiant eyes towards Michael.

"If you heal her, then that will be the end of everything. Don't make that mistake. You already messed it up by your selfish need to pursue her. If you don't stop you will bring damnation to us all, including her."

Lucifer growled, "Shut up!"

Michael's lips pursed into a thin line, for once being quiet. Lucifer looked back at Charlie, the glow from his hand had stopped. Rolling his eyes, he scooped her up in his arms.

"I think we need to find someplace a bit quieter, without all this negativity. Don't you?" He was talking to Charlie in a soft, unbothered tone, trying to keep her from panicking.

And perhaps himself, as well.

A portal slowly opened beside him. Before he stepped through, he heard the vines snapping behind him. Looking over his shoulder, he could see an enraged Michael trying to escape his current prison.

A grin spreading on Lucifer's face, he leaned down to Charlie's ear and whispered, "Think of a safe place."

"...Carmen..." was the faintest of words that came from her lips as he stepped through the portal.

The portal opened inside of a hospital room.

"Huh. Convenient..." He mumbled as he looked around the room to spot a woman hooked up to machines. "Well, this just reeks of my brother."

The woman's brown eyes flicked open, staring right at him and then down at Charlie.

"I'll explain later, look after her, will you? I've got unfinished business elsewhere." He flashed her his best charming smile as he placed Charlie down in an empty hospital bed beside Carmen. Leaning down he placed a tender kiss upon Charlie's forehead and stepped back.

The woman in the other bed gasped but Lucifer already knew. Michael stood behind him, his flaming sword raised high and ready to bear down on him as he turned around. Panic flooded him, realizing he had to move this elsewhere, fast. Without waiting for a solid idea to fully form in his head, Lucifer lunged forward and conjured another portal sending the two immortals stumbling through.

The two appeared again on the rooftop of the Cathedral, the one place that had slid into Lucifer's mind moments before they collided. The place where Charlie had made the biggest, most amusing impression on him. Michael shoved Lucifer off him, and he watched as Michael's eyes darted around.

"It doesn't matter where you take me. I will do what is necessary to protect this world," he said, holding his sword out in front of him while he circled Lucifer. An eerie quietness filled the space around them.

"And I will do what's necessary to protect *her*." As if from the very fabric of the shadows, Lucifer summoned a large bastard sword forged of darkness. Despite its oversized shape, he held it up effortlessly. "Even if that means cutting down each and every one of you feathered assholes."

Michael lunged forward and Lucifer parried the attack. Their swords clashed, metal on metal. They've done this dance a thousand times over the eons of their existence.

Lucifer pushed Michael back with extra force, using a mix of his own strength and dark magic. The Archangel staggered, giving Lucifer an opening to advance, swiping up with his blade. Michael barely dodged the strike, feeling its chilling kiss like a whisper across his chin. A thin thread of blood seeped from a tiny cut on his chin before it healed over.

"You feeling up to the fight, brother? It seems as though you've lost your edge," Michael taunted with a self-righteous grin.

"Luckily for me, my sword hasn't," Lucifer said as he lunged again.

They danced around each other again, matching swing for swing, step for step. Pieces of the building crumbled beneath their traded strikes. They were evenly matched in skill as well as motivation. Perfect partners in a deadly dance. What would it take to beat his heavenly brother, to keep him from yet again attacking Charlie when Lucifer turned his back next?

That was a problem for another day. Today, Michael had earned one hell of a beatdown.

Chapter 27

Lucifer

SWEAT PULLED FROM LUCIFER'S brow. They'd been fighting for a while now. Metal on metal clashing like thunder to a spring storm. The citizens on the streets below may have believed a storm was coming with all their ruckus. Michael was wounded in some places, just like Lucifer. They'd each gotten a good hit or two, egging each other on until the other showed a sliver of weakness. Then they would strike.

Michael had unleashed his graceful wings during battle, countering Lucifer's bouts of dark magic. An angel's wings were one of their greatest defenses. Always the warrior, Michael had no issue using his as an offensive weapon. Still, Lucifer could tell that his dear old brother was becoming tired, each new strike just a little less powerful than the last. He hated to admit it, but even he was growing exhausted. Neither one would give up on their cause, though.

Both were insanely stubborn.

"Enough of this!" Michael spat out as he crouched down just so he could push himself off the roof to shoot high into the air.

Lucifer's eyes followed him as he anticipated the attack. Michael held out his hand as a beam of light, brighter than a thousand suns, shot out of his palm. The holy light could easily blind anything that wasn't celestial, but even for them it could give one hell of a punch.

"Fuck..."

Lucifer cried out as the light reached him, knocking him off his feet and pushing him through the roof of the building. Wood splintered around him; the wind knocked out of him. When the light receded, Lucifer caught a glimpse of the Archangel descending from the sky mere seconds before he drove an elbow right into his chest. The roof collapsed around the two sending debris spiraling down into the cathedral.

Any other being would have been finished with that move, but his dear brother was deeply arrogant thinking he could win so easily. With Michael on top, Lucifer grabbed hold of his brother's shoulder and threw his forehead into his, sending the Archangel flying back in pain.

Lucifer quickly stood, satisfied as he watched the celestial bleed from his nose. A grin spread on Lucifer's face as he launched himself forward, shoulder checking his brother into the effigy of Hope.

Michael smacked hard into the statue, pieces of wood and himself falling to the ground. Lucifer manifested his sword back into his hand as he walked around the pulpit to get to the fallen angel. Michael looked up at him, slightly dazed. Before he could get his energy back, Lucifer swiped downward with the hilt in the back of Michael's head in hopes of knocking the bastard out.

When there was no movement coming from Michael, Lucifer finally felt a wave of adrenaline crash. He fell to his knees and leaned back to rest on the dais.

To say he was exhausted was an understatement.

He studied his handiwork, sweat dripped down his temples, sliding slowly down his cheek where he wiped it away with the back of his wrist. Regaining his breath, he huffed a bitter laugh before spitting on the remains of the sculpture on the floor, the gentle visage of a woman lost to his violent outburst.

"God could have come himself instead of sending you to deal with me. See? Expendable garbage. Just like me," he said to the thrashed Archangel lying unconscious on the floor.

"Is that what you think?"

The voice brought a roll of eyes from Lucifer. Of course, *now* He shows up. "What else would you have me believe?"

"I would hope after all this time you would know better. How many lifetimes must you carry this anger? This bitterness?"

"Oh please..." he said, standing slowly. Lucifer could feel the bumps and bruises weighing him down. "You're a real jack-off, you know that? You still pretend that you are some almighty philanthropists when we both know the truth. You're nothing but a sadist. The humans are scared of me, think I am the ultimate punishment for a life of evil when it's you they should be fearing."

His eyes scanned the sanctuary but didn't see his father. Annoyed, Lucifer moved stiffly to the first pew and sat down. He leaned forward resting his elbows on his knees and stared down at the polished floor. A calm vibration warmed his face and hands, and he answered it with another disgruntled sigh.

"Trillions of people have begged for you to give them comfort, and you hide away. One wayward son destroys an ugly excuse for art, and you make a personal visit."

He lifted his eyes to find a gentle old face smiling down at him in a way that only a father could give. He wore the body of an old woman, but he knew it was him. He also knew the look he wore–that of a disappointed and exhausted father.

"Balls."

God grimaced at the vulgarity. "Must you speak in such a way? You have so much more intelligence and charm than that."

Lucifer leaned back in his seat and lifted his hand up at his sides. "What can I say? That free will you gave me is a real bitch, isn't it?"

God sighed and clasped his hands behind his back, walking to the heap of debris on the ground with a shake of his head.

"So, *pop*. Why exactly are you gracing me with your divine presence after all of this?"

"Do I need an excuse to visit my favorite son?"

Lucifer was suddenly on his feet, his hands balled up in the meat suit's crocheted vest. He shoved his father back, leaning him back over the altar on top of the dais. All sarcastic humor was gone from his features, replaced with desperation and ire. God stared up at him with that infuriating placidity that drove him mad.

"Why?"

"My boy. Does it truly matter?

"No. Why do you call me that?" He stared down into the eyes of the almighty and saw... disappointment. The problem with trying to figure out the "mysterious ways" of the almighty God was that he gave nothing away.

"Because... When I made you, I created the most special being in existence. I created you with the most important destiny."

"I was special? I had a destiny? What of your pet projects. Adam and... Lilith?" The name choked out of him, and it took the briefest of seconds for Lucifer to collect himself.

He cleared his throat, forcing his voice to cooperate. "Oh, right... we don't talk about that one. Eve, then? You made them from the dirt of your beloved little ball in the heavens. Did they not have a purpose? Before you cast them away for what? Learning truth? Your pitiful little followers believe moral knowledge to be proof of your existence—because the heavens know you won't show yourself to *them*. Yet you cast out your little pets for daring to gain that knowledge. And what about Jesus? Your sweet, pure sacrificial lamb. He let them raise his broken body on a cross because of his love for you and for your little pets. And yet, *he* is not your 'favorite'?"

"Lucifer..."

A guttural growl erupted from Lucifer, and he jerked God to his feet, bodily walking him around the dias where Michael still lay unconscious. Bloodied and bruised... but alive. He held his father so that he had no choice but to look at his other son.

"And what about him? What about your shining warrior? He would do anything you asked of him and has. Without prejudice. He was perfectly crafted by your hands and has never questioned your will. No matter the cost. He swallowed your ridiculous dogma, lapped it up like the faithful lapdog he is. The sacrifice of one for the salvation of the many. Meanwhile, I piss on your churches and show your prized pets the truth about themselves. And yet I am still the 'favorite son'?"

He released God abruptly, walking backwards to watch as he looked on at Michael. If there was any sense of pain or concern for the warrior's well-being, the bastard gave no indication of it.

"Say something you righteous bastard," he demanded, his voice thick with eons of repressed emotion.

"What is it you would have me say? That I love all my children equally? I could say as such, but it would be a pretty lie." God turned away from Michael and weighed Lucifer with a serene smile. How he wished he could wipe it away with his fist.

"They all have served their purposes. I love them, of course. With every fiber of my soul. But you are so much more than you understand." The very same sentiments he'd said to Charlie now hit him like cutting barbs. "You are not done, yet. When you are, my hope is that you will see what I see. Michael is a good soldier, but you... you are my child. Lost as you may be."

"Oh, but I am. I *am* done, father. You forged me as a bar of cold unfeeling steel to fight in a war that was yours to fight. You set me on the path to my own eternal torment and you dare to ply me with empty platitudes and false endearments!" His voice echoed within the large room, building layers of anguish around them. "Let's not forget the mission you sent Michael on."

The silence that followed was deafening. He wiped at his nose, turning his back to God so that he could not see the pain slipping from his eyes. When he turned back around, God was gone.

Lucifer snorted, waving off the empty space. "Why am I not surprised?"

He took a moment to collect himself before heading back to Charlie. He wanted to be there when she woke back up. She deserved that much. He smoothed his hands through his hair and straightened his shirt, heading to the door.

"Think you hurt his feelings?"

Lucifer spun around to find Michael propping himself up on the floor, looking a bit dazed, but alive. "He doesn't have feelings."

Michael laughed, but it turned into a cough. "Sure, he does. He has all of them. He just shoved them into all the little meatbags."

He had to laugh at that. Scratching his neck, he took a few steps towards his brother. It probably would have been a better idea to just turn around and go, but then when did he ever do the proper thing?

"How long have you been awake?"

"Long enough," Michael said. His face was completely unreadable, but Lucifer had an idea of just how the Archangel felt about what he'd overheard. He could see the wheels rolling in that brain. "You know what will happen now. You dropped the first domino. I'll have to intervene... eventually."

Lucifer nodded, looking around. "You can try."

He smirked at Michael then started making his way to the door. "Raincheck, though. No need to beat you up twice in a week. Besides, I need to go meet up with a sweet little hellcat. I wouldn't want to miss the extraordinary reprimanding heading my way."

"Be careful," Michael laughed as he tried sitting up fully. "Don't want to get chained down again. You fell for a pretty face once before, and that didn't exactly end well the last time if I recall."

Lucifer stopped at the door and chuckled under his breath. "Yes, well... we're working our way up to chains. See you 'round, Michael."

All he heard in reply was a booming laugh as he stepped through the door.

Chapter 28

Beep. Beep. Beep. The noise was absolutely annoying. Charlie had no idea where it was coming from, but it kept droning on and on. She moaned in protest as it got louder, bouncing off her eardrums relentlessly.

What did she do to deserve to be tormented so? With such a diabolical torture, she must have been back in Hell. Great. She died and wound up *there*.

She could only imagine what Lucifer would have to say about that. Would he be pleased? Or annoyed that she'd gone and got herself murdered?

Charlie did everything she could to lift her arm up, but it felt like a wet, soggy noodle. Sleep had built around her eyes, crusting over and making it hard to pry them open. Forcing her body to cooperate, she finally managed to wipe the crust away from her eyes.

After her eyes managed to focus, she realized she was in a hospital room. That discovery drew her eyes to her hand and found an I.V. taped to it. The incessant beeping that had guided her back to consciousness came from the monitor tracking her vitals.

Well, on the bright side, she wasn't dead. Though she sure as hell felt like she was.

The last thing she could honestly remember was being stabbed. Her hand mindlessly moved to the wound in her abdomen. Surely, someone like Michael wouldn't have missed... would he?

"Well, if it isn't Sleeping Beauty."

The familiar voice surprised Charlie, and she followed it to find Carmen wobbling her way into her room donning her own hospital gown. Charlie quickly scanned her over, noticing the bruises scattered across her features like spots on a dalmatian. "What the hell happened to you?"

"Nuh-uh, you don't get to ask questions yet."

Charlie instantly shut her mouth, her lips pressing together. She couldn't help but roll her eyes. Carmen looked probably as bad as Charlie did, but *Charlie* was about to get an earful. She could just feel it in the air, like the moments before a violent storm.

"What the actual fuck did you get yourself into?" Her usually stern face held an unexpected edge of fear Charlie had never seen before. Carmen looked behind her to make sure none of the nurses were coming before she got closer.

"Not only did you just appear in my room with some guy like David fucking Blain, but then I saw Detective Noir appear behind you with a fucking fire sword. He was just about to cut you into two equal pieces then *poof*, they were both just gone. I thought for sure it was the drugs, but I don't think the hospital has anything that can make you trip out that bad."

Charlie blinked a few times, trying to think of something to say. "Well... Umm... you know about angels and demons, right?"

Carmen's eyes narrowed slightly, "You getting religious on me now?"

"Hardly," Charlie huffed. "At least, not exactly."

"Okay, Brant, how about you stop beating around the bush. You know I can't stand watching you try to lie. It's like watching a drunk virgin on their wedding night. Just... sad."

She wasn't wrong about that. Whenever Charlie tried to pull one over on her, Carmen was always quick to call her out on it. She shifted uncomfortably in her bed, unsure how to say what she was going to have to say. "You're going to think I'm crazy."

"Try me."

Charlie took a deep breath, bracing herself. "That man that brought me here, he's Lucifer. As in the actual Devil, Lucifer."

Carmen didn't say anything. She simply stared at her, as if waiting for her to continue or to hit her with the punchline. When it was obvious she was doing just that, Charlie continued.

"I don't know how, and I don't know why, but he dragged me into his little grudge match with his brother—" a thought struck her then. She shot a glance back up at Carmen. "You might know him as Detective Noir."

Carmen's eyebrow rose at that. Good, so she followed along.

"Noir? Is Lucifer's... brother?"

Charlie nodded. "Yup. Michael. As in Archangel Michael."

Carmen snorted at that.

Fine, so she wasn't going to believe her. Charlie had expected as much. Had she not been there to see it herself, she'd probably have had the exact same reaction.

"Him and Brian were trying to keep me away from Luci—"

"Brian?" Carmen sat up sharply, as if remembering something important, but whatever she had intended to say washed away on a wave of pain.

Once she had gathered herself again, she asked, "Why would Brian be working with him?"

Charlie shrugged. "It's fucked up, isn't it? This right here-," she lifted her arm and winced, pointing to the bandage covering her stomach, "was a gift from the angel himself. And here I thought we were supposed to be afraid of demons and shit."

"Just imagine what they would do to you if the good guys do this shit," Carmen said, sitting down in the recliner.

"Actually," Charlie said, a soft smile forming, "they aren't that bad. Some boundary issues, maybe. But the ones I met at Lucifer's place were kind of nice. At least *they* didn't try to cut me open."

Carmen blinked wide eyes at Charlie, as though she were having trouble processing.

"Are... Are you being serious right now? Or are you fucking with me?"

"What do you mean?"

"You went to Lucifer's place.... You mean Hell?"

For some reason, hearing it out loud hit differently. Especially coming from her best friend. She had been in Hell. Wow, was this really her life?

"Yeah. Wait." She looked at Carmen a little closer. "Aren't you going to call me crazy? Isn't all of this *completely impossible*?" Charlie prodded, staring at her.

Carmen stared at her for a moment before her eyes darted away.

"Carmen. What do you know?"

"I don't know any—"

"Don't you dare fucking lie to me, Vega!"

"Am I interrupting?" Lucifer's voice called from the doorway.

Both women turned around to find him looking between them, a large stuffed bear and an obnoxious bouquet of wildflowers spilling out of his arms. Charlie gave him an annoyed look at his interruption, but Carmen looked relieved.

Taking advantage of a clean getaway, Carmen moved to Charlie's bedside and looked down at her, lowering her voice. "First heal. Then we'll talk about things."

Charlie wasn't happy, but with Lucifer now in the room, she agreed that Carmen leaving would be for the best. "I'll hold you to that. Don't forget, I have friends in low places..."

She smirked up at her, knowing that if she told Camilla she wanted to see her, the little girl wouldn't rest until Carmen brought her to Aunt Charlie. She couldn't hide from this one.

"Yeah, yeah," Carmen said, bending over to kiss Charlie on top of the head. "Just get better, then we will talk."

Charlie glanced up to find Lucifer staring, head tilted, straight at Carmen's ass. "Who's your cheeky friend?"

Carmen turned around, clutching her hospital gown closed behind her.

"Savor it," she said with a glance to Charlie. "Love you, *hermana*."

"Love you," Charlie said back.

They both watched her leave the small room, then stared at each other, the awkward silence filling the space between them. What could she say? She didn't even remember him bringing her here. The last thing she could remember was running from Michael, the flowers, him stabbing her...

"You look a lot better than when I left you. Lots more color, little less death rattle," Lucifer said, setting his gifts on the nearby table.

"What happened?"

"Ah, right. You probably don't remember much. Too busy dying, I understand." He smiled down at her, something strange passing behind his eyes. Before she could get a read on it, he quickly turned his attention to the machines hooked up to her.

"Lucifer, cut the bullshit."

He clasped his hands behind him, almost as though he were physically restraining himself. "Right. What happened was I came back home, and you were gone."

Charlie bit her lip, a wave of shame hitting her. She had been so angry with him; she hadn't been thinking straight. Looking back at it now, she was embarrassed. He had told her it wasn't safe, and obviously, he was right. She left, and she nearly got killed.

"Don't worry about it," he said, and she realized he was giving her his full attention once again. Whatever he was seeing on her face, he was reading her like a book. "I was fooling myself to think you wouldn't do exactly what you did. It's one of the things I enjoy most about you. Though it will be the death of you one day. Or me."

A soft chuckle escaped him, and Charlie's cheeks turned a shade of pink. "Anyway, when I discovered you had flown the coop, I knew I needed to find you. Something told me you had gotten yourself into a steaming pile of trouble."

He held his forearm up briefly in a silent gesture. Charlie looked at the mark on her forearm and sighed. He'd felt everything she had when Michael and Brian trapped her. Every ounce of terror, of pain, had pumped out of her and into him through their connection. What would that have been like being on the receiving end and not knowing what was happening on the other side?

"I'm... sorry."

"Hmm?" Lucifer turned to look at her again, he'd been looking at the machine.

"Don't make me repeat myself."

Another chuckle came from him. He finally sat down beside her on the bed. "I won't this time."

A small half-smile formed on her face. All that anger she held when she last saw him simply melted away. She wondered if that was a good idea or not, letting him off so easily. It was all his fault, wasn't it? The smile faltered as she looked away again.

"What's wrong?"

"I still don't understand." She shrugged her shoulders, "Michael said things... many things that I don't understand. But out of all of it, all I still don't get is why me? Why was the target on my back?"

"I don't know—I *didn't* know," he said, cutting her off as she opened her mouth to call him out. "Not until our little trip to my place. Then... it all started making sense."

"What did?"

"You ask why you? Why did Michael try to kill *you*, why is all this strange happening, why was it you that got attacked that night? It's quite simple actually. I don't know who captured my hellhound, but when he escaped, he must have been looking for a way home. The fact that it came to you... usually, hellhounds only come to creatures of the underworld. Beyond that... I'm not sure."

"But it didn't *come* to me. It attacked me."

Lucifer waved that off, "Contrary to popular belief, hellhounds are not bloodthirsty beasts that will attack any being it crosses paths with. They only attack in self-defense. Or..." He stopped as if an epiphany struck him.

"What?" Charlie asked, feeling her anxiety spike.

"To protect their masters." Lucifer took her hand in his, looking down at it as though seeing it for the first time. "Tell me, Charlie. Have there been any other strange things happening since your visit to Hell? Other than your sudden green thumb."

"Green thumb? What are you talking about?" The bouquet of wildflowers was suddenly thrust into her hands. They both stared at the flowers, waiting for them to do something. When nothing at all happened, Lucifer looked more than a little disappointed.

She lowered the bouquet onto her lap, giving him a soft smile. "I guess not, huh? Any other ideas?"

He was still staring at the flowers as if they were a puzzle. Whatever he had expected to happen, he didn't seem to be content with the result.

"Look, Lucifer, I appreciate you trying to make sense out of all this for me. But I think it's just time to accept the fact that it was a freak acci—"

His lips were suddenly crushed against hers, taking her by surprise with a squeal. His hand cupped the side of her face as he kissed her, and she felt a strange sort of tension break. His breath was sweet, his touch tender.

When he pulled away, she was almost disappointed. "...dent."

His hand was still on her face as they tried to catch their collective breath. She wasn't sure what had driven him to do that, and she more so wasn't sure how she felt about it. It was nice. It was confusing.

"Well, will you look at that," he said.

She opened her eyes. "Huh?"

He grabbed her hand and helped her lift the bouquet of flowers, and her eyes went from heavy with euphoria to wide with surprise. The flowers tripled in size, blooms erupting from buds that had barely been the size of a pebble moments before.

"As I said," Lucifer said, clearing his throat. "Anything else?"

Charlie couldn't take her eyes off the still-growing bouquet. She set it down on her legs carefully, as though she were afraid it might reach out and bite her and tried to think. "I, uh... I don't know. I guess... I have been seeing things–people."

"What kind of people? Going to have to be more specific than that."

"Dead ones," she blurted out.

"Ah, yes," he said, smiling. "Man, I really liked that old woman."

Charlie wasn't sure who he was talking about at first, but then it hit her. The old woman at his place. The one who she had let escape.

"Abby kept saying that it was really interesting that I could open the doors, but no one ever explained why. What is the big deal about it?"

"Well, people like you—humans—don't usually have the power to see spirits, let alone give them passage in the underworld. That means you are something quite special."

"And that is?" She was starting to tire of him dragging this on. "If you know something, then spit it out. I'm sick of the head games, Lucifer."

"A creature of the Underworld, Charlotte. What some circles might call a Chthonic." Lucifer's eyes were full of wonderment at this revelation.

"You realize that's impossible, right?" Charlie said a little too quickly.

Lucifer lifted an eyebrow, his smile firm. He plucked a single magnificent rose from her flourishing bouquet and after a quick sniff of its fragrance, he held it to her. "There's a lot of impossible things happening lately, wouldn't you say?"

Charlie couldn't help but feel a little embarrassed at her outburst. He was right. Of all the things she'd witnessed, was it really hard to accept such a thing?

"You're not wrong there." She half grinned. "Still doesn't mean I have to accept that."

"Believe it or don't. It doesn't mean it's not true, Charlotte."

"Stop calling me that..."

"Calling you what?"

Charlie gave him a side glance which provoked a chuckle from Lucifer as his hands shot up in defense. "Apologies. Or I guess I should say, 'sorry, Charlie.'"

Her smile matched his, and for the first time in days, there was a sort of ease in her shoulders. There were so many questions still hovering around in her head, questions that needed answers, but at that moment she just wanted to get some rest and enjoy the calm.

"Knock, knock," a cheery voice called from the doorway.

A nurse entered the room, stopping for a moment seeing her visitor, but her well-practiced smile stayed in place. "Oh, well hello there. Ms. Brant, it's nice to see you awake and smiling. I'm here to take your vitals before the doctor sees you."

They both turned to look at the nurse, but it was Lucifer who spoke first. "Ooh, vitals. That should be fun to watch."

"I don't think so," Charlie said, flatly. "You can wait until I call you. After I get out of here. You are on a growing list of people who owe me a long talk."

Lucifer shrugged and stood. "As you wish. I will hold my breath then," he said with a wink. "Take good care of her. And see if the doctor can do something about that stick up her ass, will you?"

Charlie chucked the wildflowers at his head, but he caught them with an expert flourish. He grabbed the empty hospital cup on her tray and walked them to the sink, filling it and placing the flowers inside it before placing it on the tray in front of her.

"That would indeed be my cue to leave. Goodnight, Charlie."

The nurse moved and blocked her view of him, but she could hear soft laughter passing through the door. "Yeah, Goodnight. Luci."

Epilogue

Five years earlier

Smooth, sultry jazz leaked in from the other room as she sat at her mirror, running her a brush through her dark hair with careful precision. She loved when he was in this kind of mood. It wasn't often her husband was able to let the aches and pains of his day-to-day roll off his shoulders, so she cherished it whenever she could. The rich timbre of his voice sang along with the record, the sound smoothing over her skin like a warm embrace.

Gods, she wasn't looking forward to her coming departure. With Spring at their doorstep, their time together was running out and she would rob her beloved of these rare moods for another six months.

A soft sigh of disappointment escaped her, and she shook her head, attempting to shake off the sudden feeling of overwhelming sadness. No, she would not allow herself to waste such precious little time left in sadness. She could be sad after.

A soft purr vibrated behind her, and a cold nose bumped her elbow, making her nearly drop the silver brush. A dark snout pushed into the opening of her arm until it could lay its massive head in her lap.

"Pushy boy," she said with a laugh, scratching the animal's ear softly. "Are you missing your brothers? Hmm?"

She laid a gentle kiss between its eyes and pushed him off her, turning so she could face the beast. Her attention honed in on the large scar running up the center of his chest, examining it closely before giving it a loving rub.

"You look like you're pretty well healed up. You should be fine to go back to them."

Her heart ached heavily remembering the state of her poor pup when he hobbled into the palace. His ear had been clipped off, his chest poorly stapled shut from Gods knew what, and a gaping hole in his shoulder. His dark blood had left ghostly stains on the floors around them. Never had she seen him in such a horrific state. Whoever had done such damage to him was going to have Hell to pay... quite literally.

With a soft pat to his head and another kiss, the beast flicked his long tail and licked her cheek before bounding away. If he could rejoin his brothers, she was sure he would finish healing. At least she could only hope. No one had ever hurt him so badly before and it made her extremely anxious not knowing what had happened. What could manage to do such damage to such a powerful creature.

Just add it to the list of things to look into when she went back to her mother's.

She stood and moved to the large bed, tossing her dressing gown aside, but stopped suddenly as a gut-twisting knot pulled at her stomach. One hand gripped her belly, the other braced on the carved bedpost, and a cold dread swept over her entire being. The soft jazz in the other room ripped to a halt and the bedroom door blew open, her husband filling the door frame. They stared at each other in unfiltered panic.

"Did you feel that, pet?" he asked.

Oh, she felt it. Like a frigid wind blowing through her very soul. The rawness of her husband's face pained her. He looked lost, unsure how to feel but she knew exactly what he was feeling because it matched the storm raging inside her.

"I did. Something is wrong."

She stared at him for a heartbeat, silently begging the fates for it to not be true. Her feet were carrying her before her brain had a chance to fully grasp the motion. She rushed to the mantle, praying she wouldn't find what she feared when she got there.

In the center of the ledge lay a mirror. Floating an inch or so above it, a beautiful white Asphodel was in full bloom. It was truly the most perfect specimen of the flower, a tall stalk adorned with many white starbursts. But beyond its natural beauty, a shimmer of something else sparkled on the edge of its existence.

It looked unmarred, flourishing beautifully as it had been for twenty-nine years. For the briefest of moments, a smile of relief nearly took hold of her lips, but it was short lived when she saw the star-like blossom lying on the mirror beneath the flower.

This shouldn't be happening. They had been so careful, so purposeful in their choices. But there it was... an ember. The smallest spark reigniting. Her violet eyes welled with tears as she stared at her husband. Tears of longing, of despair, and of fear.

"It's started."

Thank you
FOR READING!

If you enjoyed *Dance with the Devil*, please take a moment and leave us a review! You can find us on most platforms.

If you want to see more follow us on our socials:
MadisonChaseBooks

We also have a newsletter and cool sneak peeks through our website:

www.madisonchasebooks.com

Road PLAYLIST to Hell

Falling Apart *Skyler Grey*	**Trouble** *Cage The Elephant*
Moth *HELLYEAH*	**Mr. Sandman** *SYML*
Natural *Imagine Dragons*	**Come As You Are** *Nirvana*
Wicked Game *Ursine Vulpine, Annaca*	**Don't Speak** *No Doubt*
Sugar *Sleep Token*	**A Little Bit Off** *Five Finger Death Punch*
Running Up That Hill *MEG MYERS*	**Dead Weight** *PVRIS*
Die Trying *New Medicine*	**Dial Tone** *Catch Your Breath*
Pomegranate Seeds *Julian Moon*	**And More...**

Harley escaped the monster who claimed to love her, but the scars he left behind run deeper than she thought. Will she conquer her fear—or become the very thing she fled?

Explore our other stories set in this universe!